Man of Honor

T0352256

Man of Honor

Battle Scars, Book 3

DIANA GARDIN

FOREVER
YOURS

New York Boston

Forever Yours
Hachette Book Group
1290 Avenue of the Americas
New York, NY 10104

forever-romance.com
twitter.com/foreverromance

First published as an ebook and as a print on demand: August 2016

Forever Yours is an imprint of Grand Central Publishing.

The Forever Yours name and logo are trademarks of Hachette Book Group, Inc.

The publisher is not responsible for websites (or their content) that are not owned by the publisher.

The Hachette Speakers Bureau provides a wide range of authors for speaking events. To find out more, go to www.hachettespeakersbureau.com or call (866) 376-6591.

ISBNs: 978-1-4555-9478-8 (ebook edition); 978-1-4555-9477-1 (print-on-demand edition)

For Mel and Shan, for loving me
unconditionally throughout all these years.

Acknowledgments

Through Christ I can do all things.

To my superman, Tyson. True love isn't a fairy tale. It's a battle every day, and I'm blessed to be fighting through it with someone as strong and steady as you. Thank you for picking up my slack around the house and with the kiddos when I'm a crazy woman on a deadline. I will always love you.

To my busy bees, Carrington and Raleigh. Thank you for being patient with Mommy when I am just letting you run around like maniacs while I type away on this computer. You're always in my thoughts and I do it all for you.

To my mama, Inez. Thank you so much for passing on your love of books. It meant everything. You are and have always been my inspiration.

To my crew, the Fab Five: Crystal, Emilee, Beth, Christy, and Maria. Without you hot mamas and our girls' nights, our girls' trips, and our group texts, I would go stark raving mad. I'm infinitely blessed to have you in my life, and I hope Dare keeps your hubbies happy for a while! Love and kisses, Kitty.

To my BFF of the South, Natalee, you are truly one of my favorite people on this planet. Thank you so much for being the first one in line to buy each and every book, and for your unwavering love and support. With each new hero I write, I can't wait to see what you'll think of him. I heart you.

To Stacey Donaghy. What a lucky day it was when you agreed to be my agent. I'm still not sure how it happened, but I'm so thankful it did! Your hard work and positive words, especially about this book, are incomparable. I would not want to navigate this publishing world without you, because what I've learned with you by my side can't be traded. Every time I write something new, I can't wait until you read it, because you're my biggest cheerleader. Thank you!

To my editor, Leah. You were the first traditional publishing editor to believe in my work, and this has turned into such a wonderful working relationship. Your expertise only makes my work better, and I'm so glad to have you in my corner.

To my Forever Publicity Team. Thanks for helping to get the word out about my books. We will keep climbing!

To the rest of the team at Forever Romance. Thank you for all the hard work you do in order to make authors look good. You are all so spectacular to work with!

To Tracy Comerford. You are a one-woman wrecking team. You were one of the earliest reviewers to love my books, and I'm lucky enough now to be able to call you so many things: friend, reviewer, publicist, and even my trusty PA from time to time. Your time is so valuable, and the fact that you spend some of it on me and getting the word out there about my books blows my mind. You're uber talented and knowledgeable about the book world. Can't wait to see where BMBB goes from here!

To my critique partner for MOH: Marie Meyer. We share so many things: a writing group, a publisher, and a genre. I admire you and the beauty that is your writing so very much! Thank you for your advice and the encouragement you gave me on this book. Love you, girl!

To my warm and fuzzy writing group, the NAC. Kate, Ara, Marie, Bindu, Meredith, Jamie, Jessica, Sophia, Marnee, Missy, Laura, and Amanda. I found you guys when I was already well into this biz, and now I don't know what I ever did without you. I wouldn't trade any of you, and I can't wait for the day when we can all have dinner together. Remember, I would cut a bitch for any one of you.

To my mentor, Rachel van Dyken. All I can say about you, love, is that I'm learning from the best. You probably don't even know what your advice and friendship mean to me, but you are invaluable. I love you to pieces!

To the Dolls...Best. Reader. Group. Ever. You guys are so awesome, and I love sharing snippets and pics with you on a daily basis! I hope that one day I get to meet each and every one of you.

To the Diana Gardin Review Team. Thank you for willing to read and review my books early. Your effort means so much, and I appreciate you all for your time and effort!

To the bloggers and readers who find this book: THANK

YOU. Thank you so much for reading, purchasing, reviewing, and spreading the word about the Battle Scars series. Without you, what would I be? You make this possible, and I want to hear from each and every one of you soon!

Man of Honor

1

Drake

My palms itch, and I clench my hands into tight fists, trying to force the uncomfortable sensation away. The tingling merely changes course, shooting up my arms and giving my entire upper torso the sensation of being eaten alive by pissed-off fire ants.

I hate this fucking place. I hate this fucking *day*.

My eyes are grainy. I dig my fists into them, trying hard to root out the tiny granules of sand I know aren't there. It's just what happens when you've been up for a solid thirty-six hours. I sigh, my chest swelling with the pent-up air before I force it back out of my lungs with a loud *whoosh*.

Blinking a few times, I stare around me. Sitting in the pews surrounding mine is a sea of faces. Some I recognize from another lifetime, some I don't. They're all wearing the perfunctory look of extreme sadness one is supposed to express at a time like this. But I can probably count on one hand the number of people who truly loved her.

Because she was so goddamned hard to love.

For me, it was obligatory. She was my mother.

After the short service, in which the minister said a few words about the woman everyone in this small Georgia hole knew as the town drunk, I stood at the front of the church beside the closed casket. A long line of people waited to greet me. I nodded at each person who slugged by. There were some, like old Ms. Ebbie, who used to babysit me when my mom was on a bender, and Jim Tucker, who owns the grocery store, who wrapped their arms around me.

Fuck. Did I ever even tell Jim how grateful I am for all those times he let me clean up aisles in his store just so I could take home a meal for me and Ma?

From the kind and sympathetic look in both Jim's and Ms. Ebbie's eyes, I realize it doesn't matter whether I ever actually said it.

They knew.

Everyone in this tiny godforsaken town knew. Without their help—the handouts that they gave me and the times they'd peel my mother off the floor at Boondock's bar—I wouldn't have made it out of here alive. They saved me first.

The army did the rest.

I hadn't even noticed the fact that my eyes had glazed over until my vision clears as there's a timid tap on my shoulder. I focus on the wizened, kind face of my high school shop teacher. The lines around his eyes are more pronounced, but other than that he looks exactly the same as he did the day I graduated eight years ago.

"Mr. Harris. Thank you for coming." My voice sounds as though I haven't used it in years.

His knowing gaze is enough to place an enormous lump in my throat, but I swallow it down like a shot of hard liquor. There's no room for weakness in my life. I learned that a long time ago.

"You doing okay, Drake? I'm sorry that it took something like this to bring you back to town."

Nodding, I bow my head in shame. "I should have visited. Sorry, Mr. Harris. Everything you did for me back then…"

He pats my shoulder, clearing his throat and looking me straight in the eye. "Did what needed to be done, son. Every kid deserves some lookin' after."

He did more than that. He was the first person to put a wrench in my hand. The first man in my life who ever gave a shit. He gave me goals, put the army on my radar as a chance to break free from here.

I owe the man my life.

"You stayin' or goin'?" he asks gruffly.

I glance at the coffin and cringe. "Going. Right after she's in the ground."

He releases a heavy sigh before nodding. "Can't say I blame ya. Imagine you got a life wherever you are now. Carolina, is it?"

A small smile touches my lips. "Keepin' tabs on me, Mr. Harris?"

Patting my shoulder again before he begins to walk away, he grunts. "Somebody has to. Maybe use a phone every now and again this time. You hear me, boy?"

"Yes, sir."

He pauses and then looks back at me. "I'm proud of ya, Drake. The hand you got dealt? No-count daddy who ran when you was just a baby, mama who drank herself silly…" Mr. Harris shakes his head, scowling. "Wasn't fair for a good kid like you to have to deal with it. But you done good, boy. Despite it all."

The lump is back.

Tenfold.

He shuffles off, leaving just a few more townsfolk to greet me and give me their condolences. It's so strange to accept them. Although I'd been sending my mother a percentage of my income ever since I first left home, I never could bring myself to come back and face it all again. Looking down at the shiny, cherrywood casket brings all kinds of regret bubbling to the surface. I should have come home. I should have done more than just send her money. I knew that she was drinking herself into the ground. I should have done more for her.

Should.

Should.

Should.

Too late now. She's gone. All I have left is the life I've built for myself back in Lone Sands, North Carolina. Small cottage on the beach. Full-service auto shop I started and built from the ground up. A few friends I call family.

I have to move forward with my life.

I know that. But then why do I feel so empty?

The Challenger races up the interstate, seemingly just as charged up and ready to unwind as I am. Rather than sorting through Ma's things and packing up her house to sell myself, I hired a packing company. Dredging up those memories and digging around in that part of my soul would accomplish nothing. I'm done with Blythe, Georgia.

From its spot in the cup holder, my phone catches my eye as the screen lights up. *Guess I never turned the sound back up after the funeral. Just as well. I don't feel like talking to anyone.*

Curiosity forces me to check the caller ID.

Dare. Dude's been blowing up my phone all day.

But today…I can't even force myself to check in with the one man who's like a brother to me. Dare Conners and whatever he has to say can wait until I'm back in the right headspace. I know he'll understand.

I place my phone back in the cup holder and continue driving, way too fast, back to North Carolina.

A couple of hours later I'm breezing into the town limits past the old wooden WELCOME sign and breathing an enormous sigh of relief. But I bypass the turnoff that'll take me to my house and instead head for one of my favorite places in the world. The day of my ma's funeral has come and gone, and night has fallen. Pulling into a parking spot, I shut off the Challenger's ignition and step out into the night. Even in late January, the air here is moist, if also chilly. I take a deep breath, letting salty oxygen fill my lungs again. Exhaling, I stride up to See Food and let myself inside the restaurant.

Bypassing my usual table, I pull up a stool at the bar and focus my gaze on the plentiful choice of bottles behind Lenny. The middle-aged restaurant owner lifts a brow. "Rough day, Drake?"

Grunting, I nod. "The roughest."

"Hungry?" Her eyes are kind as they search my face.

"Could always put away a basket of your coconut shrimp, Lenny." I find a smile somewhere deep inside and lay it on her. "And why don't you go ahead and pour me a stiff whiskey. Neat."

Now her eyebrows pull together and lift toward her hairline. "Must have been a really bad day."

She busies herself with a bottle of Jack and I take a minute to glance around me. On a Friday night in the middle of winter, See Food isn't as packed as it would be during tourist season. But it's busy with the local crowd, and the few waitresses are bustling around in jeans and boots. See Food's laid-back atmosphere is what draws me here, and the second-to-none seafood is what keeps me coming back. It's warm, it's familiar, and right now it has the ability to make me forget for a little while.

The crowd tonight is easy, not rowdy. Full of men who want to drink and girls who want a good time. There's no live music at See Food in the winter, so the notes floating out from the speakers is a playlist of low-key Southern rock mixed in with country hits.

I'm almost desperate with the need to get lost. Burying my mother dredged up all kinds of darkness I thought I'd buried a long time ago. It's swirling around inside me now like silt in the ocean.

Churning, churning, churning.

When Lenny slides my drink toward me, I grip the glass in one hand and take a long, burning swallow. As the amber liquid slides down my throat I close my eyes and grimace.

Never wanted to be like her. And having a drink right now doesn't mean I'm turning into her. It's just been a rough day.

"I'll have what he's having."

The sugary sweet voice comes from right beside me, and when I open my eyes I see that its owner is anything but. A bleached blonde dressed to impress has sidled up next to me at the bar. She leans over the shiny wood, her enormous tits nearly falling out of her low-cut top. My eyes slip down her body to take in the tight black leather pants and spiky heels. When I meet her eyes, the bright blue irises are sparkling with knowing allure.

"Hey there. Mind if I have a seat?" She puffs her red lips out in a pout. "Doesn't seem to be anywhere else to sit."

Out of the corner of my eye I see Lenny roll both of hers. I nod toward the empty stool beside me, indicating that she should sit if she wants to.

The blonde's lips curve into a seductive smile as she hops up. Her thigh brushes mine and my dick springs to attention. My body responds to hers like it knows exactly what comes next, and it's eager to get to the finish line.

I glance at the blonde again, and she bats her lashes at me. Making up my mind, I nod to Lenny.

"Her drinks are on me."

Lenny tries and fails to hold in her sigh. "Sure thing, Drake."

"Drake?" The blonde leans over my arm, dragging a long fingernail across my inked skin. "Nice name."

I down the rest of my drink and shove my glass back toward Lenny, wordlessly asking for another. Shaking her head while giving me the side eye, Lenny obliges.

It's going to be a long night.

2

Mea

Order up!" Boozer barks as his bald head appears above the food window in the kitchen of See Food.

"Got it!" I put down my glass of Sprite and pick up my plates of food, balancing a large tray while arranging the four heaping platters of seafood on top, then push through the swinging kitchen door backward and enter the bar area. I've only been working here for about a week. I'm still thanking my lucky stars that Lenny and Boozer hired me without any experience. I need all the money I can stockpile if I ever want to get my yoga studio up and running.

In this century.

Breezing past Lenny, I bump her hip gently with mine where she stands rinsing glasses at the sink behind the bar. "You good?"

She smirks at me. "I should probably be asking you that, doll."

Shooting her a sassy wink, my tray wobbles slightly, and Lenny catches one mug of beer just before it tips off the edge. Groaning, she grabs my shoulders to steady me. "Lord, girl. You might be the death of this place."

I scoff. "Please. Berkeley did it, and she's ten times clumsier than I am."

Lenny smiles, half-moon wrinkles forming around her lips. "Berkeley had years of practice. You're meant for greater things than this old place. Just like she was."

I glance down. "Maybe. But for now, this place is saving my ass. And so are you." I lean over and kiss her cheek before brushing past her toward the high-top tables surrounding the bar. Hearing a throaty giggle, I whirl around. My chocolate brown curls slap me in the face as I zero in on the curvy blonde poured into her clothes at the bar. Yep, she's the source of the giggle. Rolling my eyes, I start back on my path.

But something catches my eye and my steps stutter, then freeze.

The blond chick has large, spectacular, and most likely fake, breasts. They're currently squished up against a solid brick wall of a man. First my eyes follow the veins in his muscular forearms, exposed by the white collared shirt he's wearing, sleeves rolled up. Then my gaze wanders to the open collar, where the thick, winding lines of ink swirl up toward his neck. And that neck…muscular and thick, just like the rest of his perfectly sculpted body.

A body I know very, very well.

Lastly, my eyes land on a face that simultaneously makes my blood boil and my toes curl. Olive skin, mostly smooth except for the scar near his left temple. Short brown hair so dark it's nearly raven. Square chin, covered in perfectly rough scruff. Straight nose with a slight rise in the top. Deep-set eyes the color of the warmest caramel.

Perfect male beauty. Rough and deep and dark. There's so much story behind those eyes that I never learned. Eyes that are currently, hazily focused on the tits rubbing against his muscled arm.

Goddammit.

Drake Sullivan.

It's not like I never run into him. I see him quite often actually, because my best friend and his are getting married in two months. We cross paths because we have to, not because I want to.

My past with Drake? It's complicated. When a man gives you the best one-night stand of your life and you ruin everything by running out on him and never speaking to him about it again, things are bound to get tricky. Every time I see him, a slow burn of attraction sizzles just beneath the surface, and I do everything I can to pretend it isn't so.

Because I'm not in the market for a boyfriend. It's the last thing I need in my life.

It's not like I didn't know that See Food is his favorite hangout. He only lives right down the beach, for Pete's sake. I just wasn't expecting to see him *now*. And certainly not with that slut pressed against him like white on rice.

Dammit. I don't want seeing him with another woman to affect me like this. I don't want it to affect me at all!

My heartbeat thumps wildly in my chest as I watch him. I

want so badly to tear my eyes away, but I just can't. He's clearly tanked. His eyes are glassy, and he's tilting slightly sideways on his stool. Which is completely at odds with everything I know about Drake. He's always calm, cool, and collected. He's always in control.

The dude is a freaking ex-army Ranger. He's someone others can depend on.

Well, most others.

Suddenly, Lenny's face is directly in front of me, replacing my view of Drake and the Blonde Bombshell.

"Um, hello…Mea? What the hell is wrong with you, girl? You're about to drop that tray!" Her voice is more concerned than angry, and that's just so typically Lenny that a lump suddenly forms in my throat.

Horrified at the thought that I might actually cry for no reason and in front of anyone else, I blink rapidly and swallow hard.

"Oh, uh…right. I'm on my way to table twenty-three with these. Just…sorry."

"I've gotta run to the office for a minute." Her last sentence pulls me back around to face her. "After you drop that off, can you hang behind the bar for a few until I get back?"

Slowly nodding my agreement, I turn on my heel, and doing everything I can to avoid dropping the tray of not-quite-hot food, I scurry in the opposite direction of the bar. I drop off the food at my table and then take a second to gather myself.

This is where I work. I have a job to do, and I'm not going to let the sight of Drake Sullivan and some flavor-of-the-week stop me from helping Lenny when she needs it.

They both glance up as my rag swirls the bar top in front of them. "Everything okay here?"

Drake's bleary gaze meets mine, and then his eyes widen in surprise. "Mea? What…what are you doing here?"

I prop my hip up against the bar and send him a smirk. All the while, my heart beats like the wings of a trapped butterfly inside my chest.

Drake looks…hell, he looks damn good. He's traded in his usual T-shirt for a white button-up, and the dark ink winding around his forearms catches my eye.

"I work here, Drake." I'm proud of how well I'm able to keep the tremble out of my voice.

Why is he affecting me so much? Maybe it's because of the woman. My gaze slides to her.

"We're fine here." Her high-pitched voice sends me a very clear signal. *Step off. He's mine.*

Which, of course, only makes my smirk grow wider as my eyes slide back to Drake. "Y'all let me know if you need anything, k? I'll be behind the bar until Lenny gets back."

His eyes drinking me in, Drake lifts his chin once in acknowledgment.

The fact that he hasn't looked at his drinking buddy once since I've been standing here makes me smile as I move on down the bar to check in with other customers.

I can feel his eyes burning into me as I chat and refill drinks. When Lenny returns, I take the opportunity to head for the front door. A quick breather is all I need. A chance to catch my breath and gather my thoughts.

For just a minute, I need to be as far away from Drake fucking Sullivan as possible.

The night drags by. Despite my best intentions to keep my head down, serve my tables, and get through the night without snatching the blonde off her barstool or elbowing Drake off of his, my eyes continue to track their movements from wherever I am in the restaurant. Drake's been different than his usual self—he seems almost down in the dumps—oblivious to everything, including the blonde for the most part. I can tell from the time she's invested in him that she thinks he's taking her home tonight. But, watching Drake way more closely than I should, I'm not so sure he's on the same game plan as she is.

He accepts her attention, but he doesn't dish out any of his own. Mostly, Drake's eyes are trained on the drinks that he keeps slugging down like they're going out of style.

Except for the occasions I can feel their searing gaze on me.

Blondie's getting impatient with his lack of attention despite all her efforts.

A small smile quirks at my lips when she literally begins to pout. That's the moment when Drake decides to glance up from his drink. His dark gaze nails me to the spot, instantly freezing my movements as I'm caught up in his stare.

Do you know that expression *time stands still*? You know, the one they only use in chick flicks and romance novels?

Yeah, I now understand what it means. It doesn't mean that the second hand on your watch stops ticking. It doesn't mean that everyone around you pauses, grotesquely frozen in whatever activity they were engaging in. No, it's not like that at all.

When time stands still for me at that moment, it happens because Drake's gaze meets mine, and the intensity of it as recognition dawns on his face levels me. Flattens me. Roots me to the spot where I stand. And even though everyone and everything continue their normal goings-on around us, the thread that holds us together at that moment stretches taut, and I can't tell how much time passes.

Do seconds tick by? Minutes? An hour?

Hell if I know.

Drake's previously watery gaze sharpens in that moment, perfect clarity reflecting in his eyes. Awareness sizzles along my skin, tracing the path that my nerve endings draw, and there's absolutely nothing I can do about the effect he's having on me.

Not a damn thing.

I hold my ground. Neither of us moves a muscle for at least ten seconds, and I have the uncontrollable urge to move toward him. He blinks, and I take that moment to flee. I don't want him to see me so unraveled. I don't want him to know that seeing him liquefies my insides, turning me into mush. Escaping through the high-top tables in the bar area and around the long wooden high-top where Lenny is filling a glass with something dark and frothy, the kitchen door swishes shut behind me and I lean against the wall. My chest rises and falls with my heavy breaths, and there's only one thought running through my mind at top speed.

Holy shit. Holy shit. Holy shit.

Because if I'm honest with myself—and it's not very often that I allow that to happen, not when it comes to this—Drake Sullivan has had this effect on me since the moment I laid eyes on his gorgeous self. And I've never been able to stop it.

Ignore it? Yes. I can ignore it with the best of them.

But stop it from happening? Never. And I'm pretty sure that he doesn't have the first clue as to how he affects me.

I intend to keep it that way.

I need to keep my eye on the prize. And that prize has nothing to do with a sexy, deliciously dark man like Drake.

3

Drake

The back of my neck prickles.

I rub it, trying to ease the sensation out of my muscles, but it's surface level. I learned a long time ago to trust my instincts, because not doing so could get me, and the entire team of men around me, killed. So instead of ignoring the feeling, I lift my eyes from my highball glass to glance around the bar area. It's easy to find her. I've been keeping track of Mea's exact placement in the bar all damn night.

The sight of Mea Jones standing behind the bar earlier stopped my breathing just as fast as a chokehold would have.

I see Mea around a lot. My best friend, Dare, is marrying her best friend, Berkeley, in just a couple months. As best man and maid of honor, we have to be in the same room from time to time. We share a tight-knit circle of friends that neither of us is willing to give up. But Mea avoids me like the plague when she can, and I know it's because our past together is sticky.

But tonight, something's different. She's just standing there, staring at me from her place on the restaurant floor just outside the bar area. Her petite body is tight and stacked, and my big palms itch at the thought of running them over every curved inch of her. What she lacks in size—hell, she can't be taller than five foot two—she makes up for in attitude. She's got miles of it, and is never too shy to put someone in their place.

But right now? She looks like someone just punched her in the gut. And those big, dark brown eyes are wide and tentative, something Mea is most definitely *not*. She looks…vulnerable. Like she needs something from me.

God, at that moment, even in my inebriated state, I wish I could give it to her.

My eyes scan her, because I can't fucking *help* it. It's January, and she's a girl with half a brain, so no tight tank top like Tina, the blonde beside me. No, she's wearing a casual long-sleeved shirt that dips into a deep V, showcasing just a tease of the perfect set of tits I know lay just beneath. My cock stirs to life again just looking at her, but I force my eyes to keep moving upward and focus on her face.

Her gorgeous, flawless face. Skin the color of the richest caramel. Lush, pert lips set in a perpetual pout that chicks usually have to pay for. And then her hair, fanning around her face in a mess of wild, wild dark brown curls.

Wild. Free. Untamed.

That's Mea to the hilt.

She's always been like a little tornado, a force to be reckoned with who sucks everyone around her into her orbit. She's all power, tucked into a tiny, sexy frame.

Fuck.

I blink, shaking my head to clear it, and when I open my eyes again she's gone. Like a ghost, she's disappeared, probably into the back somewhere. Anywhere she doesn't have to see me. Or talk to me.

It's what I've been dealing with when it comes to Mea ever since Dare moved to Lone Sands two and a half years ago and started dating Berkeley. They went through plenty of ups and downs in their relationship, and Mea and I were there for them every step of the way. Me on Dare's side, Mea on Berkeley's.

The one night I spent with her? The one where she blew my fucking mind and then just walked away? That happened shortly before Dare arrived. I've been living with the memory for three damn years.

The second I saw her again all I wanted to do was pull her into my arms. Touch her. Love on her.

Taste her.

But when she looked at me, it was with venom and acid and I was so shell-shocked by it I never asked her why. To this day, I have no idea what turned her against me so absolutely.

And now, not only are we going to have to costar in this wedding event in March, she's apparently also working at my favorite hangout.

Fuck.

"What?"

Right. The blonde. Tara? I must have said that last "fuck" out loud. She's looking at me the way an orderly in a mental hospital looks at a patient.

Shaking my head, I put my hands to my head and rub my temples. I'm so fucking tired. Why'd I think it was a good idea to come out and get tanked? And how the hell am I gonna get home?

Sighing, I signal to Lenny. She walks over, wiping her hands with a rag. Raises a brow in my direction.

"Close me out, Len."

She nods. Glances at the chick glued to my side. "Hers, too. On my tab. And then call her a cab, will ya?"

Nodding again, Lenny turns to the register. "What about you, big guy? How you gettin' home?"

I stand so I can pull my wallet out, and then groan as the liquor in my stomach sloshes around. A wave of nausea hits me, and my head threatens to split my vision in two. Blinking rapidly, I take out a few bills and toss them onto the shiny bar top.

"Guess I'll be walking tonight. The cold air should help."

I know I'm slurring, but there's nothing I can do about it. I'm drunk as fuck, and damn if I'm not ashamed of myself for it. This has never been my thing. Losing control like this…it's not me. I just needed to let loose after the previous seventy-two hours from hell.

But now I'm straight fucked.

The bar's gone pretty quiet around us. At this hour, the crowd is gone and the staff is starting their closing duties. The blonde, finally realizing we're not going home together because that's the absolute *last* thing I need, turns around in a huff and flounces away. She's a little unsteady on her feet, but I watch to make sure she makes it to the door okay. The cab should be out there for her.

"You're welcome for the drinks," I mutter and turn back to Lenny.

"I can call Dare," she offers.

I shake my head vehemently at that, and wince at the pain it causes. Shit, how many whiskeys did I have? I'd lost count somewhere around eleven o'clock.

"Don't do that, Len. I'll be fine. Let me just—" I attempt to make my legs move me toward the front door, but they end up getting twisted around, and I stumble, nearly falling on my ass.

"Boozer!" Lenny hollers. "Get out here!"

Her giant of a husband appears instantly from the kitchen. He takes one look at me, shakes his head and frowns. "What the hell, Drake?"

Shrugging, I chuckle. "Rough day, Boozer. You don't wanna know."

He sidles up next to me, holding up one side of me, not grunting with the effort, because he's as big as I am. "Where am I taking you?"

I'm about to open my mouth to answer him, when instead a sweet, sassy voice from my other side does it for me. "You can put him in my car, Booze. I got him."

Boozer glances at her and scowls. "You don't got shit."

Mea pulls herself up to her full height, which makes me grin, and narrows her eyes at him. "*I said* I got him."

Boozer looks like he doesn't know which one of us is annoying him more right now, but he and Mea work together to help my pathetic ass walk to her car. Boozer pushes me in on the passenger side, where I feel like a sardine crunched into a small aluminum can, and closes the door. I lean my head back against the seat, taking deep and steady breaths in through my nose and out through my mouth.

My eyes are closed, so I only hear Mea when she gets in beside me.

Without a word, she starts her ignition and pulls out of the parking lot.

The silence is thick but the last thing I want to do is piss her off, so I stay quiet and just concentrate on breathing and not throwing up. Because I'd never live it down if I did.

"Where are we?" I ask when the car rolls to a stop. Opening one eye, I check our surroundings.

"Your place. Because this is where you live." Mea speaks slowly, like she's talking to a kid. I guess I deserve it.

"Thanks. I can take it from here."

"Sure you can." She rolls her eyes, sighing in total exasperation. "Stay right there, you big idiot. I'll help you."

This time I watch as she scoots around the front of the car, her hair billowing out all around her. She walks with her shoulders back and her head held high. Proud, proud, proud.

Whatever can be said about Mea Jones, she's not weak. She's smart, she's strong, and she's tough as nails.

And when she grabs my arm and begins tugging me out of her car, I try my damnedest not to snort with laughter. I help her out, lugging myself up and out and trying not to lean too heavily on her while we walk from her car parked in my driveway to the front door of my house.

I glance at my keys, then glance at the lock. Realizing this task might just be harder than my numb mind can handle at the moment, I hand the keys to Mea. She throws me a heated glance, busies herself with unlocking the door, and we both lurch into the living room. She kicks the door closed behind her and we both collapse onto my couch with triumphant exhaustion.

"I'll give it to you, Mea," I pant. "You're tiny, but you're strong as a goddamned ox."

"And I'll give it to you, *Drake*," she shoots right back, full of sass and snap. "You've usually got your shit together, but right now you're a big hot mess."

I throw my head back and roar with laughter. "Yup. Can't argue with you there. But you know what? That's kind of what happens on the day you put your mom in the ground."

Silence. My eyes are still aimed at the ceiling. *Why'd I say it?* It's the last thing I want to talk about, and I know Mea couldn't give two fucks. She's made it clear where she stands when it comes to me. Now I've gone and gotten myself drunk, let her drive me home, and I'm shooting off at the mouth about my dead mother. How much more pathetic can one dude be?

So the shock that jolts through me when she lays a hand on my arm jerks my head right up off the back of the couch. The place where she touches me is tingling with warmth. I marvel at the way the delicate contours of her hand contrast so perfectly with the tough ink marring my tanned skin.

With a single touch, she has the power to unhinge me.

Still.

When I glance up at her, her eyes meet mine, and it's like fire and gasoline. Someone just dropped a match into the pool of liquid fuel, and we're both in serious trouble. I get a little lost in her stare, because it's just so damn beautiful. Hypnotic.

"I'm sorry, Drake. I didn't know."

I nod slowly, afraid that if I move too fast she'll pull away. But she doesn't. She just sits there with an understanding in her eyes that lets me know this isn't pity.

It's compassion. And it causes a pain in my chest so fierce I use my free hand to rub the spot in agitation.

"Yeah," I answer her, my voice soft and rough. "We weren't close or anything. But it sucked, you know? Going back to a town I never wanted to see again. Remembering. It sucked."

She stares a moment longer, and then pops off the couch like a jack-in-the-box. I miss her touch immediately and pull my hand back into my lap. I'm being so stupid right now. This chick hates me.

And I don't need the grief that would come with trying to change that. I decided a long time ago to just let it be.

"Where are you going?" I ask, expecting her to say good night and flounce right back out my front door.

She pauses, headed toward the kitchen rather than the front door. Turning her head, she gives me a sexy smirk that I don't even think she means to be sexy. Goddamn. She's trouble. Always has been.

"When you've just buried your dead mother, you shouldn't have to drink alone. So I'm going to find the strongest liquor you have in your bar, and then I'm going to catch up to you." She turns on her heel and marches out.

The second I think I've got Mea Jones figured out, she throws me for a completely fucking loop. And that should make me crazy. It does. It makes me feel like the wheels are about to come off.

But when she's the one riding beside me...I kind of don't mind it.

4

Mea

I'm not sure what I'm thinking. All I know is that the sound of his voice when he told me about his mother, the shards of pain that sliced straight through the middle of it, and the anguish in his eyes pulled me toward him like a magnet. Leave it to me to be attracted to all the darkest, most tortured places inside of a guy rather than the light and the warmth. At that moment, when he blurted out what was hurting him, he was vulnerable and sad and *beautiful.*

Painfully beautiful.

So painful that it made my insides ache for him. So beautiful that it made the very core of me burn for him.

I don't know anything about Drake, not about his family or his background or his past. And this bit that just slipped out drew me closer to him than the one night that my body had been wrapped around his. I'd never wanted to *know* him before.

I don't want to know him now, do I?

I thought I knew everything I needed to know about the quiet, good-natured, ridiculously sexy ex-army Ranger. But maybe there's more to him than I ever imagined.

Of course, I'm the last person who should be delving into anyone's personal life or dark past. I have my own ghosts that haunt me every single day. Just trying to make myself better and accomplishing my dream of opening my own yoga studio is what I need to be focused on. Not my painful past. Not Drake's, either.

So why am I now digging myself in deeper? I can't answer that. It's unexplainable. But I know that at least for tonight, I need to be here for him.

I grab a bottle of tequila—go big or go home, right?—from the cabinet underneath the bar in the dining room and two shot glasses.

Drake's eyes widen when I reappear in the living room, and he leans forward with his elbows on his knees. He's completely wrecked.

I hold up the bottle. "Found some!"

With a crooked smile that jump-starts my heart in a way I don't want to analyze, he gestures toward the spot next to him. "By all means, sweetheart. Give it your best."

I plop down beside him and narrow my eyes. "Was that a challenge, Sullivan?"

His eyes twinkle with amusement. "I think I'll lose every challenge with you, Mea."

Nodding firmly, I pour myself a shot. "You're damn right about that."

Knocking it back, I relish the burn of the liquid. I'm no

stranger to tequila. Or any other type of liquor, for that matter. There have been a lot of nights in my life that I've just wanted to be numb. To forget.

But this isn't one of them. This is for Drake.

Smiling broadly, I take a second shot. "No chaser."

He raises a brow. "Impressive."

After the third shot in quick succession, I sit back and raise two fists in the air. "I think that was a good start. At this rate, I'll be where you are in no time."

He smiles, a real, genuine smile that turns his face into the purest form of light. For a second, I'm caught by it, frozen in the depth of his sunshine. How can one man be full of so much light one minute, and so much darkness in the next?

It's the first time I've realized that usually when he smiles, it's hollow. His normal smirk shines only a fraction of the light that this full-watt grin does.

What's Drake Sullivan been hiding behind that easy smirk?

As the alcohol begins to send signals of pleasant numbness throughout my arms and legs, I lean back against the cushion and pull my legs up to my chest, facing Drake. I study his profile, noting again just how attractive he is right before he turns his head and meets my gaze.

"Why are you doing this? I thought you hated me."

I squirm, discomfort settling hard in the bottom of my stomach. My tongue is looser now after three shots of tequila, and I speak without my usual guard. "I don't hate you. I just..." My voice, already set in a whisper, fades away into nothingness.

Drake leans toward me. His forehead wrinkles and his eyes go all soft in concern. He reaches out, but when I flinch away his hand drops down beside him. A flicker of understanding crosses his expression, and I close my eyes so he doesn't see any more of what I'm trying so desperately to keep behind my high stone walls.

"Mea...I didn't hurt you that night, did I?" His voice is heavy, like he's already carrying the weight of my past pain. His gaze burns into mine, like he needs the answer to this question more than he needs his next breath.

I shake my head, wanting to reassure him. "No, Drake. It was...me. It's always me."

He just keeps staring, and I need to ramble on. "I have rules, you know? When it comes to being with men. I don't do anything more than a one-night stand. So seeing you again, after...it surprised me. I didn't expect to ever see you again, much less have you so embedded in my life."

He nods slowly. But his expression stays soft as he scrutinizes my face. "Rules...about sex. Why would you need those, Mea?"

The energy that constantly keeps me moving buoys me and I pop up from the couch and begin to pace. Drake's eyes follow me, burning into my skin and burrowing deep inside me where I don't want him to go.

"I just do. Okay?" My face is defiant as I halt and face him once more. Silently, I dare him to ask me more so I can either fly out the door or completely shut down.

Instead of pushing, Drake nods and pats the couch beside him. "You promised me a drinking partner." He picks up the bottle and lines up two shots. Grabbing his, he glances at me, as if waiting.

With just another moment of hesitation, I return to the couch and grab the shot. Drake holds his up toward mine and we clink. Then we both down the liquid courage in one gulp.

An hour and two shots later, Drake's big body is sprawled out on the floor beside the couch and I'm giggling uncontrollably at his imitation of my old roommate Greta's fiancé.

"All those Navy SEALs are the same." Drake laughs, low and throaty. The sound of it does something chemical to my insides, making them melt in reaction to the sound of his voice. His forehead wrinkles as he adopts a comically stern expression, eyebrows pulling together. "I can swim three hundred miles in a hurricane! I'm a SEAL!" He punctuates his statement with a wild fist pump, and I dissolve into a fit of laughter. In my inebriated state, I roll right off the couch and onto the floor, landing directly on top of Drake. His hard, muscly form breaks my fall, strong arms instantly wrapping around me securely.

For a moment, neither of us moves. His caramel-colored eyes turn molten. My eyes drink in every detail: his full lips, jagged scar, imperfect nose. Impossible male beauty up close and personal. My insides turn to Jell-O as my limbs betray me, beginning to tremble as all of his hard places line up with my soft ones in what seems like a dream. His eyes hood as a storm begins to brew within them.

Jerking into action like a rubber band snapping back, I half-crawl, half-walk backward on my hands and feet. Kneeling a few feet away, I attempt to take a deep breath. But the alcohol working in my system prevents my head from clearing the way I need it to. I can't be taken in by all of Drake's gorgeousness and the pure sexual energy that exists between us. I'm in control here.

Who am I kidding? And what am I thinking? Sacrificing my control to cheer up Drake?

Drake sits up with slow and careful movements, eyeing me like a trainer would approach a cornered jungle cat.

"I…I think I need to go." My words come out in a rush.

Drake shakes his head. His eyes are kind but his words are firm. "Not happening, Mea. You're in no shape to drive, and I'm in no shape to take you. You can stay."

I shake my head just as firmly. "That's not a good idea."

Drake sighs. "I'll sleep on the couch. You take my bed. You don't have to worry about anything with me, Mea. You're staying."

My eyes dart from his sincere gaze to the hallway where I know his bedroom lies. I only hesitate for a second before I agree. "Okay. I'll leave first thing in the morning."

Because we're both too far gone to worry about changing sheets and other niceties, Drake walks me to his room and I fall back onto his bed. I open one eye to watch him. He stands in the doorway, both arms hanging on the doorjamb above him, his white dress shirt long since unbuttoned, the rippling abdominal muscles and toned chest ripe for the viewing. With a big swallow, I squeeze my eyes shut once more just as the room begins to spin.

"I'm gonna put some water next to the bed. Drink it."

I open my eyes and scowl. "Bossy."

He only chuckles as he walks away, and then I'm lost in the darkness as sleep pulls me into its arms.

5

Drake

When I open my eyes the next morning, my first thought is that my head fucking hurts. My next thought is a question: *Why the hell am I sleeping on my couch?* Then my brain snaps back to last night and Mea's flawless face and sex kitten little body. I groan at the tent my instant erection creates in the blanket thrown over me.

Just the thought of her. That's all it takes.

Last night is the closest I've been to Mea since the one night we spent together years ago. And just like that, my brain flashes back to the memory I've kept locked away in a secret compartment of my mind, labeled "Best Night Ever."

Her full lips quirk upward in a seductive smirk as she plants two small hands on my bare chest and shoves. Allowing her to think she could actually move me with her strength, I fall backward onto my bed. Propping myself up on my elbows I lean back and stare at this sexy goddess standing in front of me.

Without a word, she slips the straps of her tank top off of her slender shoulders. My eyes rivet to the creamy caramel skin as it's exposed. My fingers curl as I suppress the urge to rise up and touch her. It's obvious she's running this show.

In the hottest fucking striptease I've seen in my life she removes the skimpy top and the skintight jeans painted on her legs. She's so small and petite, I know my hands could wrap twice around her tiny waist. I can't wait to put that thought to the test.

When there's nothing left but a simple black bra and panty set, she walks toward me. Each step is deliberate and steady, and the sight of her confidence mixed with the portrait of her nearly naked perfection would be enough to bring me to my knees had I been standing. She stops just in front of me. She scrunches her lips to one side as she studies me.

"Strip," she orders.

Not needing to be told twice, I make quick work of removing my jeans. My shirt was dumped somewhere in the living room, and I'm not wearing underwear tonight. The evidence of the way she turns me on springs free, and her eyes glaze over in the semidarkness of the room.

I crook a finger as I slide back on the big bed, beckoning her closer. She obliges, following me. Her round tits bounce as she crawls toward me, and the first thing I do when she reaches me is unhook the clasp of her bra. Cupping her fullness in one hand, I kiss the plush skin of her breasts. She sighs, dropping her head back and straddling my lap. My ready and willing cock twitches in response as her hips move restlessly against me.

When I lift my head from her chest, her eyes meet mine. The heat in them matches the fire blazing a path through my veins as we stare each other down. She's using her eyes to send me a message, one I can't quite decipher. Finally coming to some kind of silent decision, her lips finally meet mine for the first time.

She tastes like mint chocolate with the barest hint of forever.

Forever? *I've never attached that word to a woman, never. I only met this girl today. For all I know, I'll probably never see her again. But something inside me tells me she's something to remember. Something to spend time on. She's special.*

When we pull free, we're both out of breath and she gasps as my hips jerk underneath her.

"Condom?"

Nodding, I reach over and grab a foil packet out of my nightstand drawer. I hand it to her and she tears it open with her teeth. I'm hungry for her when she grasps a firm hold of my shaft and rolls the protection on me. She leaves her hand where it is for a moment, staring down as she strokes me. A litany of curses fly from my mouth and every single muscle in my body goes rigid. Her touch is going to undo me. Never have I been in danger of coming just from one stroke of a woman's hand.

She glances up at me, and there's a mixture of awe and concern in her eyes. "You're big."

Pride fills me and I shoot her a crooked grin. "Big and all yours tonight, baby."

A look of determination changes her expression and I don't have time to take a full breath before she lifts her ass and sits down hard on my dick. We both moan at the sheer ecstasy we feel as our bodies meet for the first time. She stills, closing her eyes, and my arms come up to cup the back of her neck. My hands are so big that my thumbs caress her face.

"You. Feel. Perfect." The words are clipped and short because I'm in serious danger of busting a nut before she does, and I just can't have that.

She begins to ride me, slowly at first and then faster. Her tits jiggle, her head flies back as she goes wild. I can't handle the sensation of her moving on my hardness mixed with the way her inner muscles are grabbing a hold of me like they'll never let go. Combine that with the way she looks right now, so free and wild, wild, wild.

I just wanna bottle this moment up and save it forever.

When she's coming, I know it from the way her whole body trembles. Just as she flails in my arms I let loose a growl of possessiveness I don't even know I'm feeling. Before I know it, I have her under me and I'm driving into her. She's making little noises beneath me and I close my eyes as I come, letting out a shout. When I'm spent, I roll off of her and lay down beside her, breathing hard and heavy with exertion.

"That was…" I can't find the words. I glance over at her and see her staring straight up at the ceiling. "You okay?"

Instead of answering, she rises off the bed and starts getting dressed.

"Hey," I protest, sitting up. "You don't have to go."

She shakes her head, chocolate brown curls flying everywhere as she pulls on her jeans and then the sexy heels that stopped me in my tracks at the garage.

As she makes to leave the room, she turns back and tosses a good-

bye over her shoulder. "Thanks. That was the best oil change I've ever had. You get an A for your service."

Then she's gone. Just like that, the girl I know I'll see in my dreams for months to come disappears.

I'll always remember her name though. I'm the one who ran her check card through the machine when I rang her up at the garage today. Mea Jones. *I'll probably never see her again.*

For some reason, that thought almost brings me to the brink of devastation.

Shaking my head to clear the memory, I haul up off the couch and walk down the hallway to my bedroom. The bed is empty, but neatly made.

Mea's gone. Again.

With a heavy sigh, I head off to the shower. I have to open the garage in a little over an hour.

"Boss man!"

Hoover Stone tosses out his usual greeting as he enters the garage through an open bay door. I lift my chin in greeting and he breezes past me to put down his stuff inside the shop. I've already opened the office, turning on the two customer service computers and starting the pot of coffee that's free for customer use. My shop is on the small side, but it's open and airy and modern, with red leather chairs and a black-and-white checkered floor. I have glass-top side tables scattered around with magazines. It's a place where people can be comfortable kicking back while they wait for their car to be serviced. I even added free Wi-Fi last year.

The garage is big, with eight bays. I have four full-time mechanics working, but the way business is going I'll probably have to hire one more by summer. I'm getting my station ready, organizing the tools I'll need today, when Hoover returns along with Javier Sosa and Will Reeves.

Dare used to have one of the full-time mechanics positions here, too. I hired him when he first moved to town, knowing he'd need a place to work while he got his feet under him. Leaving the army is always an adjustment process, and helping guys out when they're first discharged is a passion of mine. I'm proud to say that all the guys working in my shop, with the exception of Will, are veterans. Will was still just a kid when I hired him, a teenager with no one at home who gave a shit about him. He was into cars, which I discovered when I found him outside a restaurant one night trying to boost mine. Instead of another charge on his record, I gave him a job. He never looked sideways at a car again, and now, at twenty-three, he's a damn good mechanic and my shop manager.

Now Dare's gone, having found his calling as a security specialist for a big-time firm in Wilmington. Our friend Greta, who used to live with Dare's fiancée Berkeley and Mea, just happens to be the daughter of the man who owns that security firm. The fact that my friends are slowly pairing off, settling down, starting their families…it's not lost on me. I see it happening.

And yeah, maybe sometimes I wonder if it'll ever happen for me.

The guys are all kidding around with each other as they walk to their own tool stations and start getting ready for the day. Will stops beside me and leans against my black metal cabinet with an iPad in his hands.

"What's the day look like?" I ask him, shoving my tool drawer shut.

Will shrugs one shoulder and glances up at me. "Pretty full. Appointments back-to-back till one, and then another round starting at three. I'm guessing we'll have more than a few walk-ins too for oil changes and tire rotations."

My glance strays longingly toward the last bay, where my new baby stands waiting for me to find the time for her.

Will grins. "She's beautiful."

I grunt my agreement.

"She" is a run-down Yamaha XS 650 sport motorcycle with plenty of chrome and black leather. Restoration is really more Dare's thing, and he's been helping me get her back into riding shape. But I like to tinker around with her during my down-time at the shop. Today it looks like I might not have the chance.

"I'll get to her if I can." I tear my eyes away from the bike.

Putting the tablet down by his side, Will scrutinizes me. His bushy blond brows furrow as he frowns. "You okay, boss? Looking rough today."

I snort. "Thanks, Reeves. Guess I didn't get enough beauty rest last night."

I popped three aspirin this morning for the raging bitch of a headache I woke up with, but I still feel like shit. Snapshots of my mom's funeral chase each other through my brain, and I wince. The thought comes to me from nowhere as I fight to bury the memories where they should be. Deep down in the darkness where I put everything bad.

Would she be dead right now if I had done more? If I had come home to check on her? Sent her to rehab? Made her move in with me here in Lone Sands?

They were all ideas that had crossed my mind in the past. But my mom was an addict. And as I kid, I couldn't force her to get help. I just had to watch as she succumbed to bender after bender. I had to keep myself clean, fed, and clothed when she was gone for days at a time with some dude she barely knew, or when she was passed out cold on her bathroom floor.

She was my mom and I loved her, but she put me through hell growing up. And I wonder now if maybe that's the reason I didn't try harder to save her once I was an adult. When it's all said and done, I'm a big dude. I could have forced her to come with me, made her get help.

I check back into the conversation with Will halfway through one of his sentences. "…arrived yesterday. All we gotta do is put 'em together."

I squeeze my eyes shut for a minute, trying to get my stuff together. I have a business to run. There's no time for looking backward. "Put what together?"

Will shakes his head at me. "Man…whatever family stuff you had going on during your personal leave must have really shook you up. I said the new rolling docks for the garage floor."

I nod and start moving toward the shop. "Yeah, we'll get to it. I'm heading to the office to crack down on some invoices and accounting. Come get me if you get slammed or if you have a problem."

He salutes me. "Roger that."

With a breath of relief, I retreat to my office in the very back of the shop. I move down the bright, white-tiled hallway past his and hers restrooms. Just before the exit door at the end of the hallway, I turn right and close the red office door behind me and face my black polished desk and matching leather chair. Sinking into it, I drop my head in my hands and just take a minute to get my bearings. I already can't wait to head straight to See Food tonight when I'm done here.

I need a stiff drink. I just need to make it through to another day.

At this moment, I don't really care how I make that happen.

6

Mea

From my place against the wall just outside the kitchen, I stare with stupid disbelief. Drake's big body is hunkered over the bar in front of a tumbler.

He's dressed more like himself today in faded jeans tucked into black combat boots. His gray tee sports a vintage muscle car on the front. His black leather jacket is hanging over the back of his stool. I breathe an unbidden sigh of relief when I notice there's no bimbo parked next to him tonight.

He's alone.

And his gaze has been focused on his drink for the last hour I've been watching him.

Lenny slides him a second glass of whatever he's drinking, and she raises her eyebrow at me. I know her silent question is: *What gives with him?*

But I'm not Drake Sullivan's keeper. I helped him out last

night because I didn't want the idiot to drown in the ocean on his way home. But two nights in a row?

I'm not the one who's going to listen to his sad story every night.

With that thought comes a niggling sensation of guilt. Drake is obviously hurting. He lost his mom this week. I have no idea whether they were close, but it seems to be dragging him down. He might even be drowning in his mourning.

I know how tough the guy is. He'll get through this. I mean, he's been to war. He served as a Special Forces soldier for heaven's sake. He'll make it through the loss of his mother.

But my feet are drawing me forward without my permission until I'm standing beside his stool.

I pull out the one beside him and climb up into the tall seat.

Glancing up, Drake's honeyed eyes brighten. "You again."

Narrowing my eyes, I snap back. "Shouldn't I be saying that to you? Two nights in a row at the bar, Drake?"

But even as I'm fussing at him, the electricity he awakens in me starts to buzz all along my skin. It draws me in, making me lean forward so that I inhale the smoky, spicy scent that is Drake. He smells like woodsy masculine soap and the ocean. There's also the faintest scent of motor oil clinging to him like fog to the sea.

I breathe him in and I'm instantly intoxicated. It evokes all kinds of memories from that night three years ago that I've tried my damnedest to erase from my mind.

I don't want to forget that night because it wasn't the greatest sex I've ever had. It was definitely that. I experienced a physical connection with Drake I never had before, and never have since.

But then…it all fell apart. I left that night because I had to. Otherwise I would have lost myself in front of a stranger, and that's something I would never allow to happen.

"So," comments Drake. "Interesting coincidence. That night, three years ago?"

Oh my God, does he read minds, too?

"…You know, the one where you disappeared on me? I kinda had déjà vu this morning."

I sucked the corner of my bottom lip in between my teeth, a habit I can't help, and notice his eyes zero in on my lips. I immediately stop biting it and thank the good Lord for my bronze skin tone. Maybe he can't see the blush I am most definitely feeling.

Shrugging it off, I twirl a strand of curly hair around my index finger and turn around on my stool so I'm facing away from the bar.

"Nothing personal, Sullivan. I don't do morning-afters."

He nods, swirling his drink around in the glass. "Point taken. Do you do go-out-to-dinners?" He looks up from his drink and looks me straight in the eye. I'm stranded there in his gaze, held by the intensity and sincerity in those warm, warm eyes.

I'm caught so off guard, I start to stammer. "Um, what? Wait—what? Uh…"

Chuckling, he leans in until his lips brush gently against my ear. The shock of the slight touch sends a jolt of heat through me, and I shiver visibly.

Drake notices my reaction and grunts, nuzzling his nose against the shell of my ear. "You smell like heaven. Just dinner, Mea. Say yes."

My pulse is pounding in my ears, my heart hammering against my ribs like a caged animal fighting to be free. Why does he have this effect on me? No guy ever has this effect on me. I'm always completely in control when it comes to the opposite sex. But with Drake, that control flies right out the window whenever he's around. And when he gets close…holy hell frozen over. I'm a fucking mess quivering before him.

He pulls away but not far, and his stare burns as I try hard to remember how to breathe. *What is he asking me?* For a date? I don't date!

"Drake…"

He shakes his head slowly from side to side. "Stop thinking, Mea. Just say yes. Dinner…that's it."

"I need to get back to my tables." The words fly out of my mouth and I practically leap off my stool to hurry back to work.

Safely back in the kitchen, I lean against the wall and try to control my breathing once more. He's under my skin, somehow. I thought I flushed him out of my system, but there he is again, wreaking havoc on my body and my emotions. And when will it end?

Maybe if I just give in to him, go to dinner one time, that'll be the end of it. I don't have to touch him. I don't have to let him touch me. Just dinner.

"Order up!" Boozer barks at me from the food window. Grabbing ahold of the two plates and placing them on a tray with two drinks, I back out of the kitchen. As I breeze past Drake, I mutter my answer.

"Yes."

He glances up, surprise and a genuine grin lighting up his face. *God, he's beautiful.*

And I'm in deep shit if I can't learn to control myself around him.

By last call, Drake is in much better shape than he was the night before. Sipping on three drinks throughout the night wasn't nearly enough to intoxicate his big, strong frame, and with a cocky grin on his face, he watches me flit around, closing out tables. A grin I'm so, so tempted to slap right off of him.

My last table is full of a group of rowdy guys clearly out for some boys' night fun. Throughout the night they became rowdier and more annoying, but despite my size I'm always able to handle myself. Anything else is unacceptable, and I make sure to stay in control at all times. I move around the table, smiling at the guys while handing out checks as their flirty banter reaches my ears. Stopping beside one particularly mouthy member of the group to put down his check, I'm frozen in place when he grabs my wrist and pulls me onto his lap.

Quicker than I know what's happening, I'm thrust back into a time I never, ever want to remember.

The dinner table is quiet as usual. The lamp that hangs overhead gives the only light source in the room. Mikah shovels food in his mouth like it's his first meal of the day. But I can't eat. I stir the green beans around on my plate without putting any in my mouth. I keep glancing at Mama. I scrutinize her out of the corner of my eye, trying so hard to remember the last time I heard the sound of her voice. She prepared this dinner, but she did it like a robot.

I remember when it first started. When pieces of her started to drop off and float into the cold Kentucky wind. My dad would snap at her, trying to force her back into this day and this time. But she never stayed long. Then he started taking her to doctors. She would come home with medication after medication until finally a psychiatrist was able to make a firm diagnosis: dysthymia. A constant, withering form of depression that no medication could stave off for very long. She completely withdrew from daily activities. My father threatened her, so she would continue to keep the house. But the fun-loving, vibrant woman I knew as my mother? She was gone.

I can very vaguely remember a time of smiling photos. Of her attending my dance recitals. Of our faces pressed together, her wild curls identical to mine. My mixed heritage was sometimes a sore spot for me growing up in Kentucky, and when I came home in tears because someone had made fun of my skin color or my name or the fact that I had a black mama and a Spanish daddy, she knew just how to comfort me. Chocolate chip cookies and love was all she said I needed. She was the one who taught me to hold my head high and be proud of who I am.

Looking at her now, it's hard to keep hold of those memories. I'm sure they're all but nonexistent for poor Mikah. He's only two years younger than me, but he was so little when she began to disappear. He might never remember her the way she was.

"Eyes on your plate!" My father's slightly accented English broke me from my reverie and I snapped my eyes back to my plate.

"Eat!" he barks. "Your mother worked hard to prepare this dinner. Eat it. Now."

My stomach is churning with turmoil, but I obediently stuff a bite of chicken and rice into my mouth. Mama doesn't move at all, just stares off into a distance that the rest of us can't see. But I can feel his eyes on me.

My father.

My room, the very last one in the back of the house, is utterly black at night. But at twelve years old I have no reason to be scared of the dark. My room is my safe haven. It always has been.

My bed is the place I crawl into when the loss of my mama is too much. My pillows catch my tears. My blankets protect me from the pain. I am completely at ease and safe in my room, the way a bear cub is secure and protected in its cave.

I pictured Mikah, most likely fast asleep in his own cave. At night, I didn't have to worry about my little brother. During the day, he got into fights at school. He's hotheaded and temperamental, and suffers from ADHD. I'm his voice of reason. I'm the person he comes to when he feels alone. Which is a lot of the time. Daddy is too wrapped up with Mama and her medications to worry too much about us. Which is good, because when he is worried about us it's usually to tear us a new one when we've done something wrong. Or when we've done something he deems wrong, even though we're just doing what other kids do.

I sigh, content in my safe haven, turning over in my warm, comfy bed as my eyes drift closed.

What was that? A soft click causes me to peek over my shoulder. A sliver of light slices through the darkness in my bedroom as the door slowly opens. But my bedroom door doesn't open at night. My little cave stays warm and dark, and that's the way I like it. That's what I've come to expect.

The door closes again and I sigh in relief. Daddy must have been checking on me. Or maybe it was Mama?

Like a lifeline, hope floods me as I picture my mama opening my bedroom door to make sure I'm safe and cozy in my bed. The way all mamas do for their children at night.

"I know you're not asleep."

Daddy's voice, close to my ear. Only it's different than usual. Heavier, full of something dark and moody.

I'm startled as I turn over again and blink up at him in surprise. "Daddy? What do you need?"

He kneels down beside my bed and leans on his elbows, staring at me. All I can see in the darkness is the glow of his eyes. It's dark to make out his expression, so I struggle to understand what's happening here. Why is he in my room?

When he speaks again, his breath coasts over the front of my face. It's warm and smells sour. I don't know what that smell is, but it's something I have never smelled before.

"You know I wouldn't have to be here if your mother were well. She's gone, you know. And it's because of you and your good-for-nothing brother."

Tears immediately spring to my eyes. But I fight them back, because nothing ever gets done if you cry about it. My mama taught me that. "That's not true. Mama is sick."

He swipes a hand over his eyes, and I wonder if my big, strong daddy is crying. Surely that's not possible. I've never, ever seen him shed a tear. But I understand that even through his meanness, he *must be going through a hard time the same as Mikah and me.*

"No, Mea. If it weren't for the stress of raising two kids, she would have been able to fight it. As it is, she can't be my wife anymore. Not in all the ways I need her to be. Do you know what that means?"

I shake my head, the large lump forming in my throat making it impossible to speak. Then I remember that he probably can't see the motion, so I release a strangled, "No."

A noise escapes him. It sounds like a sob, and it rips me apart inside. My daddy is hurting. The same way Mikah and I are hurting.

"What can I do, Daddy?"

Then I feel his hands on me. They are rough and fumbling, and all of my muscles go rigid at the same time my blood turns to ice in my veins.

His next words chill me from the inside out. "You can take her place. I need this. Do you understand?"

On the inside, I'm screaming as he rises from his knees and climbs onto my bed. But on the outside, I can't make a single sound. I've been struck mute. God, how I wish I was struck unconscious as well.

My eyes are so wide and my breathing so harsh and fast. I shake my head from side to side, but he ignores me. The pain and the shame fight for the top spot in my heart. He thinks he needs this. But does he know he's shattering me into little, irreparable pieces?

After tonight, my room will never be my safe haven again.

When I snap back to the here and now I'm still on the drunk Neanderthal's lap and he's pulling me back against his chest. His paws are all over me, and I'm in serious danger of hyperventilating. I try to gather my composure, because this isn't me. I'm not weak. I am in control.

I am in control.

But then why do I feel so utterly out of control? Dizziness and nausea settle in my belly at the same time, and without even thinking twice about it, I look toward the bar, where I know Drake is sitting.

He's turned all the way around in his stool, his eyes narrowed and focused on me. As soon as I meet his gaze, something intense and taut passes between us. I swear he reads the expression in my eyes because he's up and by my side faster than should be humanly possible.

Damn, the guy is *big*, but he's also *fast*.

I'm off the drunk guy's lap and in Drake's arms before anyone can say a word. He squeezes me to his side and looks down at me, his eyes gentle and soft.

"You okay?"

I'm still in kind of a frenzy and my brain isn't working right. All I want to do is get away. Get a breath of fresh air. But instead, I drop my head against his chest and snuggle in closer.

I hear him speaking, his voice low and rumbling. Risking a peek through the crook of his arm I see the table full of good-timers has gone silent as they stare at the hulk that's just become my savior. On his best day, Drake is a scary man. He's big and intimidating, and it's not even the scar on his face or the tattoos lining his arms that tell a would-be opponent to stay away. It's the air he carries with him. Like he's seen plenty of death and even been the cause of it more than once. Danger rolls off of him in droves when he's not being the big teddy bear our friends all know and love.

"I swear to God, if she wasn't under my arm right now, I'd make you pay for touching her." His voice is low and menacing and directed at the man who pulled me onto his lap. "But as it is, I'm going to put her first. Pay your tab and get the fuck out. Before I change my mind."

I hear the scraping of several chairs, and by the time I look up again the table is empty. Then Drake turns his full attention on me. His eyes are searching, his hands softly caressing my face as he bends down to search my eyes. "Want to get some air?"

I nod, thankful he knows what I need and that I don't have to say it. Without another word he's towing me beside him out the front door and I welcome the cold January air as it hits my face.

And I have to admit it to myself.

Drake Sullivan just became more than a past mistake.

7

Drake

I wouldn't have stepped in unless I knew she needed me to. I know Mea well enough to know that she's nothing if not damn independent. She doesn't want some guy swooping in to save her. Ever. So I watched, with itching palms, as that bastard pulled her without her permission into his lap. I waited for her to get control of the situation. And then it seemed like she blacked out or something. Like she wasn't even there in the moment. I don't know what she was thinking about, but when she came back to herself she looked for me.

She looked for me.

And I needed no more motivation than that to eat up the space between us and pull her into my arms. When it comes to Mea, some sort of caveman instinct kicks in. I know she's tough and she wears a coat of armor most of the time, but something tells me it's a front. There's more going on in that woman's head than anyone knows.

She was so shaken up after that, Lenny told her to go home and relax. Len also sent me a pointed look that told me not to let Mea out of my sight until I was sure she's okay. So that's how she ended up in the Challenger beside me.

"Where can I take you?" I glance sideways at her as I rev the big engine and pull out of See Food's gravel lot.

She looks small, even smaller than usual, huddled in the passenger seat of my car. She's staring out her window, her hands clasped in her lap. She looks tired, so tired that even her normally defiant curls seem limp and spent.

"Mea?"

She looks at me, and the expression in her eyes is hollow and wrung out. I reach over to take her hand in mine without another thought. Hers is cold, but her fingers curl around mine. The simple touch does something to me. It kick-starts my pulse, sending it thumping in my chest. It causes my stomach muscles to clench and my merely interested cock to strain against my jeans.

But the look in her eyes? That carves out a piece of my heart.

I answer my own question. "You're coming back to my place."

She just nods, her eyes turning back toward the window.

After the quick ride to my house, I pull into the drive and hop out. When I open Mea's door for her, she startles.

Had that asshole done something else to scare her so badly? I can't fathom that; he was just some drunk dipshit. I know Mea well enough to know that some guy manhandling her a little bit in a bar wouldn't rattle her this much. I'm pretty surprised she didn't deck the dude herself. That's just the kind of girl she is. A tough girl.

But tonight she was stuck. She was lodged somewhere between terrified and overwhelmed, and she couldn't pull herself out. What could have made her react that way?

We walk silently into the house and I close the door behind Mea. She stands there in tight black jeans with black motorcycle boots, a sparkly red sweater, and a black leather jacket. She's hotter than an August afternoon, but all I want to do right now is make her feel safe.

"Tired? Hungry?" I ask.

She shakes her head, crossing her arms over her chest. The gesture doesn't seem sassy or surly like the usual Mea, though. It's more like she's closing herself in, protecting herself. She curls inward, something I've never seen her do except for when she was leaving me the night I met her.

"I'm just…" She sighs, trailing off.

Without another word, I lead her back toward my bedroom. As I'm turning down the covers on my bed, I glance at her and see she's still standing in the doorway.

"I'll get you something to sleep in." My voice is gruffer than I want it to be. I just can't stand seeing her like this. It hurts.

"I'm…I'm okay you know, Drake." When I look at her she lifts her chin the slightest bit, and the determined gleam is back in her eyes. I almost sigh with relief until I see that her hands are still trembling. "I always am."

I walk slowly forward until I'm standing right in front of her. She holds her ground beside the bed. I take both of her shaking hands in my own and hold them close to my heart. I don't talk until those thick-lashed dark brown eyes are staring into mine.

Inside them flecks of emerald green are swimming in the chocolate.

Deep, deep, deep.

Deep enough to drown in.

"No, you're not okay. And it's fine for you not to be okay sometimes, you know? I know how strong you are…we all do. It's not something you have to prove. Not with me."

She struggles. I can see the battle happening within her. It's clear in the way she tenses her jaw, in the way her expression turns pleading and needy, in the way her fingers squeeze mine. She's drawing me in at the exact same time that she's pushing me away. I wish I could read her struggle. I wish it were a book I could open and devour, page by page. So I could understand. So I could help.

When I'm with her, I forget to drown in my own pain and failure. I just want to absorb hers.

She closes her eyes, and the connection is broken. Dropping her hands, she wrings them together and takes a step back. She falls onto the bed. Glancing around the room, toward the floor, anywhere but at me, she whispers.

"I don't want to kick you out of your bed again."

I grunt. "Doesn't matter. It's yours if you need it."

She nods, and then looks directly at me. "Thank you, Drake. For…all of it."

Nodding, I turn and leave her alone in my bed.

Again.

A scream cuts through my sleep and I bolt upright on the couch. I'm instantly completely alert, my eyes searching the darkness of my living room. My back is ramrod straight, my bare feet planted on the carpet. *The fuck?*

And then I remember Mea.

Another scream slices me up, and I'm up and in the bedroom in seconds. In the doorway, I reach out to the dresser and flick on a low light. It's enough for me to assess the situation in a glance.

Mea, tangled up in sheets, is thrashing in the bed. She's asleep, but her breathing is coming in gasps and she's sobbing.

"No, no, no!" Her voice is a sound that I'll never forget. She's terrified—no, she's *horrified*. She's fighting off an invisible attacker with her hands and her legs and even her teeth are gnashing in her mouth. My heart sinks to the floor, and something inside me cracks wide open.

I cross the room and climb onto the bed. I wrap my arms around this tiny but strong, trembling girl. From behind, I stroke her wild curls and wipe the tears from her face. And I squeeze her to my chest until she stops rioting in the sheets. Her body arches at first, fighting against my hold, until I use my voice. I don't recognize it; it's gravelly and raw, but it's all I have.

"Mea. Shhh…baby. Shhh. You're safe. I got you."

I say the soothing words over and over again until she goes rigid in my arms. And then she sags into me completely, her back flush against my front, and her tears are no longer sobs. She's just crying quietly.

"Oh, baby girl…*fuck*. Who hurt you?" The rasp in my voice is heavy with pain. Her pain, my pain. I don't even know the difference anymore. She wraps both hands around my forearms, holding on to me.

And I just hold her while she cries.

At some point, I bury my face in her hair. I inhale, smelling something fruity and so utterly feminine it makes me instantly hard. But I ignore my body, because I can't get the sound of her screams out of my head.

I don't know how long we stay like that. Her breathing evens out, her chest rising and falling underneath my arms. I refuse to let her go.

"Drake?" Her voice is small. Normally, everything about Mea is larger than life. But right here, in this moment, she's miniature.

"I'm right here."

She inhales. It's a long, deep, shuddering sigh that moves her entire body.

I have questions. So many fucking questions. But somehow I know she's in no way ready to answer them. So I just ask one.

"Who knows, Mea?"

I need to know that there's someone in her life that she can count on with this. Someone she can turn to, talk to while she's falling apart.

"I…I don't usually have the night terrors anymore. But after the guy in the restaurant tonight…I just, I know that's why."

I'm relentless, because I need to know this more than I need my next meal. "Who knows, Mea?"

Who have you told about what happened to you?

"My brother, Mikah. That's all."

I blow out a harsh breath. That's not good enough. She needs to depend on someone in her inner circle. I can't believe she's never trusted her best friends with it. But then again…I went alone when I went back to Georgia. Sometimes the moments you lived alone, you want to keep that way. They're too utterly private and monstrous to lay at anyone else's feet.

But she can lay it on me. I can take it.

I curse softly under my breath. And then my lips meet her neck, because they need to be touching her. I keep my hands still, but I press soft kisses against her even softer skin. Over and over again.

She shudders against me. And her hands squeeze me tighter.

"You need to trust someone, Mea."

She nods, her soft curls tickling my chin. "I...can't. Not with this."

A few minutes tick by, and when I speak again, my lips are against her skin. "When you're ready...you can trust me. With anything."

She doesn't answer, and I don't know if that means she's declining my offer or whether she just isn't ready. Either way, I'm not giving up on her. Because she needs me, whether she knows it or not. She needs *someone*.

When her breathing evens out again this time, I know she's asleep. I stay awake a little bit longer, remembering. Remembering what she sounded like, what she looked like thrashing in covers tangled by her fear. It's a sight I never want to see again. But somehow, I know her pain isn't over. Just like mine.

I fall asleep to the sound of her breaths, the feel of her heartbeat, and the sweet smell of her hair.

8

Mea

When my eyes blink open, I think I must have accidentally fallen asleep underneath a bear. I'm warm, much warmer than I usually am when I sleep, and the light is so dim it could be called cave-like. I'm torn between wanting to snuggle in deeper and hibernate and wanting to leap up in fear of the unknown.

Then the bear grunts in its sleep and pulls me tighter, and I realize instantly what must have happened.

Drake crawled into bed with me during the night.

Why would he do that? *Oh…*

Last night's horror show flashes through my mind like a film, reel after reel of mortifying moments from the night before. I can't believe I had a night terror while sleeping in Drake's bed. I actually woke him up…he must think I'm a complete whack job.

Since when do you care what anybody thinks of you?

Behind me, Drake's rock-hard body is completely molded to mine. I can't remember the last time I slept next to a man.

Wait...that's because it's *never* happened. As something warm and gooey begins to spread through my chest, something molten and fiery makes wetness pool between my legs. Sucking in a sharp breath, I squirm and twitch.

It's not that I'm a stranger to sexual attraction. I've never shied away from bringing a guy home from the bar if there's a connection. I decided a long time ago that the way my father marked me wouldn't be the thing that ruined me. I made sure, after years of cowering in fear of the man and then of the memories of him, that I was going to take control of the part of me that he stole.

I am in control.

So why, with every inch of Drake pressed so firmly against every inch of me, do I feel so utterly out of control?

I can't see his face, but the warm puffs of breath skate across my neck as he breathes. He's still sleeping. But sleep doesn't stop his body from reacting to mine. The evidence of his awareness is very blatant against my back, and all I want to do is push my hips backward to meet his.

In a corner of my mind, I'm terrified about giving in to this pull I can't ignore with Drake. It's everywhere all at once; it's in my mind and my body and my soul. It lives in me. But something happened the first time we had sex that sent me running, and my head tells me not to ever let it happen again. Not to get that close. With anyone.

I sigh as Drake's hand caresses my stomach where the shirt he loaned me has ridden up. The simple touch sends a wild rush of sensation along my skin. My breathing becomes heavier, because I can't help it. This is a purely physical reaction to this particular man's proximity. Never have I wanted to just give myself over to a guy. But everything about Drake right now is surrounding me. His manly smell, his strong, hard body. In contrast, his hands are gentle where they touch me.

I know he's awake when his lips meet the soft skin just below my ear. A needy moan escapes me, matching the needy ache between my thighs. My hips begin to move on their own, restless.

Restless.

Restless.

Behind me, Drake tries to suppress a groan. He does a shit job of it.

"Mea, sweetheart. If you want me to be a gentleman this morning, then you need to stop wiggling around against my dick."

His voice is rough, raw, and so delectable I want to swallow every word he says. I want to lick my way around his perfect lips before diving deep into his mouth to taste him.

Something is seriously wrong with me. I've officially lost my everloving mind.

With a heavy breath, I nod. Speaking right now isn't an option.

With one quick movement, Drake flips me onto my back so that he can look me in the eyes.

His assessment is blazing. His beautiful honeyed gaze roams from my half-lidded eyes to the pert peaks of my nipples showing through the thin tee, to my bare legs. I'm still having trouble catching my breath, and Drake's eyes zero in on my face once more.

Slowly, his hand, resting on my hip, slides up my body. When he grazes the side of my bare breast, the shirt hitching up with his hand, I bite my bottom lip to avoid crying out. And *dammit* I can't keep my restless hips still.

Drake's eyes widen. "Are you needy, sweetheart?" He scoots closer, his nose caressing the skin of my throat. I throw my head back and clench the sheets with my fingertips as his hot, wet tongue licks my neck. When he pulls back again, his gaze is pure hunger.

"Do you...do you need me to take care of you, baby?"

I bite my lip again.

Drake pulls away. "Mea. I'm not going to do anything that might hurt you. If there's something you need from me, you *need to ask.*"

I suck in a breath. I might burn up from the inside out if some part of him isn't touching some part of me in the next few seconds.

But when I look into his eyes, seeing the evidence of his own need and weighing that against the obvious way I'm feeling...I can't deny it. Not this time.

"Drake..." My voice is nothing but a whisper. "I need you."

A slew of curses fly from his mouth as he stares into my eyes. Seeing what he wants, his hands make quick work of removing the shirt I'm wearing. Underneath, there's nothing but black satin boy shorts.

"Fuuuuck. I've been sleeping beside you all night, and you were wearing this? I'm a fucking idiot."

I send him a small smile. "Now you know."

He nods, dipping his head low to trace a path with his tongue around the fullest part of my breast. I push toward him, helping him aim for the part I really want him to focus on. When he pulls one pebbled nipple into his mouth, I gasp. The pleasure is intense and immediate. He settles there with his mouth so hot against my skin, nibbling and sucking like he missed his last meal. When he's completely worked over one breast, he just moves on to the next. Drake is a man who used to run missions for a living. And it seems that right now, his mission involves me and driving me as insane as he can.

For me, sex has always been about achieving the greatest high possible in the shortest amount of time. I've never wanted to spend time with a guy before. And I've never been with a man who wants to spend time making me feel good. I've never allowed it to be that way.

Without me even realizing it, I've turned to completely face him. My hands are rubbing at the top of his head, the sides of his face, cupping him and pulling him closer. I want everything he's giving me times ten. My body is screaming for more.

More, more, more.

With his mouth still teasing, licking, tasting my breasts, Drake's hand begins a descent, smoothing softly against the skin of my chest and my belly. The ache between my legs grows unbearable. Pausing to look up at me, Drake smirks.

"I know what you need, Mea."

Thank God, because I'm not sure how much more of this teasing I can take.

His palm rests flat against my pelvis bone while his fingers drift downward, rubbing along my slick folds.

He groans. "So wet. So ready."

When his middle finger finds my throbbing clit, I think I drool a little as a moan finds its way out of my throat. He circles the sensitive spot with his finger, teasing it, loving it. Then he dips two fingers inside of me, which makes me cry out and him exhale a curse.

"Drake." My voice has dropped to a needy whisper. I don't know how to tell him what I need, but I need it so bad it hurts.

He looks up at me. "I want to taste you. Can I eat you, Mea?"

Oh, God. Dirty words falling from Drake's mouth should be illegal. I buck my hips in response. "Please."

Dragging my panties down my hips, he follows them, kissing a trail over my stomach and hip bones as he goes. He throws my underwear over his shoulder and settles himself between my legs, placing both of them over his huge, broad, bare shoulders. All my muscles tense in anticipation, and the first swipe of his hot tongue on my even hotter flesh nearly sends me into overdrive.

"God. You taste so goddamn good."

His words alone could make me come. I'm clenching, my muscles vibrating frantically as my body struggles to find a release. He allows his tongue to dip inside of me and then brings it back to my clit, making tiny circles that send sparks of fire through my core. I want to explode. No, I *need* to explode.

But I also want to push Drake away. Falling apart like this, completely exposed to him, will make me the most vulnerable I've been since...

No, I can't do it. I try to pull away.

Drake holds me steady, lifting his head. He reads the expression in my eyes.

"Mea…" His voice is soft, and he keeps his eyes locked on mine. "I will never hurt you. Ever. Just wanna please you, baby. Let me. You're safe with me."

I exhale, slowly lying back against the pillows and closing my eyes.

"Open 'em, sweetheart. See me. See me."

I do what he says, meeting his fiery gaze. There's nothing threatening in his eyes. All I can see there is need, and sweetness.

He won't hurt me. I'm in control.

I cry out as I burst. Drake catches each and every piece of me that comes apart. Some are physical, and he laps me up with his tongue.

But some of the pieces are so much more. And he's right there to catch those, too.

Drake Sullivan catches all of me when I fall, and I've never trusted anyone to do that before. Something in me shifts, changes, breaks, and is reconfigured.

Drake pulls me into his arms and holds me as I tremble, coming down from a high I never even knew was possible. His arms are strong and sure. Strong enough to catch me. Safe enough to keep me warm when I should be freezing, out in the cold and alone.

9

Drake

I fumble through my brain, trying to come up with the logistics behind what's happening right now. Mea is lying against me, her arm slung across my chest while her legs are all tangled up with mine. She's bare. Her skin shines in the now-bright light of day, its toasted caramel color in direct contrast to the nearly black of her wild, wild curls splayed out on the pillow.

She's gorgeous.

The most beautiful thing I've ever seen. The time three years ago we spent together definitely marked me, more so after she left without a word and treated me with cool indifference ever since. But this Mea? This Mea that I know intimately, that I've spent time with outside the bedroom, that I've seen vulnerable and tender?

This Mea blows my fucking mind. She changes every game that's ever been played. She can end me. And I welcome it.

I rub my hand against her bare arm, gently drawing a path

from shoulder to wrist. The sunlight filtering in through the window tells me it's late morning. Which means the time we spent together in the early morning was about six hours ago.

Her skin under my rough, calloused hands is like satin. I didn't know it was possible for skin to be this fucking soft. It melts more than just my hands. Something inside my chest is turning soft, too.

She stirs. Either I woke her up with my constant need to touch her, or the bright light streaming in is the culprit. Either way, she turns her head and bats thick black lashes at me. Her eyes are actually sparkling in the light, and it seems like the deepness inside them goes on for miles.

"Hi." My voice is sandpaper.

Her smile is crooked and tiny. "Well, this is a first."

I quirk an eyebrow. *Is she talking about waking up in my bed? Because she's done that before.*

She's completely unfazed by all of the things that freak girls out when they wake up for the first time next to a guy. She isn't covering her mouth, not that I care about morning breath when she's this sexy lying beside me. She doesn't reach up to check her hair, or try to leap out of bed and apply makeup before I see her face. No, not Mea. She's not shy. Never has been.

"My first time waking up in bed with a man." Her voice is nonchalant, but her eyes tell a deeper story. There's nothing shallow about this girl. No matter how light and carefree she makes herself seem, there's always miles of depth beneath the surface.

Miles, miles, miles.

It could take a lifetime to get to the bottom of it all.

"So how does it feel?" I ask. My voice is cautious, because the answer might not be what I want to hear.

She smiles and stretches. That's when I notice the tiny dimple that dents the top of her left cheek. It's adorable.

"It feels...different." A shadow crosses her expression, and as she finishes stretching the sheet falls away from her naked breasts. She doesn't bother to cover herself back up. I like that.

"Is it something you want to repeat?" I don't realize I'm holding my breath waiting for her answer until my lungs start to burn. I can't believe I care this much. Mea has put me through the wringer since we met. But something deep inside tells me I can handle more. When it comes to her, I can always handle more.

She meets my gaze with a steady one of her own. "It might be, Sullivan. But I'm not going to be like other girls; I don't do clingy. I have a lot of my own shit to worry about. Like saving money so I can open the space I plan to rent on the Upper End as my own yoga studio. It's all...it's all I have."

Her voice drops to a whisper at the last, and my chest constricts. I cup the side of her face. "I can handle that. I don't do clingy, either. And I also have my own shit to worry about." *To drown in.*

She nods as she sits up, taking the sheet with her. Her tiny movement somehow seems big in my bedroom, her curls whirling around her like an unseen wind is tossing them around. Wild.

Again, I'm reminded of a tornado. She could suck me in if she really wanted to. But where will I end up when she spits me back out again?

"Cool." She bends down to grab her clothes and begins to dress. "Then we keep this casual. And our friends don't need to know anything. I don't want to steal any attention away from Berkeley while she's in the home stretch for the wedding."

I nod, stretching my arms above my head. They reach the headboard. "Sounds good to me."

She pulls on her black combat boots, stamping each foot before tying up the laces. "Okay then. Can you take me home?"

I rise from the bed, taking note when her eyes roam hungrily over my naked body. I'm pretty sure that whenever she's in the room, my cock will jump to action, and now is no different. My soldier stands at attention, and her eyes stray to my very blatant erection.

I watch her with amusement on my face. Damn, I could get used to her staring at me like she wants to eat me for breakfast.

Because that's exactly how I stare at her.

"I teach…" She trails off as I bend over to grab my jeans.

"Yeah?"

She clears her throat. "I teach yoga at the gym at noon. I have to get going."

I dress quickly, smirking at her. "Then let's get you to work on time."

I haul ass straight to the garage after dropping Mea off at the grill to get her car, then following her to her place. It was the first time I'd seen where she'd been living ever since Greta, her old roomie, moved into her fiancé's house. Mea couldn't swing the rent at her old place without Greta, so she'd moved into a tiny studio that was really just the upstairs in someone's cottage. She had her own walk-up entrance, though, so it wasn't too bad on privacy. But when I stood at the door and glanced in, something tweaked me. Her place is tiny. Too tiny. And sparse. She doesn't have much, and I know that every spare penny she makes is going toward opening her own business. But *damn*. She needs more.

It's still bouncing around in my mind when I walk into the shop. On the back wall, my own name in big, red block letters greets me. The sight usually makes me smile, but I'm too bogged down in my thoughts to see it today. DRAKE'S AUTOMOTIVE. My pride and joy.

Will saunters over to me, a shit-eating grin on his face. "Well, shit, boss. I can't remember the last time you let me open the shop and gave yourself a morning off."

My scowl doesn't deter him or wipe the smirk off his lips. "Had things to do."

It shouldn't be possible, but Will's smile grows even wider. "Yeah? Like what?"

My frown deepens, and when I aim it at him he takes a step back, raising his hands in surrender. "All right, boss. Don't lose your shit. I get it. It's *private*." Giggling like a little girl, he walks back toward the Corolla he's rotating.

Marching back toward my office, I run into Hoover. I jerk my chin in his direction, reaching out a hand so he can clasp it. "Stone."

Hoover nods back and pulls me in for a one-armed hug. "Good to see you, boss. You good?"

Nodding, I lean against the wall, propping my foot up behind me and folding my arms across my broad chest. "Yeah. Lemme ask you something. You ever let a woman get in your head?"

Hoover, ever thoughtful, rubs his hand across his gnarled beard and mimics my position on the wall across from me. "Can't say I have."

Hoover Stone is my most recent addition to the team at D.A. He's nasty with a wrench under a hood, and he knows cars like Santa knows toys. He's a little rough around the edges, but what man who's been to war isn't? He's as tall as I am, but not quite as bulky, and his long dirty-blond hair is gathered in a ponytail at the back of his neck. The fullness of his beard is something to brag about, and he's always casual in a pair of boots and jeans. Today, his coveralls are situated at his waist.

"Never had time for women. There was the army, and then training to rise up in the ranks. Chicks were for entertainment and getting my needs met, you know? Never got one stuck in my head. Guess it's just as well."

His thick Alabama drawl makes his words come out slow, but I never let that fool me. The man's sharp, and I value his quiet opinion.

I push off the wall. "Sucks when it happens."

A smile appears behind his beard. "Roger that."

We go our separate ways, me into my office and Hoover toward the garage.

Pulling up today's appointment schedule on the computer, it's clear that the boys can handle what's rolling in today. I pull out my phone to text Dare. Maybe we can get some work done on my baby today, see about bringing her classic ass back to life. I think an afternoon filled with chrome and oil is exactly what I need.

A few hours later finds Dare and me doing just that. I'm sitting on a wheeled auto stool with a wrench in my hand while Dare crouches beside the rear fender. We've been working in silent camaraderie for a solid half hour before Dare speaks.

"You dealing with something, Drake?" He keeps his eyes on his work.

Dare knows me well, probably better than anyone. We were in the field together as Rangers, and when I retired we kept in touch. When he cut the army loose, he came to Lone Sands to start a life. He even stayed at my house for a while until he got on his feet. He's closer to me than any brother would be.

I grunt in an affirmative.

He glances up with a frown. "Oh yeah? So drinking your weight in whiskey at See Food every night is dealing?"

With a roll of my eyes, I blow out a breath. I scrub my fingers across my forehead, probably dragging greasy black streaks there in the process. "You keeping tabs on me now?"

Dare shakes his head, lets out a chuckle. "Don't have to. This tiny town you brought me to knows how to talk. I know Mea poured you into her car one night and brought you home. How'd *that* go?"

Since he's been here, Dare has observed the dance Mea and I do at every meeting. It's been different lately, though. She clearly doesn't hate me like I thought, but I still don't know what I originally did to send her running.

"It went all right." I figure with an answer that vague my best friend won't be able to read too much into it.

I thought wrong.

"Yeah? Drake…tell me you didn't fuck her. Berkeley says Mea seems off, and she can't figure out why. If you screw her up even more, I'm gonna get my ass handed to me by my fiancée."

I level my gaze at Dare. My expression is dead serious, because I don't want there to be any mistaking my next words. "You can tell Berkeley not to worry. Mea is safe with me. And as for fucking her, I don't think that's anybody's goddamn business."

Dare whistles low and long. "Defensive, are we?" He studies me closely, too close. I glance away and begin twisting my wrench on the bolt that's holding the front fender on the bike.

After a minute, I can feel Dare's eyes leave me, and I can breathe again. He goes back to work, and so do I. There's no more said about it. But that doesn't mean thoughts of Mea aren't swirling around in my head like mist. She's not quite solid; I don't think I can catch hold of her yet. But at some point, she's going to be standing right in front of me, open and ready. At least that's what I hope will happen. And when it does, will I be ready to lay it all out there? For her? Or will my own demons be dragging me under, to a place I can't come back from?

10

Mea

I glance at the speedometer. As usual, Mikah drives way too fast through the back roads that lead to the western side of Brunswick County.

We're headed to our aunt and uncle's house. We aren't close, but we keep in touch because Aunt Tay and Uncle Wes took us in when we had to leave our home in Kentucky as teenagers.

"Slow down, Mikah," I admonish him from the passenger seat. "I want to get there as a whole person, not in pieces."

Mikah glances over at me. The rap music blaring from his radio should drown him out, but his voice resonates with me like no one else's, and I hear every word.

"You're barely a whole person as it is, little sis."

Glaring at him, I clench my fist and wave it in front of his face. "You little brat! I've taken you down enough times for you to *know* size doesn't matter. Call me 'little sis' again and I'm gonna pound your face."

Mikah chuckles. At six feet tall, my little brother isn't so little anymore. He's the one person I would do anything for, and I proved it when I was fourteen and we moved to another state to stay with our aunt and uncle. We might fight every time we're together, but I'd do anything for him, and him for me.

"So what does Tay want to talk to us about?" Mikah drums one hand against the steering wheel as he drives. His short black curls, darker than mine but still so very similar, bounce as he does. We look so much alike. His complexion matches mine, and he has the same wide, full mouth. But Mikah's eyes are the darkest, deepest green. I've always envied him those eyes, and they gain him no shortage of female attention. Skipping the college route, he became a longshoreman in Wilmington after he graduated high school a couple of years ago. But the girls on UNCW's campus still found ways to get his attention whenever he attended their parties.

"No clue." I rest my head back against the cloth headrest. "But it must be important. We usually only go there on holidays."

He nods, or his head is bopping to the beat. I'm not sure which. We talk easily for the remainder of the twenty-five-minute ride, and when we pull into the long gravel driveway at the farmhouse where I spent my teenage years and Mikah lived since he was twelve, I let out a sigh.

I always have mixed feelings returning here. My time at the farm was pleasant, because my aunt and uncle are kind. But the memories are always tinged with shadows and fear. While living here, I underwent several years of intensive therapy because of what my father put me through. And my aunt looks so much like my mom, I had a hard time dealing at first. I threw myself into school, becoming a member of the cheer squad and became best friends with Berkeley, but I had to watch my brother struggle to find his place.

We're both fighters, but Mikah's more of the scrappy kind. And it showed with every suspension from school he received. My aunt and uncle tried their best, but they weren't our parents. And we all knew it.

My aunt comes onto the white, wooden wraparound porch. Her smile is tight, but even with the addition of some gray strands in her curly hair and extra lines on her face, the resemblance to my mama is striking. The only difference is the fact that my Aunt Tay can smile freely. That was something her sister forgot how to do long before she died. Seeing her feels like someone dumped a bucket of ice water on my head, and while Mikah bounces up the steps to greet her, it takes me a little longer to drag myself closer.

"It's good to see you both." Aunt Tay's greeting is warm and genuine, and she ushers us inside the refurbished farmhouse to sit in the great room.

The house is beautiful, with accents of both old and new. I remember thinking when we first moved in that it seemed like someone else's fairy tale. After what I'd gone through, I never felt like I deserved any of this. I was dirty, stained.

Used, used, used.

The inside hasn't changed much. White bead board covers the walls, light wooden beamed ceilings with cavernous heights. The furniture is casual and tasteful, but the place has a lived-in appearance despite its style. I choose a spot on the khaki sectional sofa and kick off my shoes, tucking my feet up beneath me. Mikah sits a few feet away, spreading his legs wide and placing his forearms on his knees.

"So what's up, Aunt T?" Mikah's voice is deep and rumbly, and always manages to sound jovial and nonchalant at the same time. I envy the carefree way he goes about his life. It's what I try to do, but mine is fake. His is real.

My aunt sits down across from us on a plush ottoman and begins wringing her hands.

I glance at Mikah. *Never a good sign.*

"It's about your father."

Well, leave it to Tay to get right to the point. Just hearing those words cross her lips, *your father*, makes my insides begin to tremble, turning me in a mess of goo. I clench my muscles together, trying to get control of the shaking. Hot tears spring to my eyes, and I blink rapidly to try and keep them in. *Why?*

Lately, he seems to be everywhere. I've tried to keep thoughts of him buried deep for years, but all of a sudden they're popping back up to the surface again, dead bodies that won't stay sunken.

"What about him?" I can't disguise the tremor in my voice.

Mikah, his face hard and set, grabs my hand and squeezes it. I know what he's saying without using words. *I'll never let him hurt you again, Mea.*

He thought he was protecting me all those years ago. But it would have made things so much worse. So I did what I had to do in order to protect us both…

I lay in bed, my sweat suit causing me to roast but also giving me a sense of false security. My knuckles are white, clenching the covers as tightly as I can. Each muscle is taut, and I've been like this for hours. Hours.

Waiting, waiting, waiting.

Please, not tonight. Dear God in heaven, if you're up there...if you can hear me? Please. Just not tonight.

I pray the prayer over and over again. I'm not sure why. It's never saved me before. At this point, I don't know what could save me. There is no longer anything behind my mother's eyes. In the last year, they've gone completely vacant. It's like she's stopped living, but her body still functions. The kids at school don't understand why my mom doesn't come to stuff like the other parents do. They don't get why Mikah and I never invite them over to play. And Daddy's so controlling, we wouldn't dream of asking to go to someone else's house.

We're the town weirdoes. And that's the least of my problems.

The blackness in my room gives me no warning that the doorknob is turning. It's silent, and I don't know he's coming until I see the sliver of light from the hallway. Then it's gone.

Which means he's in my room.

I can hear his heavy breathing as he stands there.

Watching. Watching. Watching.

I'm holding my breath, but the tears are already streaming down my cheeks.

My stomach is so tight it hurts, all my muscles coiled and aching from overuse.

You are strong. You are strong. You are strong.

When my initial prayer mantra fails, that's always the next one.

Because I am strong enough to handle this. It hurts, and it twists my thoughts into things dark and abysmal, but I am strong. I am in control.

When he grabs my ankles and yanks me around, flipping me so that I'm facedown, I scream. I never scream, he told me not to, but I can't help it. This is new. He's never flipped me over before. He pulls down my sweatpants and underwear and slaps my bottom as hard as he can. The sound makes my stomach curl. Bile rises in my throat when he touches me, spreading my legs apart. His weight crushes me, my face mashes into my pillow.

Then his voice is in my ear, and it's like grease coiling around in a skillet. Slow, oily, and hot.

"Told you to shut your mouth. You like this, just like your mother used to. You're gonna like tonight even more. Shut up, if you want to tell me how good it is, you whisper."

I can feel him fumbling around, hear the ragged sound of his zipper as he pulls it down. And then he pounds into me, and I scream again. Oh, God. I'm not strong enough for this.

Then my bedroom door creaks open. The light flips on, and there's a sleepy eleven-year-old Mikah rubbing his eyes. Almost twelve, he's halfway between a boy and a man. He's tall, but gangly. His voice is just starting to change, and he's outgrowing all of his jeans and sneakers.

Horrified that he's going to see me like this, I hiss at him. "Get out Mikah! Go!"

My father doesn't say a word. But he backs up off of me and rises to his knees.

Mikah doesn't move. I watch as his face flits between sleepy, con-

fused, horrified, and then finally to rage. Blinding rage that he can never come back from. He surges into the room, pulling my father off of me and throwing him to the ground. Standing in front of me, he gulps heavy breaths.

"You're touching my sister! No…No! Fuck you, you bastard! Don't you ever touch her again!"

"Mikah," I whimper. "Please. You have to go."

Because I'm afraid. I don't know what this monster will do to my little brother now that he knows. I have to protect him. I have to be in control.

Our father zips up his pants and stares at us, his eyes moving from me to Mikah and back again. Finally, he turns and heads for the door as if nothing happened.

"You'll both pay for this later. I can promise you that." And then he's gone.

We hear his bedroom door shut just down the hall.

Then Mikah flings himself at me. I can barely move I'm in so much pain. And the blood…the blood is all over my bed. Mikah goes for towels and he helps me clean up.

He sleeps with me in my bed that night. Just before we drift off, he murmurs beside me, "I'll never let him hurt you again, Mea."

I keep the thoughts to myself, but I know it's me who can never allow him to be hurt.

The very next day at school, I go to my guidance counselor. And I tell her everything. It changes our lives forever.

Tay's lip curls in disgust. She never met my father. When he and my mother married, he moved her away to Kentucky and she never kept in touch with her sister. We'll never know if it was her choice or his, but Mikah and I had never met our aunt and uncle until the day they picked us up from the state care system.

And then my father was found guilty on all counts of child sexual abuse.

"He's been an exemplary prisoner. He's undergone hundreds of hours of therapy and counseling over the last ten years that he's been behind bars. And now he's up for parole."

I just sit there. I'm not sure if *stunned* is the correct word. More like *frozen*. Chained to my seat. Distraught.

But Mikah, always needing to move, jumps to his feet and begins pacing the room. "How's that possible, Aunt T? I mean, can't we go and tell them there's no way in hell that monster should be out of prison ever?"

She nods miserably. "You could. You could go to the prison in Kentucky in two months for the hearing if that's what you want to do and plead for his continued containment."

That's absolutely the last thing I want to do. I never want to see his face again. I *can't*. That will most definitely spin me out of control, and I can't allow that to happen. Not while I'm in the same room with that man.

Mikah is looking at me like he's ready to jump a plane to Kentucky right this second.

"I'll…think about it," I say quietly to Tay. She nods. She understands completely, I can see it written all over her face.

"Let's go, Mikah."

His mouth clenches tight, but he follows me to the front door and out to his souped-up Tiburon.

"That's it?" he asks as he slides behind the wheel. "I mean... I'm with you, Mea. Whatever you want to do. But don't you have more to say?"

I stare out the window as he begins the drive down the country roads back toward the shore that I've grown to love.

I have no words.

11

Drake

January flies by in a blur, with me working at the garage, fixing up my Yamaha, and then sliding into See Food every night for a drink. Or more than a drink.

But one morning, I wake up to a phone call from Mea.

"Hey." My scratchy morning voice is in full effect. "What's up?"

The sexy rasp of *her* sleepy morning voice lights a red-hot flame inside me. I'm instantly awake.

"We have things to do today. You're not working today, right? I'll swing by in a half hour."

Sitting straight up in bed, I squint at the phone, like that's gonna help me understand what she's talking about. "What do we have to do?"

The smile in her voice reaches out and hugs me. "Our best friends are getting married in a couple of months. We have a party to plan."

Sinking back down into the softness of my pillows, I sigh. "Oh, right."

"Drake? You just laid back down, didn't you?"

Chuckling, I swing my legs around and stretch. "I'm up, Mea. See you in thirty."

I've just walked into the kitchen, freshly showered and dressed, when she knocks at my front door. When I open it, she waltzes in with two large cups in her hands.

She thrusts one in my hands. "Coffee for you, green tea latte for me."

She settles in at the kitchen table. Sipping the bitter black liquid, just the way I like it, I follow.

"Good morning to you, too. Thanks for the coffee." I take the seat beside her.

And the she pulls out a fucking binder. A *binder.*

"This," she says, her voice full of pride, "is full of possible bachelor/bachelorette party activities." Her voice is pumped.

Not sure what it is with women and weddings. It's like candy or something. They all get high just thinking about them. Trying to bite back my groan, I slide the binder toward me.

She starts chattering away, talking through the ideas she has for the event, and I get lost. In her excitement, in her energy, in the way her teeth sink into her soft lips as she scans her notes.

"See?" Her voice is all bubbles and giddiness. "They have this code-breaking place in Savannah. Wouldn't that be fun if we had to break out of this scary room by solving clues and stuff?"

I just stare at her. "Pretty sure we're gonna be drunk most of the weekend. Breaking codes is like work for the security guys. So I veto that idea."

Her dark eyes narrow on me. "Pretty sure I didn't give you veto power."

I lean in, dropping my voice to a whisper. "Pretty sure you're not the boss of me."

Her eyes dart down to my lips before flashing back up to my eyes. Her small, pink tongue darts out to lick her lips, and I can't stop the reaction my body makes. "Fuck."

"Bar crawl." I grind the words out, my teeth clenched tightly together just like the rest of my muscles. Her looking at my lips isn't exactly an invitation for more.

But *damn* do I want that invitation.

"What?" She looks confused.

"Bar crawl. It's what we should do one of the nights we're in Savannah. Laid-back and fun. Split up the guys and the girls for the night, then meet up at the end of it."

Her eyes light up as she turns a page in the binder and jots something down. "That's a good idea." Looking up at me, her bottom lip juts out just a bit.

She's trying to kill me right here in my kitchen.

"But I still like the code-breaking idea."

I lean in, studying her gorgeous face, taking advantage of the closer distance. "How about we save that for another weekend? One where we're not all likely to be three sheets?"

With a smirk, she taps the end of her pen against her lips. "I might be willing to take that deal."

"Let's talk to Dare and Berkeley about what activities *they* want to do while we're there, and next time we get together we'll book some stuff. Sound like a plan?"

She nods.

I reach over and close her binder. "Good, because I'm hungry. Let me take you to breakfast."

Her lips pull into a distracting smile. "I'm in."

In the following weeks whenever Lenny sees me rolling in to See Food she slides my tumbler toward me and pours my whiskey neat. Sometimes we chat, sometimes she's too busy with other patrons.

Mea works there waiting tables six nights a week, so I see her every time I come in. Seeing her whipping around the place, grabbing orders and dropping off food, chatting with the customers, makes my mouth water. I want *more* of her. She always stops by, has a seat on the stool beside mine, and we talk about life and shit. I tell her about my bike and she tells me about her studio. She's already leased the space, now she's saving money for licenses and equipment. It shouldn't be long now; she's thinking maybe early fall she'll be able to open the place. The way her face shines when she talks about it is enough to make my heart grow a size bigger. There's just something about the wild girl…when she's happy she makes everything around her seem that much brighter.

One night in the middle of February, we both get to talking about the wedding, which is now just a month away.

"So we all set on plans for the bachelorette weekend, right?"

I stroke my chin slowly. "You mean the bachelor weekend?" I shoot her a wink. "Yeah, that's coming up in two weeks, ain't it?"

She nods, leaning onto the bar top with her elbows. She wrinkles her nose. "I still think it's a mistake, doing it together. I mean, there's no way I'm gonna be able to get a pack of strippers for Berkeley now that Dare will be around."

"Oh, was that your plan?" I tweak one of her long curls. "Watching naked dudes dance?"

She rolls her eyes at me. "It's called a bachelorette party for a reason. She's saying good-bye to the single life. In other words, she's saying good-bye to all the fun."

I study her. Her lips are pouting out in a painfully adorable way and her hands are cradling her delicate chin. "That's what you think? That settling down with someone means all the fun is gone?"

She doesn't answer aloud, but her thoughts are written in the conviction of her expression.

"How much fun have you been having lately being single?"

She cuts her eyes away from mine, and that's all the answer I need. Chuckling, I elbow her gently. "So, not much."

She turns to me with a challenge in her gaze. "I've been busy. But I'm not too shy to take a guy home from a bar, Drake. I could pick any single guy in this place tonight and have him wrapped around my finger in a heartbeat."

Now my dick is straining for some attention. At the same time, my blood is rushing in my ears at the thought of her bringing some random asshole home from the bar with her. "No deal. I don't need proof. I know you're a wild girl."

She nods firmly. "And don't you forget it."

I lean in closer. "But you wouldn't really want someone else, sweetheart, would you? Not when I'm sitting right here waiting on you."

She visibly shivers, and I grin, pulling back just a little to see her all hot and bothered.

As I watch, she schools her face, and I realize she's not going to show me all her cards no matter how flustered she is. Not unless I have her alone, and under me.

I finish my drink, and then I lean in again. "So you want to come home with me tonight?"

She takes a glance around the quiet restaurant and bar. It's Thursday night, so it's entirely feasible that the crowd went somewhere a little livelier tonight. Either way, Lenny is wiping down the bar and it's only just after eleven, and I can see the other waitress leaning a hip against one of her male customer's tables, clearly shooting the shit.

"Hey, Len." Lenny raises a brow at Mea, who is placing her hands on her hips. "Are you gonna have to roll this one outta here under your arm again?"

Lenny gives me a quick glare, but I know underneath all the sass she's worried about me spending so much time in front of her bar.

"Nope. Not tonight. I think he stopped at three."

I give her a proud grin. "Sure did. Had some eye candy to keep me busy." I wink at Lenny.

She harrumphs. "Don't play me, soldier. I know the eye candy sure as hell ain't me."

Mea jerks her hand toward the door. "Mind if I go ahead and dip out? Silverware and ketchups are done."

Lenny pats one of Mea's cheeks like a grandmother might. Only Lenny is tougher and about ten years younger than most grandmothers I know. "Sure."

I settle with Lenny by throwing a bill on the bar and tuck Mea under my shoulder as we walk toward the door. All of her curves seem to melt whenever they touch me, and I pull her just a little tighter. Peeking up at me from under my arm, she shoots me a mischievous grin. It has me so stiff and aching it's hard to walk straight. My body answers to this girl like she's the only one with my number.

"Huh. Didn't think you'd actually say yes to my proposal." My smile is aimed down at her.

She's busy texting on her phone. "Oh, I'm not. Not yet, anyway."

I pull up short as we reach the Challenger. "So I'm just taking you home?"

The thought brings with it a surge of disappointment. I haven't had Mea alone in weeks, and I've been missing all those miles of creamy, light-brown skin laid out before me. Tonight I was planning on treating her like a dessert buffet, because that's what it's like when she's naked and in my bed. Like I have the most delectable selections of sweetness anyone could ever taste. And one night with her, even though we didn't have sex, wasn't enough. I'm not exactly sure when I'll get enough of her, but I haven't had my fill, and I'd like to see how far this fascination with Mea goes.

"Nope." She giggles as she climbs into the passenger seat. I can't help palming her ass as I help her in, and she narrows her eyes at me as she settles in her seat. Kneeling beside her, I hold her gaze with mine. Her eyes are huge in the darkness, and that hair is pulled up into a pile of curls on her head tonight, some tumbling down around her face like some kind of dark little angel. Just looking at her sitting in my car, I feel something inside my chest shaking around a little.

"Then what exactly did you have in mind, wild girl?" My voice comes out husky because of all my dirty thoughts, and clearing my throat won't do a thing. I watch her eyes darken as her pupils dilate in response to something I said or did. I like it.

Damn, I like it a whole lot.

I trace the rough pad of my index finger down her cheekbone. Her skin is always so soft, and I don't want to stop touching her. She closes her eyes as my finger draws a trail down to her jawbone, sketching the curve of her face until I reach her lips. I drag my finger along the bottom one, and then she opens her mouth.

She opens her eyes, watching mine widen in surprise.

She gently sucks my finger inside the perfectly wet heat of her mouth and closes her lips around it.

Fuuuuuuck. A rumble emits from my chest, and she allows my finger to pop from her mouth with a sinful smile on her face.

She leans forward and whispers, "Don't put your fingers where they don't belong if you don't want them to end up wet and hot."

She knows. She knows she's undoing me, because it's right there in her devilish eyes. Pulling back slightly, I smirk. "I like hot and wet."

Her smirk widens, and I like the fact that she can take every single thing I give her. And she can give it right back.

"I want to go dancing."

The sentence pops out like we weren't just being extremely dirty, and I have to switch gears in my mind and my pants before I can answer.

"You want to go...dancing. Really?"

She nods. "Already texted Berk and Greta. They'll be at Boots."

Boots is a local bar with a small dance floor that plays both pop and country, and it's not exactly my thing. But the look on her face as she thinks about spending some time with her friends and shaking her ass makes me get on board with the plan real quick. Plus I can sit and have a beer with Grisham and Dare while I watch her.

In the back of my mind, something nags at me. It might be the fact that I already downed three whiskeys here at See Food, but I drank them over time and I'm still sober. So I don't need to listen to the little voice that tells me I'm drinking way more than I used to.

It's irrelevant.

My mom's dead. There's nothing I can do about that now. There's no going back and saving her. So I'm dealing with it, and the whole shitty situation is going to be temporary. I can handle it.

On the drive over to Boots, I offer Mea a sideways glance. "You're not worried about what our friends are going to think when we walk in together?"

She shrugs her thin shoulders. "They're either going to think I've lost my mind, or that I've finally found it. Either way, I don't care."

Smiling at that snippet of straight-up Mea honesty, I pull into the parking lot of the bar.

When we walk in, we scan the small crowd until we find our friends. They've snagged a table near the patio door, and we head in that direction. As we draw closer, I place my hand protectively on the small of Mea's back, and she lets me. Melts into my side like butter. When I glance down at her, she gives me a sultry look that tells me this is going to be a good night.

Four sets of eyes are locked and loaded on us as we approach, and Berkeley's lips tilt up in a small smile when she notices my hand on Mea's back. Greta doesn't even try to hide her grin.

"Hey, you two. Didn't expect to see you together." Berkeley is practically shining with excitement for her friend, excitement that I'm pretty sure I can't live up to. Dare gives me a silent nod, his expression mirroring what I'm thinking.

Sighing, I take a seat beside my best friend and Mea takes a chair beside hers. It just so happens that hers is two seats away from mine, and the loss of her warmth beside me when she goes is monumental. Meeting my eyes across the table, hers turn down at the corners, and I'm wondering if she feels it, too.

I shoot the shit with Dare and Grisham, asking them how work is going. They're both security professionals on Greta's father's tactical team at his company, Night Eagle Security. It's a pretty sweet arrangement, especially coming from military Special Forces backgrounds like they both do. Grisham was a Navy SEAL until he lost his foot to a bomb in Syria. It was rough for him at first, adapting to life back in the States knowing he was going to have to leave his SEAL days behind. But then he got together with Greta and met her dad. Everything sort of fell into place from there.

I'm glad they both love the job, but I wouldn't trade my garage for any of it. I left my Special Ops days back in the desert, and the only mission I want to be a part of now is one that involves chrome and grease.

I can't help watching Mea across the table. She's chatting quietly with Greta and Berkeley, all three girls' heads put together. Long blond waves, glossy raven locks, and wild, wild curls all put together in one spot. They're a beautiful sight. But almost like she can feel my gaze, Mea glances up, and when her eyes meet mine a flame ignites inside me and shoots off like fireworks. She smiles, not her usual bright and shiny smirk, but an almost shy grin that tells me she's feeling all kinds of emotions she doesn't understand when it comes to me, just like I am when it comes to her.

I toss her a wink, and her tongue darts out to lick her lush bottom lip. That's all it takes to send visions of her lying naked in my bed spinning across my vision.

Grisham leans over, his voice quiet. "Sparks are flying. You for real when it comes to her?"

I frown, glancing away from Mea to meet his gaze dead on. "I don't know what this is yet. But I'm not planning on bringing more hurt into her life if that's what you're talking about."

His blond brow lifts. "*More* hurt?"

There it is. After the way I saw Mea the night she was trembling from nightmares and tangled up in my sheets, I knew right then and there that something in her past had hurt her. Had changed her. Had made her into the strong, yet closed-off girl she is today. But no one else knows what I saw that night. There's no one she's let in to that degree. Not even her best friends. So I know that I won't be someone who causes her to fall apart again. I could never do that to her.

"You don't have to worry about her," I tell Grisham, my voice gruff. "When she's with me, she's safe."

He nods once, my admission clearly enough for him.

The thumping tones of a song that the girls love, something popular on the radio, begin, and they jump up to dance. Mea exchanges one last fleeting look with me before she's swept away, and I zero in on her in the crowd. Around the hazy conversation of Grisham and Dare, I watch Mea as she shimmies her stuff on the little circle of wood. When a crowd of college-aged dudes begins to crowd in around our ladies, both Dare and Grisham start to pay attention. Our conversation drops as we take in everything that happens on the dance floor.

The girls are oblivious at first, just dancing in a circle and laughing at whatever silly move Berkeley dishes out. Mea's the true dancer of the group; her body seems to move like a sultry snake to whatever rhythm the music plays, and it's a damn sexy sight. The problem is, it's a sexy sight to more than just me. One guy in particular, all decked out in his collared shirt and backward baseball cap, doesn't seem to know any better. He swerves behind her, looking for his best way in. When Mea puts her arms up over her head to sway to the beat, he steps into her personal space and places his hands low on her hips. She instantly freezes.

Now usually, I'm not a jealous guy. I've honestly never claimed a girl as my own, so there's never been any reason for the envy to take over. But the memory of what happened when the guy at See Food grabbed her, combined with a spark of rage at another man's hands on her body, have me out of my seat before I know what I'm doing.

It takes me about four strides to eat up the distance between me and the dance floor, and then I'm forcibly stepping between Mea and the college D-bag.

"Fuck you, dude. I don't see your name written on her." College boy clearly isn't happy with the way things are going down. His friends are nowhere in sight, and Dare and Grisham are standing right beside me. Not that I need 'em.

I flick my hand back toward the tables. "You should have looked a little closer, then." He opens his mouth to spit back, but then I pull myself up to my full height and advance on him. He looks up at me, and then out at the sheer width of my body before taking a couple of steps backward.

"It's cool, man." He raises his hands and turns away.

Berkeley is grinning from ear to ear at my streak of green, but Greta is eyeing Mea with concern.

"You okay?" she asks over the thump of the music. "You don't look so hot."

Glancing down at Mea and stooping a bit so I can see her face, I notice that she's lost some of her color. When I rub my hands down her arms, they've broken out in goose bumps, and I can feel the slightest shiver in her muscles.

It's so similar to the reaction she experienced at See Food, and my brain rockets into overdrive to try and compensate for it.

"You ready to go?" I ask her, my voice low and close to her ear so that she can hear me.

Looking up at me with wide eyes, she nods.

I bark a quick good-bye to Dare and Grisham, while Mea gives a weak smile and wave to the girls. Then I'm grabbing her hand and making our way out of the bar as quickly as I can without picking the little thing up and running with her.

Once we're seated in the Challenger, the quiet is eerie compared to the noise of the bar. But I can finally really assess her without all of the distractions. Her face is glowing orange in the light from the dashboard, and when I gently take her hand in mine, she doesn't pull it away.

"Are you ready to talk?" I ask, keeping my voice quiet so I don't startle her.

A thousand emotions cross her face all at once, and every single one of them makes me want to pull her into my arms and never let her go. I don't know where this protective instinct is coming from. I mean, sure, I served in the army where it was my job to protect people. But this is different. It's my personal mission to make sure that at any given time, Mea isn't hurting or feeling pain. I carry her happiness on my shoulders, and it's a load I know I can bear for miles.

"I think…" In the silent car her whisper screams at me. Or maybe it's because I'm so completely tuned in to her that to me, her whisper will always seem like a shout. "I think that when I'm ready to talk about it…you could be the one I tell."

We stare at each other for a long minute after that, neither of us speaking, but her hand clutches mine.

"Can I…" She trails off. Her eyebrows knit together and the little frown lines on her forehead tell me she's reconsidering what she's about to ask.

God, at that moment, with her eyes so big and bright in the darkness of my car and her hand so tightly squeezing mine, I'm pretty sure I'd swear to give her the world.

"Anything, sweetheart."

"Would you sleep beside me again tonight? The nightmares are coming…and when they do, I don't want to be alone."

If you had asked me a year ago how it felt to have your heart broken, I would have told you some sad story about growing up with a mom like mine. And then about how it felt to know that I left her by herself as soon as I could get out. It's been eating me up alive since her death, knowing that maybe I could have done something to change her life, but I didn't. I just left and never looked back. Made something of myself, but didn't reach back to pull her up with me.

But now…hearing Mea's request?

I'm shattered.

This…this is how a heart breaks.

And I'll deny her nothing.

12

Mea

Wow. This place is super nice." I turn in a slow circle in the living room, stopping to focus on the floor-to-ceiling windows overlooking the lush and fancy Forsyth Park.

The three-story, white brick home Berkeley's parents rented for us is right in the heart of the Savannah's historic district. The picturesque street is lined with huge old oak trees draped with Spanish moss. The streets are always occupied, either by cars, people, or horses and carriages. It's my first time in this city, and its energy is invigorating me in a way I essentially needed.

As a group, we take a tour of the house. Our shoes echo across the maple hardwood floors as we take in the ornate walls covered in colorful hues of wallpaper, the gorgeous, comfortable furniture, and the accented ceilings. On the ground floor is a large eat-in kitchen with a center island. The cabinets are white and detailed, and there are stainless steel appliances for all the cooking we won't be doing over the long weekend. There's also a great room with a flat-screen TV above a redbrick wood-burning fireplace. Comfortable seating lines the room, and there is one wall of bookshelves filled to capacity. A dining room completes the floor, laid out to the max just like the other rooms.

The second floor has four bedrooms, each one beautiful. I find myself falling in love with the "lavender" room. The huge four-poster bed is lined with a lavender and white patchwork quilt. White wallpaper with small purple flower buds just gives me a feeling of whimsy—something brand-new and exciting.

I want to do so much yoga in this room.

"Mine." I sigh, rolling my suitcase in with me and flopping backward on the bed.

Berkeley laughs and scans the room. "Yeah, this is perfect for you. Want to stay here and get settled while the rest of us pick our rooms?"

I nod, sitting up on the bed and perching cross-legged. The rest of the group files out of the room. All except for Drake, who leans against the walnut wood doorway with the coiled, quiet confidence that makes him so damn sexy. He studies me.

We were a three-car caravan on the way down to Savannah. I rode shotgun in Berkeley's Escalade, with Greta, Grisham, and Berkeley's friend Olive, who works with her at the interior design firm. Also squeezed into the third row with her was Dare's friend Ronin Shaw, who also works special security services at Night Eagle. Ronin and Olive were smushed in pretty tight in the backseat, considering all of the luggage, but neither of them seemed to mind. They were either giving each other sideways glances or talking quietly together. It was kind of cute, and it makes me wonder if maybe there's some chemistry between them that will one day catch fire.

The car in front of us, Dare's big red Ford F-250, housed the rest of the guys. Drake rode up front while Jeremy Teague, another security specialist and ex-army dude from Night Eagle, and Dare's brother Chase rode in the back. Chase's wife, Shay, would have come, too, except she's very busy taking care of their toddler at home.

After everyone else is gone from my room, Drake sizes me up. "You want me gone too, sweetheart?"

Ohhh, Lordie. Every single time the word *sweetheart* rolls off his tongue, shivers roll up and down my body like they're riding a current of heat. His deep, dark voice just does something sinister to my insides, and it's not the kind of sinister I want to run from. It's the kind I want to dive into and roll around in.

"Well, I dunno, Drake. What's everyone gonna think if we share a room?" I grace him with a coy smile from my spot on the bed.

Like a stealthy predator, he moves farther into my new bedroom. "Don't give a fuck what anyone thinks, baby. Only care about making sure I'm the one warming your bed at night."

Drake in my bed…the thought brings flames of heat creeping into my cheeks. I like him there…he's been there for me a few times since the night I asked him to sleep beside me. It doesn't matter who's bed we're in…I feel comfortable sleeping beside him. Safe. Protected.

And it scares me to death. Depending on him could be dangerous…but I haven't been able to stop myself from walking right into his arms.

I suck in a breath, and creep backward on the bed. I'm still not sure I'm ready for everything this big, sexy, deep and dark man is willing to dish out. "I have an idea. Why don't you go and pick a room. You can keep your stuff there, and I'll keep my stuff here. But if there's ever a time during the night that we want to be together, well…" I trail off suggestively.

I want to be with him in the worst way. But that's what scares me most. Being with Drake, giving him all of my mess-up bits and pieces, might pull me so far apart I'll never be put back together again. And my head's a mess, thinking about the possibility of having to see my father again. I still haven't given my aunt an answer about whether or not I'll attend the parole hearing. I've been wanting to talk to Drake about it, but I haven't found the right words. And now the hearing is only two weeks away.

Drake backs up. "Sounds like a plan. I'll see you later."

He disappears from my room, and I sigh a sigh that could be heavy with either disappointment or relief.

I'm just not quite sure which.

I spend a little bit of time unpacking and admiring my room until the evening sky tells me I should be getting dressed for dinner.

For the first week of March, it's unusually warm. It's not a surprise, considering the easy winter we've had down south. So I put on a little black dress. I leave my hair free flowing and wild, and apply a bit of makeup. Mostly bronzer, to give my face a slight shimmer for the evening in Savannah.

By the time I make it downstairs, everyone is already there. They stand around the island in the large kitchen, discussing the dinner reservations we have for tonight at an exclusive restaurant in downtown Savannah.

"I think we can walk there from here," Dare is saying.

Greta looks at him like he's lost his mind. "In these heels? Ain't happening, man."

Berkeley giggles. "Maybe we could take a couple of carriages? I've always wanted to ride in one!"

The way Dare looks at her in that moment needs no words. He'd move heaven and earth to get her whatever she wants. And I know without a doubt that we'll be riding to the restaurant.

From where he's standing by the wet bar, pouring himself a drink that I know to be whiskey, Drake turns and meets my gaze. The temperature in the room instantly rises two degrees just from one look alone. I nod toward the glass in his hand and he shrugs as if to say, *We're here to party, right?*

Frowning slightly, I try to remember the last time I saw him *without* a drink.

In the few years that I've known Drake, he's never been much of a drinker. He would be the guy who when out with his friends would nurse one or two beers the entire time. Not until that first night a couple of months ago at See Food—the day of his mother's funeral—had I seen him with a glass of straight liquor.

My frown deepens when he raises his glass to me.

Sidling over to where he stands, I nudge him with my shoulder. The damn mountain of a man doesn't even budge. "Starting the party early?"

He gives me an amused glance. "It's a party, isn't it?"

I shrug. "Is it? We're just getting ready to go to dinner." I scan our group. Everyone is getting ready to walk out the door.

"Guess I better finish this, then." Drake downs his whiskey and places his hand on the small of my back. As soon as he touches me, heat radiates through the fabric of my dress and straight through my skin. Heat flushes my face, and my eyes hood as I look up at him.

Leaning down, his lips brush the shell of my ear, and my knees wobble slightly. "You look amazing, tonight, sweetheart. Really beautiful."

He's decked out in all black. Black sweater that hugs the bulge of his biceps and gives just the barest hint of the chiseled beauty of his chest and abs. Charcoal gray slacks. Drake never wears slacks, but it's nice to know that when the occasion calls for it, he can fit the bill. The pants fit him just right, and I already can't wait to watch him walk out the door so I can ogle his perfect ass. He's missing his usual black combat boots, instead rocking really nice black suede brogues.

"You clean up nice, Sullivan," I mutter as I follow our group out the door. His chuckle, rumbling behind me, chases the shivers up and down my spine.

The restaurant Dare and Berkeley have chosen is actually a renovated historic mansion. The Olde Pink House is straight up not my usual scene, but I can always appreciate good food. The charm of the place has mesmerized me. Completely pink on the outside, the inside is gorgeously redone in the style of the old South. Tons of molding, dripping chandeliers, and old hardwood floors make this a building I want to explore for hours. As I'm studying the menu, my eyes widen, because I definitely have not budgeted for this type of place. I really have no business even sitting here. I'm not sure what to do. Order an appetizer only? Just one drink and a salad? At these prices, one drink and one entrée would mean I can't pay my utility bill this month. I continue scanning the menu, trying to be as nonchalant as possible while I'm having a minor panic attack inside.

Jeremy Teague, who I've learned is kind of a jokester, whistles. "Whew! You trying to break the bank on dinner the first night, huh, Conners?" He glances at Dare and winks, letting his buddy know that he's kidding. Jeremy shakes his head, his short blond ponytail bobbing against the collar of his starched white shirt.

No kidding. Fire forms a blush in my cheeks, but I'm once again grateful that my skin tone most likely hides it. That and the flickering candlelight in the center of our table. Berkeley gushes that she can't wait to sink her carnivorous teeth into a steak, her fiancée agreeing wholeheartedly. Greta, a foodie and a whiz in the kitchen herself, is comparing each item on the menu in great detail while Grisham listens closely, happy to follow her lead. After all, she's the one who introduced the boy to grits.

Drake leans over, his movement subtle and smooth. "So what do you think looks good, sweetheart?" His voice, meant just for me, makes a flurry of wings beat frantically in my chest. I react to him like a schoolgirl, and it's a fact that would usually annoy the hell out of me. But at this moment in my life, with Drake, it seems right.

His large hand lands on my thigh, and it feels like it could wrap fully around my flesh if he only squeezes. I swallow hard as I peek over at him. "Um, I love a good salad with some kind of protein in it. Chicken or shrimp, maybe. But—"

At that moment, the waitress arrives to get our drink orders. I sigh, and Drake appraises me. His shrewd glance narrows as everyone orders what they want to drink.

"I'll have a whiskey, neat, and she'll have a sangria."

The table stares at Drake, and then at me. Chase snorts, glancing back down at his menu to cover his laughter. Ronin Shaw, who also works with Dare and is more reserved than Jeremy, gives me a curious glance.

There's been more than one friendly gathering that we've both attended where conversation has flowed easily between Ronin and me. With his dark brown hair curling around his ears, bright green eyes, and his olive complexion, he's completely gorgeous in a way that stands out in a crowd. But it's been a while since the last time we talked, and I haven't been able to see much past Drake for over a month now.

I mean, hell, I *do* love sangria, but Drake ordering for me? It causes my blood to boil with irritation at the same time it soaks my panties with lust. What the hell is this man doing to me?

I clear my throat. "Thank you, Drake." The sangria was one of the special drinks the server announced when we were first seated, and I thought it sounded delicious.

"Yeah, girl. Can't wait to try that sangria." Berkeley covers her grin with her hand, and I shoot her a warning glare. She's sending me a mixed message and she knows it.

The other members of the group who don't know Drake and me that well go right back to their conversations, but Berkeley, Greta, Grisham, and Dare continue to dart curious glances in our direction.

"I hate being the center of their attention," I hiss quietly to Drake.

He grins, suddenly reaching around me and pulling my chair closer to his. I gasp. "Know you do. Might as well give them something to stare at." He bends down and inhales at my neck, sniffing deeply and running his nose along my skin. My thighs instantly squeeze together as my toes curl in my peep-toe pumps.

Oh, my God. If he keeps doing shit like that, I'm not going to make it through this dinner.

"Dinner's on me," he whispers, moving a tendril of hair away from my ear so he has more access.

I shake my head. I want it to be firm, but he's turning me into something wobbly and gelatinous. I just want to close my eyes and lean into him and offer him as much of my body as he wants to take. Just the thought of it makes my skin flush hot and has memories of the way he worshipped me with his hands and his tongue chasing each other through my head.

Oh, crap. I actually had closed my eyes during my little trip down memory lane. It's been weeks since I've been close to Drake that way, and I realize I'm craving him the way an addict needs a high. When I look at him, he's staring at me with such lustful intensity I almost moan with my own desire. His eyes are gleaming with his secret knowledge, the knowledge of exactly what I want and how I want it.

Finding my voice, it's low and raspy. "You…you don't have to pay for my dinner, Drake. I can get it."

"Yeah, sweetheart," he says. "I think you can do just about whatever you put your mind to. But tonight, you don't have to. Let me do this."

I study him for a long moment, searching for any sign of pity or expectation in exchange for him picking up the tab on my dinner. I find none of it, and finally, I nod my assent.

"Thank you," I whisper.

Then, just to make him squirm, just to make him know a fraction of what I'm feeling, I place my own hand on his rock-hard thigh. He tenses. I squeeze. He swears under his breath. Now it's my turn to lean in. "I can't wait to see you in my purple bed tonight."

"Mea?" Berkeley's voice breaks in from across the table. "Restroom for the ladies?"

I reluctantly pull away from Drake and follow Berkeley, Greta, and Olive to the restroom. Olive's dark burgundy hair swishes in front of me as we walk, and focusing on it is what keeps me from looking over my shoulder to search for Drake.

When I enter the swanky, velvet-covered bathroom, I find myself cornered by my two best friends, each with their hands on their hips.

Hey. That's my stance. They're taking a page from my book. Lord help me.

Olive searches our faces, clearly confused. I think she thought this was an actual restroom break. The girl has a lot to learn.

I put on my very best innocent expression. "What?"

Berkeley snorts. Literally snorts. "What, my ass. What the hell is going on with you and Drake?"

Greta jumps in. "You two are so…close. Mea…did you sleep with him?"

My innocent friend sounds absolutely scandalized, and if she keeps it up I'll remind her of every dirty thing she did with Grisham before they were engaged.

"No!" I cross my arms over my chest defensively. "I mean, not recently."

Greta's hand flies to her mouth. Berkeley lets out a slew of curses. Olive's eyes widen with curious shock.

I hold my hands out in front of me. "What I meant was, I haven't slept with him *this* time around."

Berkeley stumbles back a step, her hand on her heart. I roll my eyes at her. "Stop it, Berk. There's only room for one dramatic friend in this relationship, and it's me."

Greta's deep blue eyes pierce into mine. "Spill it, sister."

Sighing, I realize I'm not getting out of this one. I'm finally going to have to tell them the truth about Drake. I gather a breath, pull myself up to my full five foot two, and let it fly.

"Three years ago, actually just a couple of months before Dare came to Lone Sands, Drake and I met at his garage and had a one-night-stand."

Greta shrieks, and Berkeley starts dancing around the restroom like she's hit the jackpot.

"I knew it!" she squeals. "I always *knew* something happened between the two of you! There was always this dark, scary sexual tension when you were in a room together." Her hands are flying around as she talks a mile a minute.

Greta is just as excited, but more reserved with her response. "It's true. I could never tell if you two were going to start throwing blows, or throw each other down on the floor and fuck."

Now I'm the one in shock, because Greta almost never says "fuck." It's getting real serious in here, apparently. Even Berkeley stops waving her arms around and stares at Greta.

Olive, completely new to this group and to this particular situation, offers me a beaming smile. "Well, he's hot and you're hot, so why not? Y'all look beautiful together."

After a moment of silence, we all burst out laughing. I can tell Olive is going to fit pretty damn well into this group already. The girl is striking. She's wearing a short dress in the same hue as her name, which looks ridiculously beautiful with her long, sleek burgundy hair. Her skin is alabaster, and her makeup is understated to complement it, with the exception of her dark red lipstick. She's obviously in shape, with long legs that rival Greta's, and toned arms. She's a stunner for sure, and I like her immediately.

I tell the girls about my one wild night with Drake, leaving out the reason I left so suddenly.

"But if it was good, then why have you acted so mean to him all this time?" Greta sounds honestly bewildered, and I don't blame her.

"He...he broke one of my rules that night. And I just couldn't deal with seeing him after that. I actually never expected to see him again, except then Dare came and he and Berkeley happened. It was like I couldn't get away from Drake after that."

Berkeley nods, her face full of sympathy. We've been friends since high school, and although I've never opened up to her about my father and what he did to me, I know she's guessed at the fact that something very bad happened in my childhood that I don't like to talk about. She's also familiar with my "rules" when sleeping with a guy.

"Did you tell him the rules beforehand?" she asks softly.

Thinking back, I actually can't recall if I did or not. Usually, when I go home with a guy, I'm very up front and open about the rules for having sex with me. I make sure they understand and are on board before anything goes down. But that night with Drake…I was so caught up…

"I don't think I did." I'm frowning, because it's so unlike me.

Berkeley smiles sadly. "Then how could you have expected him to follow them?"

I stare at her, struck with how true that question is. I never explained the rules, so the fact that I treated him like shit for years afterward was never fair. I hang my head, and Greta rubs small circles on my back.

"Well," she says. "It looks like you guys have patched things up now. I mean, from the look of things at that dinner table, we got you out of there just in time."

"Y'all were definitely about to set that room on fire," offers Olive helpfully.

I laugh, swiping a tear away from my eye. I hadn't realized I was crying. "He's pretty fucking sexy. And I think I'm probably way too messed up for him to stick around for long."

Berkeley backs up a step, giving me a murderous look. "You are one of the strongest, sexiest, most giving people I know. Don't you dare talk about yourself like you're not good enough for Drake. You two can be good for *each other.*"

Greta nods, agreeing wholeheartedly.

They might be right. But they don't know. They don't know how truly black my soul is on the inside. What happened to me all those years ago changed me. I know that I can never come back from it, no matter how well I fake it for my friends. I'm so broken inside that the second Drake is with me in that way again, with all of our new emotions on the table, he'll know.

And he'll never want to be with me again. He'll be utterly disgusted.

I can't get caught up in all the physical heat between the two of us. Because when that day comes, and he walks away from me without looking back because of what I've been through, I'll break into so many pieces I don't think I'd be able to put myself back together this time.

When we finally make it back to the table, our food has arrived. Clearly Drake listened to what I said about the salad, because the most delicious looking shrimp Cobb salad is sitting at my place. There's also a steaming loaf of bread for us to pass around, and my sangria is just waiting for me to gulp it down.

"Thank you." My tone is honest and open as I look at Drake.

He seems to understand that I'm thanking him for more than just paying for my dinner. He meets my gaze, and his arm goes around the back of my chair. His fingers gently graze my shoulder, and I'm introduced to a brand-new awareness, one I only know when I'm with Drake Sullivan.

Safety.

"You're welcome."

I dig in just as everyone else does, and dinner is almost over when I glance up from my food randomly just for a second. I see a familiar-looking blonde walking past our table with her date, and when our gazes meet she frowns slightly, and then her eyes widen. Stopping beside my chair, she exclaims loud enough for the whole table to hear.

"*Mea?* Mea Sanchez?"

Every single muscle in my body freezes, including the ones that work my mouth. I just stare at the girl, having no clue who she is or how she knows me by that name.

"Um…" *Great. And now I sound like a complete idiot.* The rest of the table is staring as well, at either the unknown girl or me.

"That's not…not my name," I stammer, finally.

And then I pray, I pray with everything inside of me that she'll just walk away.

13

Drake

I don't think I've ever seen Mea's face as drawn or pinched as it is right now. And there's a distinct terror in her eyes that makes me want to stand up and get her out of there. I don't know who this chick is, but she's shaking my girl up. And I don't like it.

The blonde waves a flippant hand, like what Mea just said doesn't mean shit. "Please." Her drawl is distinctly southern, but not from Georgia or Carolina like I'm used to. It's a different dialect for sure. "It's not like there were many Sanchezes growing up in Kentucky. And I'd know your face anywhere."

Greta's mouth drops open at the girl's bigoted rudeness, and Berkeley makes a move to push back from her seat. I see Dare strong-arming her to stay seated.

The girl's rudeness snaps Mea out of her obvious shock and she stands. "I'm sorry, I'm not as familiar with you as you seem to be with me. Where do we know each other from?"

The girl plasters on a fake smile as she sizes Mea up. "Oh,

yeah, I guess I've changed a lot since middle school. We went to school together in Kentucky. And then, right after freshman year started, and your family…" The girl trails off, but her gaze is calculating, not sympathetic. "I guess you wouldn't want to talk about that. Anyway, where'd you end up? Here in Savannah?"

Mea folds her arms across her chest. "What's your name?" She's subtle, but I can see that she's ignoring the snoot's question.

"I can't believe you don't remember me! I'm Emily Shore. Remember? We competed against each other in that talent show back in seventh grade?"

Mea works really hard to not roll her eyes; I can see that the struggle is real.

"So, if you're living in Savannah, maybe I'll see you around again." Emily's fake, planted smile somehow grows even bigger.

I decide it's time to join in on this conversation. When I stand up beside Mea, the girl's eyes shift to me and they go wide. Her smile gets even bigger, and she pushes her tits out overtly. I guess her date be damned.

"Hi, I'm Emily. Mea and I go way back. You are?"

Mea speaks up quickly. Her buttery skin flushes a deep scarlet while her eyes flash hot fire. "He's…not for you, Emily. It was nice seeing you."

Emily looks taken aback, and then her eyes narrow. "Yeah, maybe we should hook up on Facebook and catch up."

Mea stands strong. Pride swells up in me as something inside my soul recognizes a deep attraction to the very identity of hers. "I'm not on Facebook."

Emily tosses her one more fake smile. "Funny. I always thought the people who aren't on Facebook must have something to hide. Anyway, good seeing you, doll!" She pulls her date behind her and they leave the restaurant.

Mea falls back into her seat with a huff, and Berkeley starts in.

"That *bitch*. I swear to God if Dare hadn't been holding me down"—she gives Dare a dark look—"I would have punched her in her smug face. Also, I didn't know you lived in Kentucky before you moved to Brunswick County."

Mea's sigh is weary. I'm also curious about her roots, because we've never had a conversation about her past. But I do know there's something in it that she doesn't want to dig up, and I can imagine seeing a face from her past has shaken her up. I place an arm around her shoulders, and sure enough, she's trembling. I rub soothing circles down her arm, and she gives me a grateful glance.

"Can we just not talk about it right now?" she asks Berkeley tersely.

Berkeley, taken aback, just nods.

"Do you want to go back to the house?" I ask her, leaning in so she's the only one who hears me.

She shakes her head. "No way. This won't ruin our night. What's next?" She addresses the last question to the table.

Berkeley brightens. "A night out in downtown Savannah!"

I look at Mea, and her face isn't quite back to its usual sunniness. It's a little shadowed, no doubt because of the incident she just endured. She meets my searching gaze for just a second before her expression shutters and she plasters on a smile. I know she's doing it because she wants to be happy for her friends' big weekend. But I'd be willing to bet the last thing she wants to do right now is party.

But Mea agrees. "Sounds like just what I need."

I tuck her under my arm as we head down the street, moving at a leisurely pace. She fits there, which surprises the fuck out of me. I'm no small dude, and Mea is tiny. But having her pressed up against my side feels good. Feels more than good.

We decide, because of the way we're dressed, to stick close by in the historic downtown area. Ending up at a chic bar known for their signature cocktails, we pull up barstools around a high-top table and soak in the atmosphere. It's classic and contemporary, and even though the vibe is more upscale than the places I usually go back in Carolina, I dig the laid-back feel of the place. A male bartender comes around the bar to ask us if we've been to the place before and we tell him we're just visiting. He's flirty with the ladies and I get it, because they're all sexy as hell and he's gotta earn his tips. So I lean back on my stool and take it in with amusement as he schmoozes them, explaining the variety of southern cocktails they can order.

"Rule for the night," announces Berkeley. She claps her hands together, all bossy. Dare shakes his head at her with amusement, and Greta and Mea pay attention.

Jeremy gasps, pretending to be shocked. "There's *rules*? I thought this was a party weekend!"

Olive laughs.

Berkeley narrows her eyes at him. "That's *why* there's rules. This bar has tons of delicious-looking signature cocktails. No one is ordering beer tonight, got it?"

Ronin, who's usually pretty quiet, groans. "Seriously?"

Dare chuckles, brushing a chunk of Berkeley's light blond hair away from her forehead. "I'll order one, babe. Get me what you're having."

Jeremy shakes his head slowly "Dude, you are so whipped."

Berkeley snuggles into Dare's side. "Actually, Jeremy, we both like a little bit of whipping."

When Jeremy's eyes grow huge, Dare snorts out a laugh, which turns into a cough.

Mea bursts into laughter. "Whips and chains do have their place, gentlemen."

My cock twitches at her comment, and it doesn't help a bit when she lays a hand on my thigh under the table and squeezes. She's full of surprises, this one. And I just want to label her.

Mine, mine, mine.

Now Ronin turns on her, and I spy the hungry glance in his eyes. Predatory.

That shit ain't happening. I pull her barstool as close to mine as it can get and shoot him a glare. My look roars *hands off.* I can see from his knowing expression that he gets it.

With a round of cocktails ordered, we settle in for the night. Drinks, conversation, and laughter. It's a good start to the weekend.

But I can't keep my attention from the woman sitting next to me. She's funny, she's dynamic, she's a whole handful that I'm not sure I can keep up with, but I'm realizing that I damn sure want to try.

After we've had our fill, the stroll back to our rented historical house is easy and relaxed. I lag behind with Mea, because, well, I want her to myself. At this point, I don't even think it's a secret anymore. Dare and Grisham have given me a few pointed glances during the night, but I can't care less what they think. Whatever is happening here is happening between me and her, and no one else.

The thing that's really eating away at me from the inside out is the fact that she's struggling with something on the inside. Seeing that girl from her past in the restaurant tonight has awakened some demons in her, and I don't think it's the first time they've been roused. If her nightmares are any indication, she's wrestling with something. Something big.

And something inside of me, something brand-new that I've never dealt with before, wants to show her that I'm strong enough to beat them back for her. I can be strong for her. She doesn't have to handle any of it by herself.

Whatever "it" is.

As we're walking, I take her hand. She stares down at it, almost as if she's in shock.

When she glances back up at me, I smirk. "What? A guy's never held your hand before?"

Her face is completely perplexed, and with a sinking in my gut I realize the answer to my flippant question is yes. A guy has literally never held her hand before. Is it because all the men she's dated before me have been that dense, that fucking blockheaded, or is it because she never lets men get close enough to grab her hand?

Either way, a river of sadness runs through me, the current fast and strong. It seems like every time I'm with Mea, I'm drowning in some sort of intense emotion. The desire to protect her. The wanting…the sheer lust she creates whenever she touches me or whenever I look at her. The fury that eats me alive when I realize she's been hurt—really hurt—by someone in her past that she trusted.

The tumult of emotions makes me remember the feelings I used to have about my mom…so goddamn many of them. And it makes me crave a drink.

"Get used to it." I say it with simple clarity, so she knows there's no game with me. I like her. A lot. And she intrigues me.

I can't remember the last time a woman did that.

Oh, yes I can. The one who ran away from me after giving me the most mind-blowing sex of my life.

Her small hand squeezes mine. The movement is so feminine, so gentle and sweet, that I quickly look at her. It's rare that Mea is gentle and sweet. My little tornado is calming, and the fact that I'm here to witness it, maybe even being the cause of it, makes me one lucky bastard.

As soon as we walk inside the house, the others are lounging around in the great room. The girls have kicked off their shoes, legs tucked up underneath them on the couch. Mea heads for a seat next to Berkeley when her ringtone goes off.

She checks the caller ID, and then immediately veers for the hallway. I stand at the entrance to the great room, keeping one eye on her and one on the activity of our friends.

"What?" she asks. Her tone grabs my full attention.

"No," she says, sounding like she's in disbelief. "That's not right. We're supposed to have two weeks."

She listens again, and then nods. Her voice makes my throat catch when she speaks again. "It's fine. I'll be fine, Mikah. Don't worry about me. Good night."

She stands there, staring at her phone. The magnet that pulls me toward her is so strong right now I can't stay rooted to my spot. I drift toward her, but when she looks at me her eyes are stricken, and I freeze.

"Mea?"

She raises a hand, shakes her head, and flees up the stairs.

I'm left in the hallway, wondering what to do. With everything inside of me I want to go to her. Whatever she heard on the other end of the phone undid her.

Tied her up in knots. Pushed her over the edge.

But what could it have been? I know that Mikah is her brother. What did he tell her?

Enough thinking.

I take the steps two at a time until I reach the closed door of her lavender room. Knocking softly, I wait. I want to barge in, so much so that my hands are fisted in front of me against the door.

"I'm okay." Her voice is choked on the other side, and another piece of my heart breaks.

"No, you're not. Let me in, sweetheart."

There's a pause, and I can hear the rustling of the sheets on her bed. I think I hear a sob, but it's so muffled I can't be sure.

"Mea." My voice is pained.

Tortured. Tortured. Tortured.

"Go away, Drake."

I curse, pounding a fist on the door once before I turn away. She needs to be alone.

Translation: I'm not what she needs.

Heading back downstairs, I head straight for the bar and pour myself a whiskey. The liquor burns as it blazes down my throat, and I feel a false sense of relief as it goes down. Finishing that first drink more quickly than I should, I pour another.

And another.

14

Mea

They moved it up, Mea. Aunt T just called me. His parole hearing is tomorrow."

I replay Mikah's statement in my head over and over again, all while lying facedown on my gorgeous, temporary, lavender bed. It even smells like lavender.

This can't be happening. After what my father did to me, there's no way they'd just let him go, right? But he's been in prison for ten years already. Of a fifteen-year sentence. Maybe they'll decide he's served his time.

When I know the truth: there'll never be enough time in prison for him. Not even a lifetime would do.

I'm filled with a perverted sense of relief, because I don't have to go and say anything at all. The parole board can make their decision without me having to go through the turmoil of seeing my father again and speaking about him to a roomful of strangers.

I think about my mother. Not the vacant one who eventually succumbed to her desire to leave. But the one before. The vibrant one I can just barely remember. The one I hold on to so desperately in my heart. What would she do?

She'd say there's no point agonizing over something you can't change. And if there's a possible outcome that worries you, you don't have to handle it alone.

I'm tired of handling everything alone. I shield most of what I went through emotionally from Mikah, because he's my little brother. It was always my job to protect him. I never told my best friends, because how do you tell someone that your father repeatedly assaulted you? It doesn't come up in casual conversation. It really doesn't even come up in deep conversations.

I never told a man I loved, because I never allowed myself to love one.

The one man I ever loved hurt me.

I roll over onto my back and then sit up. Staring around the gorgeous room, I make a decision. This is not something I can handle alone. Whether my father is released or not, I don't want the burden of him on my shoulders alone anymore. I want to tell someone.

Taking a minute, I close my eyes and just breathe. In yoga, the deep breathing of the Shavasana calms you, relaxes you. I give myself about two minutes of the deep cleansing breaths.

And then I know who I want to tell first.

Glancing at the time, I'm shocked that it's past midnight. I change out of my dress and into comfy yoga pants and a soft tank top. Leaving my feet bare, I tiptoe out of my room and into the hallway. Downstairs is quiet. Everyone must have turned in for the night.

There's a night-light on the wall in the hallway. I follow the soft glow to Drake's bedroom door. I don't bother to knock.

Shutting the door softly behind me, I find him sprawled across his bed. I suck in a sharp breath, because there's a soft lamp on the bedside table, and I'm able to take in the fact that he's wearing nothing but charcoal boxer-briefs. His ass is absolutely perfect. I get distracted following the hard, cut lines of his muscular back to his tattoo-sleeved arms. I drink him in with my eyes, because my God he's beautiful.

He's asleep, snoring softly. He's so big, his bare feet hang diagonally off the bed. I creep up and crawl into bed beside him, circling myself into a ball at his side.

Immediately, he tucks one arm around me and groans sleepily. He doesn't turn his head to face me, but his hand is soft and warm against my ribs.

"Mea." His voice is rough sandpaper against a wooden surface, and it sends a shiver creeping across my skin.

"How did you know it was me?" I whisper.

He sighs gently before rolling his big body over and pulling me into his chest. He cradles me with both of his strong arms, and I'm so relieved to be here I could almost cry. The lump in my throat is proof of that.

"Because I feel you, baby."

His breath whispers across my face, and I wrinkle my nose. "You smell like a brewery, Drake."

"Had a few before I crashed."

I stiffen. "It smells like more than a few."

He shifts, and when I look up at him, his eyes are half-closed. He's barely having this conversation with me right now. Unease courses through my system.

"You were upset. Made me upset."

I sigh. "Oh, Drake. I told you I was okay. I just needed a little time."

Shrugging, he tugs me closer. It only takes another minute before his breathing slows and evens out.

He's asleep.

Half angry with him that I was all geared up, finally ready to tell him my deepest, darkest secret, but he's too drunk to listen, and half relieved just to be in his arms, I stay. It takes me awhile, but eventually, sleep finds me, too.

I'm standing beside the window in a Warrior pose when Drake's waking groan draws my attention. Sitting up in bed, he searches the room until he finds me. I pad over to the bed and climb in. He places a soft kiss on my head.

"You weren't a dream, sweetheart?" he asks.

Shaking my head, I don't look up. "Nope. And neither was the fact that you were too wasted to talk to me when I came in here last night."

He sucks in a sharp breath; his chest moves with the effort. "Fuck. I'm sorry, Mea."

I'm not quite sure if sorry is going to cut it.

"It's just…before these last couple of months…I don't remember ever seeing you drunk. And now…" I let the sentence hang.

With a sigh, Drake sits up, pulling me up with him. We lean against the headboard together, both lost in our own thoughts.

"Did you have something important to tell me last night?" His tone is so soft, so gentle. It's amazing he can talk to me like that, considering his size and toughness. I trace the inky lines on his forearm. There's a big, Gothic-looking cross there, with lots of tribal lines working around it to make a beautiful mural.

He cups my chin with one hand, tilting it up so that I can see his face. His eyes are red-rimmed, shadowy underneath. It makes me sad.

"Yes," I whisper.

He mutters a curse. "I fucked up. So, so sorry, baby. I want to be here for you. I do."

But now, he's going to have to prove that. So I just tilt my lips in a small smile.

I pull away from him and climb out of bed. "I'm going to go take a shower and see what Berkeley wants to do today."

As I walk out of the room, I take one last look back at him. He's sitting in the same spot, his hands covering his face.

If he wants to do this with me, if he wants to be the guy I turn to when I need someone, then he's going to have to get his shit together. I'm enough of a mess for two people.

"Seriously, Berkeley?" My voice is grumbly as I pull the black leather strap tight on my helmet. "I'm pretty sure this was supposed to be a spa day."

I glance around me, miles of Georgia's deciduous greenery reflecting the radiance of the morning sun. I can already picture the miles of dirt trails and exploratory freedom just waiting for us to rip it up. When I turn back to Berkeley, she's eyeing the acres around us with apprehension.

Worrying her bottom lip between her teeth, her voice is much breathier than usual. "This is a *couples* Before the Wedding weekend, Mea. Remember? That means we actually have to spend time with the guys. Dare's pick today was riding ATVs in the jungle."

She shudders slightly, and a barely suppressed giggle finds its way out of my throat. "Oh my God, Berkeley. Why didn't you just tell him you were scared to death to do this?"

Berkeley has a lot of talents. I mean, a *lot*. She's a gifted artist, and she hangs something of her own making on the wall of every interior design job she takes on. But when it comes to organized sports or basically anything that requires her to be physically active, she's the very definition of the phrase "hot mess."

With her helmet strapped firmly in place, one arm linked through Olive's, Greta steps up beside us. The breeze stirs her gleaming raven hair. Berkeley frowns at Greta. Her natural grace and long, lithe limbs ensure that she'll probably have no trouble handing the motored adventure vehicles we'll be riding today.

"Dammit, Greta." Berkeley's voice carries a note of annoyance. "Why do you have to be so damned good at everything?"

Greta's brows furrow as confusion puckers her forehead. "What?"

Laughing, I smooth my hand down Greta's arm. "Don't worry

about it, sweetie. Berkeley is going to hate every second of this, that's all. But it's too late to go back now, Berk."

Olive pipes up. Her deep-south drawl is super-size in this environment, and she's almost trembling with excitement. "Berkeley, it's gonna be so much fun! We can race the guys and show them how awesome we are."

When Berkeley turns a disgusted glance of disbelief on the redhead, I pat the helmet she's still holding in her arms. "Suit up, Blondie!"

Berkeley glares. But at that moment, the guys stroll up to us, looking rugged and sexy and ready to ride. None of them will have an ounce of difficulty with today's fun, and the machismo is basically rolling off all of them in virile waves of manliness. I try, I really try, not to roll my eyes, but I fail miserably.

And then Drake hits me with one of his rare super-size grins, and I'm a lost little girl looking for a comfortable place to snuggle into, and I almost cross the distance to wrap my arms around him. I clench my hands into fists and squeeze, just to force myself to stay still.

"Babe, why don't you have your helmet on yet?" Dare's voice is gentle as he takes the helmet from her hands and places it softly on her mop of curls. "There you go. You ready?"

Her smile falters.

Dare's grin lights up his entire face. Before he met Berkeley, I heard the guy was a brooder. Not anymore. "I got us a two-seater, babe. You're riding with me."

The relief that floods Berkeley's expression is comical, and we all burst out laughing.

I raise my hands toward the sky. "Praise Jesus. Now, can we get moving?"

Drake gives me a strange look. "What, like you've been four-wheelin' before?"

Strange thing about being in Georgia. Everyone's drawl seems to get stronger just from the open air and scent of peaches.

I place my hands on my hips and stare him down. "I grew up in Kentucky, and then I lived on a farm in Brunswick County. I've probably ridden more ATVs than you have, Mr. Army Ranger Extraordinaire."

Drake's eyes narrow with the challenge, and a sexy smirk curls his lips. "Want to make it interesting?"

The guys all hoot, and Jeremy raises his hand. "I'll take that bet."

Turning my scowl on him, he gives me a teasing grin and shrugs.

I might be little, definitely the smallest person in this group, but if Drake thinks I'm going to back down from this challenge he'd better think again. The stubborn adrenaline lights a fire inside me, and I stride toward him, holding my hand out in front of me.

I spit in it, and hold it back out to Drake.

The guys hoot again and I hear Berkeley's quiet "Ewww." Olive's laughter is almost musical, and Greta just shakes her head as she leans into Grisham.

"Bet I make it to the end of the first course before you do, Sullivan."

Without hesitation, Drake spits in his hand and envelops my

small one in his enormous one. Glancing down at where we're joined, heat flows into my lower belly because he tugs me close to his chest. Then, in front of everyone, he plants a soft kiss on my lips.

Leaning close to my ear, he whispers. "Just remember, I never lose."

Without another word, I turn on trembly legs and mount my ATV. Everyone around us does the same, except for Jeremy. He stands off to the side and raises one arm in air. Dare is laughing so hard he can't get the words out, but he gestures for Drake and me to pull up in front of the rest of them. Berkeley looks comfy in the front seat, though I have a feeling she's got a vise grip on her man's thigh.

I glance at Drake. He's staring at me, and when he notices my attention he licks his lips and guns his engine. A hot flash thrusts me into a tailspin for a moment, thinking about the way his tongue feels when it touches my skin. *Damn him!* I shake my head. My curls whip against my neck as I pucker my lips and blow him a kiss.

Even from a few feet away, I can see Drake's reaction to my air-kiss. His bottom lip is tugged into his mouth and his eyes hood seductively.

It's at that moment that Jeremy's arm slashes downward, and I grit my teeth and press down hard on the pedal.

It's glorious; the kiss of sweet southern air rushing past my face and the sensation of speed taking control of you. I've almost forgotten what it feels like to let go like this. I let out a scream of pure joy as my four-wheeler hits its maximum speed. When I allow my eyes to slide to my side, I see Drake is right there with me. There's a big grin on his face that tells me he, too, is having the time of his life.

Laughing, I keep my eyes on the trail and notice a narrowing of the dirt path coming up fast. Determined to stay ahead of my competitor, I gun it, and he falls behind me.

Sucker. I can't hide my happiness, but deep down inside I know that Drake let me slip ahead. I glance over my shoulder and he's trailing me closely. It only takes a few more minutes for me to reach the end of the narrow lip of trail, and that's when Drake really hits the gas. He bullets past my vehicle and reaches the end of the trail just before I do.

I can't help it when my lips puff out in a pout. We both pull off our helmets and Drake gives me an adorable smile that causes something inside my stomach to shift and flutter. "I thought I had you, Sullivan!"

He shakes his head, pretending to feel empathy for me, when I know all he really feels is euphoria. "A bet's a bet, wild girl. I won it fair."

His expression carries a hint of danger, and a sexy confidence that's all Drake. His biceps bulge through his gray long-sleeved Henley, and it pulls taut over the broad planes of his chest. I can't help it; my eyes scan every inch of him slowly. Hungrily. A gradual flame has been burning since I saw him this morning, and seeing him now, straddling his ATV, looking all windswept and sexy, it's going to spread into an uncontrollable fire really quick. His faded jeans fit him just right; I can see the strong ridges of his thigh muscles as he clenches the seat.

"Mea." My eyes look to his, startled at the sandpaper tone in his deep voice. "Get on my ride."

My eyebrows fly up. "What?"

"Get on. I won the bet. That's what I want. You behind me on this four-wheeler."

Oh, hell. The usual Mea would never allow a man to order her around. The usual Mea would usually tell him exactly what he could do with his bet and turn my back. But with Drake, I don't want to be the usual Mea.

The usual Mea is lonely, deep down. She doesn't let anyone get close enough to see the profound slices that mar her heart and the war wounds that afflict her soul. The usual Mea gets by with shallow, surface emotions that are usually enough to fool those around her and deflects questions that get too personal, cut too deep.

But that Mea is bone weary, and Drake is slowly wearing down the wall she's built around herself so artfully.

I don't hesitate. Climbing off my ATV, I walk the few short steps it takes to get to him and climb on the back. My arms go around his waist and my face lies against his back. He smells like outdoor air, pine, and scented soap.

It's becoming my new favorite scent.

His right hand reaches back, curling around my thigh with deliberate possession. When he looks back at me, there's no humor in his eyes.

"Ready?"

It's a loaded question. Am I ready to ride on the back of this ATV with him?

Yes.

Am I ready to trust him with my safety?

Yes.

Am I ready to give my body over to him, passionately and with abandon?

Yes.

Am I ready to trust him with my heart?

Not yet.

It's locked up too tight, and I'm not sure I can even remember where I hid the key. I might have buried it, along with any positive emotions or memories I have of the only other man I trusted with it.

My father.

The man who, as I'm growing closer to Drake, could be released from prison and unleashed onto the world once again.

15

Drake

I can't explain how it feels. Her arms wrapped around me, squeezing with just the right amount of pressure. The way her thighs press so tight against mine, like she's using her legs to hug me. It propels me into the future, one where I'm hovering above her perfect, naked body with her legs wrapped around my waist with that same tight press that makes me want to roll my eyes back in my head.

She's making me lose myself. I almost can't keep it together, keep us on the trail, keep myself from stopping the ATV and scooping her up. But I know I messed up last night. I don't know how I can read her so well, but I know…I *know* she needs time. She needs me to prove that I can be trusted with anything she's willing to give.

I want her to give me everything.

The expression on Mea's face last night when she got that phone call, that expression reached into my chest and crushed my heart in its devastated fist. I wanted to crawl through the phone, grab her brother for making her face look so stricken. The urge to comfort, to protect, to *claim* was so strong it was like a living, breathing thing inside of me. I've never felt anything like that before.

And the current of energy around her continued to swirl, swirl, swirl. Her tornado didn't succumb to her obvious desolation. It just got stronger, angrier, threatening to suck everything around it into its stormy center.

What could have made her feel that way? What scares her that much?

It has something to do with her past. I know that much. There's something inside of her so dark, so deep, that I couldn't reach the depths of it even if I tried. If I'm going to know, it'll be because she drags me down there with her.

But I'm strong enough to swim her up, save her from the current of the secret that terrifies her.

I just don't think she knows that yet.

Her startled shout alerts me, and I turn my head to see her small hand pointing off into the woods beside us. I cut the engine, and the ATV slows and stutters to a stop. I remove my helmet so I can hear what she's saying, and she does the same.

With one arm still grabbing my middle, she points with enthusiasm again. "Did you see it, Drake?"

Looking back at her with confusion, I shake my head. "See what?"

She sighs, a happy, dreamy look entering her eyes that I don't think I've seen there before. "It was a deer, two of them, actually.

A mom and her baby. They were so sweet, standing there, but they darted away before we got close."

I can't help but smile at her expression. The girl is seriously melting me, rearranging my insides until I don't recognize them. They're becoming all soft and sweet whenever I look at her. "The engine scared them."

Her curls swish against my cheek as she leans in closer, sniffing. "You smell so good."

Her voice has gone all low and husky, and my dick instantly jerks to attention like it's responding to a signal that only she knows. "Yeah?" The thudding of my heart is heavy, harsh, and violent.

She breathes out. "Yeah."

She lifts her eyes, big, warm, and beautiful to meet mine. I'm hypnotized for a minute, just staring into them while she stares right back. With an uncontrollable surge of *need*, my body moves into autopilot and I just react.

I tug her wrist, pulling her off the back of the bike. When she's standing beside me, a quick gasp escapes her as I pull her to straddle my lap.

And then she's mine.

Her lips are *mine*, her mouth belongs to me.

And I pillage.

And I plunder.

At the insistent urge of my tongue, she opens to me with a moan. I pull back for a second.

"Sexiest sound I ever heard, baby." I don't want to scare her, but I can't do much more than growl at this moment.

Claiming her lips again, I taste her and she's perfect. Fucking perfect. She presses against me, forcing me to go deeper, to kiss her harder. When she grinds her hips against my rock-hard cock, I can't take it anymore. Her hands sift through my hair. Rough, rough, rough.

I wrench away from her devilish mouth and grab her ass. The fact that any other rider could come along at any moment only amps me up, not slows me down. I lift her up, and when I plunge her back down on top of me she clamps down on her bottom lip with her teeth and drops her head into my shoulder.

"Drake," she whispers. Harsh, harsh, harsh.

Then she bites down hard on my shoulder.

"Fuuuuuck." My breathing is ragged, heavy.

I need this woman. I need to cover her, and I need her to cover me. I need to crawl inside of her, buried deep, and learn her from the inside out. The impression of wanting to jump out of my own damn skin and into hers is eating me up. Swallowing me whole. Burning me alive.

The not-so-distant sound of several engines pulls me back to the here and now, and I freeze. My hands are still on Mea's firm, round ass as she moves her head to glance at me. Her eyelids are heavy and she's wearing this sexy "I want you" look that could make me come in my jeans if I'm not careful.

I want to roar with the frustration of it, but instead I climb off the ATV, pulling her with me. When I'm standing on two feet again I set her down gently in front of me but I don't let her go.

Our friends, their ATVs slowing down to approach us, are just coming into view when I growl at her. "Later."

She bats long lashes at me. "Promise?"

Both of my hands lift to the sides of my head and I squeeze hard. Doesn't work. Trying to get her out of my mind is like trying to eat French fries without ketchup. Doesn't make any sense.

"Shit, man, we saw Mea's four-wheeler abandoned back there and got worried!" Dare's disapproval rings clear in his tone as he assesses me. When his eyes graze over Mea and her current state of ruffled, sex-kitten appearance his eyes widen the slightest bit. Swinging his gaze back to me, he shakes his head.

"Won a bet." I jerk my thumb toward Mea. "She's the prize."

Greta's tinkling laugh warrants my attention and I glance at her. "She's a perfect prize."

My gaze strays to Mea again, who's shifting from foot to foot with something akin to embarrassment. I smile as something strange and unfamiliar fills me up and practically lifts me off my feet. "I know."

We spend the rest of the morning riding, and when we've all had our fill we pack it in and decide to grab a late lunch back at the house and rest up for the night.

The fragrant Savannah air is light and airy with the impending spring, and the space inside my chest feels the same way. It makes me see how much grief and guilt I've been carrying around since my mother's death. And even before she died, I carried myself with the heaviness of a weighty load on my shoulders.

The responsibility of taking care of her and myself was laid on me at way too young an age. And I never really learned how to unburden myself after I became an adult. I carried responsibility on my shoulders through basic training and right into the

Ranger battalion. My brothers in arms were my responsibility. Their safety, whether or not they made it home to their parents, wives, and kids, fell on my shoulders.

It's a pattern I never learned how to change, because I never realized how much the weight of it all was crushing me.

I'm sitting at the table in the sunny morning room just off the kitchen when Dare's brother Chase plunks down in another seat. It's early afternoon, and everyone is doing his or her own thing.

When I look at Chase, he's got a shit-eating grin on his face that makes me want to punch it off.

"What?" My voice is gruffer than usual.

"I remember when it happened to me. Felt like a damn train hit me. Never saw it coming. Never saw *her* coming." His tone is matter-of-fact, like he's talking about the right way to reassemble the engine of a classic Firebird.

My brain tries to follow his random train of thought, keep up with where he's headed, but I fail miserably. Confusion is at the forefront of it all, and it must show on my face. "I'm lost, Chase. What?"

He leans forward, lacing his fingers together. Chase and Dare look nothing alike. They're foster brothers, and they share that bond like it's made from blood. Chase used to be a mess. Gambling, conning, and scheming were all he was good for. Until he met Shay. Everything changed for him from that point on, and Dare was grateful for it. He was always the one to bail Chase out, but now Chase has become the father and husband none of us ever thought he'd be.

"It happened to me the second I saw Shay. I never looked back. She was wrapped up tight in that criminal bastard Chavez's hold, but I couldn't see anything but her. Would have laid it all on the line if I had to. I see the same look on your face when you're with Mea. Like you can't get enough."

Like I'd drown in her if I could.

I avert my gaze, turning it toward the giant bay window once again. "You don't know what you're talking about, Chase. This girl...she's complicated. So am I."

Just talking about her like this with someone else is causing my blood to heat in my veins. She's in there...when did that happen? The first night I slept with her years back? The night she got my drunken ass home from See Food? Or was it the night I saw how vulnerable and fragile she is despite the strong vibes she puts out during the day?

The answer? All of those. She crawled under my skin and never left. She's seated there like it's her throne, her place to rule over me like the queen she is.

"Sullivan!" Her voice interrupts our conversation at the perfect moment and she glides into the kitchen. She's seriously the only woman I know who moves like that, like she's always floating. It's magnetic; drawing people toward her in her wake wherever she goes. "Let's talk about tonight."

Chase's muffled cough hides his amusement as I turn toward her with my entire body. "Right. You want to split them up tonight, right?"

Mea's adorable grin pulls her luscious lips up just a little higher on one side. "Absolutely. Don't you want to give Dare a *real* bachelor party, just for a night? We can meet up later if you want. I just need a couple of hours with Berkeley to get a bachelorette scavenger hunt going." She rubs her hands together like the dirty ideas are already rolling through her mischievous mind.

I can't help but smile at her. "Sounds good. We can handle Dare for a few hours, right, Chase?"

Chase's eyes are bouncing back and forth between the two of us. "'Course we can." I can see his own set of questionable plans taking shape just behind his eyes.

Mea's beautiful brown eyes hold mine for a second. The girl is as sure of herself as anyone I know, but I can see a hint of uncertainty in her gaze. As she turns to leave Chase and me alone, I grab on to her wrist and give Chase a pointed look.

It takes him all of five long seconds before he reads it and comprehends. Standing up, he slaps my shoulder and drops a kiss on Mea's cheek before he leaves the room.

I tug Mea onto my lap and she comes willingly, turning her body to the side so that her head finds a nesting spot on my chest. Moving my hand down her smooth skin until I'm holding her hand, I squeeze her delicate, slender fingers gently between mine. "What's up, baby girl?"

She runs a dark-polished fingernail over my collarbone, blazing a trail on the soft cotton of my thermal. My gaze drops to follow her trajectory; she traces the place where my heart is now beating an erratic rock song in my chest. When I lift my eyes again, hers are melted liquid pools of chocolate.

Damn. She's fucking gorgeous.

"Well…" Her lip is sucked into her mouth as she hesitates and I control myself, somehow refraining from taking the succulent flesh into my own mouth to suck.

"Well?" My voice has dropped low and rough. I can't help it, she brings out the barest, basic natural instinct inside of me to take what's mine and mark it. Procure, possess, protect.

Her head drops against me again as she guides her finger down lower. When it reaches my abdomen and she traces the lines of my muscles there, I clench my teeth hard. When she crosses the threshold between my shirt and my jeans, dipping her finger below the denim, I hiss out a whispered curse.

"Mea." She's exactly one breath away from unleashing the beast inside me. Does she know it? Is that what she wants?

I can't get this wrong. I need her to tell me what she wants. What she needs.

"Earlier, on the ATV? You said 'later.' I was just wondering how much later you meant."

Every muscle, every breath, every heartbeat I have goes still while I evaluate her words. I allow my brain a second to think it through, because I can't just plunge in with Mea. She's worth the time it takes to make sure we're on the same level, that we understand each other completely before I make any rash decisions. But damn if I don't want to rip every single item of clothing she's wearing right now off of her and plunge into her sweet, dark heat right here at this table.

When she lifts her head to glance at me again, all that thought is lost. Her eyes are the softest velvet, the deepest secret, the sweetest story ever told. And they focus on me with the intensity of someone who needs her body pleasured in a way that only I can do.

I'm on my feet then, cradling her against my chest as I eat up the distance between the kitchen table and the back staircase. She's weightless in my arms as I climb the steps, cross the hallway upstairs, and fling open the door to my temporary bedroom.

The afternoon sun is streaming in, and I say a silent prayer of thanks to whoever is listening. The first time with Mea again and I get to have her in the daylight? My cock twitches at the thought, ready to be freed from the cotton and denim separating him from the girl he seeks.

I cross the room, and place her down on my bed. She slides back a little bit, allowing her legs to hang over the side as she stares up at me. Kneeling, I pull off her boots and toss them behind me. Unbuttoning her jeans, I slide them down the lithe, shapely curves of her legs. Her skin is perfect, buttery and soft and fragrant. There're no girly floral perfumes for Mea. She's all woman and her scent reflects that. The inviting spice of amber and musk floods my nostrils, mixed with the heady, intoxicating aroma of her arousal wafting toward me from her panties. I want to bury my head between her legs, but first I want her naked.

"You're sure? This is what you want? *I'm* what you want?" I throw the questions out there in hopes that she doesn't back down. She's a fighter, I can sense that in her and I've seen it firsthand. She's been through more than enough shitstorms in her life to know when she's making a mistake. I don't want to be one of them. I want to be the opposite of a mistake for Mea.

Whatever that might be.

Her eyes, hooded with desire and locked in on my movements, lift to mine as she nods her head. "I want this. So much, Drake."

She says my name on a sigh that makes me weak. Tossing her jeans over my shoulder, I let my big hands slide up her thighs. Wrapping them around her ass, I yank her forward on the bed. "Take your shirt off. I need to see you. All of you."

She does as she's told, and I watch while she yanks the gray fabric over her head. She lets it drop to the floor beside me, and I watch with fascination as her chest rises and falls with a big breath. Her breasts, small and perfectly round, nearly spill out of her lacy white bra. Reaching around behind her back, she unclasps it and her breasts bounce free.

I lick my lips, because they've gone dry. "Fucking perfect. You know that, right? You're perfect."

A shadow of uncertainty, similar to what I saw in her expression just downstairs, crosses her face.

She really doesn't know that. Someone hurt her… before. I'm not an idiot, I figured that out. But it left her broken. She can't see herself the way I do.

The thought sends a tidal wave of rage crashing through me. I can't picture some asshole of a man putting his hands on her in order to hurt her. I don't know the details, and I hope that the day will come soon when she trusts me enough to let me in on what went down. But until then, all I want to be to her is the reassurance she's been missing.

"It's true." I don't mean to growl, but my thoughts make it impossible not to. "I'll show you."

I gesture toward the windows, where light streams in. "Baby, has anyone ever made love to you during the day? With the light shining down on all the best, secret, most beautiful parts of you?"

I know the answer before she shakes her head in the negative, and I push on, shaking my head in awe. "Because I can't tell you how happy I am that the sun is shining right now. Every inch of you is about to be revealed to me so that I can worship you the right way. The way you deserve. The way your body needs to be served."

The muscles in her legs begin to tremble beneath my hands. Her head falls against one of her shoulders, and I gently push her back so that she's lying down on the bed.

I dip my head, burying my nose between her thighs and inhaling a deep breath. Her scent washes over me, and I'm suddenly too hot to function. With a groan, I stand and reach behind my head, pulling my shirt off in one smooth movement. Then I unbutton my jeans. My dick is free the moment I unzip them, and I'm happy as fuck I decided to forgo underwear this morning after my shower. The jeans are gone, but I still want to crawl out of my own body and into hers.

Kneeling again, I place kisses on the insides of her thigh. Just before I reach the apex, I switch to the other leg, smoothing my hands up the sides of her and back down again. There aren't enough places to touch all at once. There aren't enough places to lick her, to kiss her, to taste her. I'm so limited, because I'm only a man, but I want to eat her up. In one swallow.

The tiny scrap of white cotton covering the center of my gravity at the moment need to come off. Almost like she's reading my mind, Mea lifts her hips off the bed with a frustrated sigh. I can't stop my grin as I take hold of the sides of her panties and tug them down her legs. Discarding them, I just take a second. To drink her in. Breathe her. Breathe her. Breathe her.

She plants her pretty little feet on my bare shoulders.

"Mea."

She glances down at me. Her voice is breathy and so damn sexy when she answers. "Yeah?"

"I'm gonna eat up that pretty little pussy now. Not gonna stop, not until you know exactly how you should be worshipped. You ready for me, baby?"

I pull back for a second searching her face. Because I need her to know that I'm not just asking her if she's ready to be intimate with me. I'm asking her so much more, and I need her to read it in my expression. To hear it in my voice. To feel it in my touch.

Her soft fingers land in my hair, tugging. Stroking. I close my eyes for a second, relishing the sensation. But they pop back open when she speaks.

"I'm ready for you, Drake."

I stare her down for a second, checking for any sign that she doesn't realize what she's getting into with me. I know better than anyone that with the shit going on in my head and in my heart that there is no easy road. Not with me. But she nods, like she sees me for exactly who I am.

And maybe she does, because isn't she the one who's been picking up the soggy pieces of me all over the bar for the last few months?

Dropping my head, my tongue meets her slick wet heat. She cries out, and her fingers are no longer gentle in my hair. Her feet push hard against my shoulders. I take another taste, and everything that is Mea flows into my mouth, down my throat, into my soul.

She tastes like the finest wine there is.

Her pleasure, free flowing from her core and into my mouth, is the sweetest thing I've ever savored. I treat her like she's fragile at first. Gentle swipes with my tongue through her folds and around her clit have her quivering in my hands. I can feel all of the tension inside of her coiled up in this one spot, and all I have to do is pull the cord for her to fall apart right in front of me.

When her moans are doing things to my body that I'm scared I won't be able to control, I graze her with my top teeth just before I pull her into my mouth and suck. Hard.

A slew of curses like I've never heard from a woman erupt from this tiny, debilitating creature in front of me. Her hips lift from the bed as she comes, and just like I promised I would be, I'm right there to catch her. I can tell she's still high, reveling in the stars above us, as I climb onto the bed beside her and pull her on top of me. Her body is liquid, her curves pressing against my ridges in the most alluring fucking way possible. I kiss her throat, her shoulders, pushing her hair off her face as she comes spiraling back down.

Opening sleepy, lust-filled eyes, she smiles at me. Steals my breath. Rocks my world before she touches me.

"Your turn."

I cover up my shock with a grin. "I want my turn to be inside of you."

With a sexy, satisfied smirk, she pushes up off my chest and positions herself right where I need her. Sucking in a gulp of air, I still her hips against me and reach for the bedside table. Remembering I'm not at home, I squeeze my eyes shut.

"I really hope I packed some condoms in my suitcase."

Her slender shoulders give a flippant shrug. "Go and check."

I head to my bag, searching the small pockets until I come up with that tiny foil packet. Holding it up to her in triumph, I stalk back toward the bed.

I've told her that I'm someone she can trust, and I'm more than glad I can back that up right now by keeping her safe.

"Please, Drake. I need...this. I need you."

I climb back on the bed. Knowing I'll never be able to say no to her.

I cup her face with both hands, stroking her high cheekbones with my thumbs. "Tell me something. And I need the truth, or we don't do this."

The wrinkle between her eyebrows shows her focus as she nods. "Okay."

Taking a deep breath, I ask the one thing that's been bothering me for almost three years. "What did I do the last time that sent you running? I never want to make that mistake again."

She freezes; her wide eyes focus on me and every muscle in her body tenses up. I continue stroking her face with gentle circles, telling her with my eyes that she's safe and that she can tell me anything. I can take it. I'm strong enough.

Her voice is a whisper so soft and so wretched that my heart clenches almost painfully in my chest. It's like with one look she's reaching inside me and squeezing with all her might, reducing the beating organ to useless dust. I want to take in some air, but I'm drowning in her deep, sad gaze.

"If I tell you, do you promise you won't think I'm crazy?"

Is it possible for twelve words to gut you, slice you in half like a midday meal?

16

Mea

I'm ruining this. I'm so sure of it as I watch something in his eyes turn dark and tortured. He looks pained, like it's hard for him to take a breath. My muscles, which have been frozen up until this point, allow me to move again and I make to remove myself from on top of him.

But his hands, so warm, so damn comforting, move to my hips to hold me to him. "I don't want you to go anywhere, Mea. I want to know what you have to tell me."

I search his face for any sign that he doesn't really want to hear any in-depth descriptions of my own personal brand of crazy. But his face is nothing but determined, sincere, and fierce. *I wish I knew what he's thinking. What is he fierce about? What did I say that obviously physically hurt him?*

It should be awkward, having a conversation with a man while you're sitting naked on top of him. Or maybe it shouldn't be, but it always would have been for me in the past. There's nothing but comfort and warmth right now, sitting with Drake. His hands, cupping my face with thumbs rubbing my cheeks so tenderly, make me feel safe and secure. The hard swell of his erection beneath me reminds me that he wants me still, in spite of the talking we've been doing for the past few minutes. The intimate and intense burn of his gaze on my face makes me feel important and *heard. Seen.*

He sees *me.* That thought has my mind whirling in a thousand different directions. I tilt my head to one side, leaning into the roughness of his palm as I wonder, marvel, at this fact. No one, aside from my brother, has ever really *seen* me.

Not the way Drake does.

This feels important. Momentous, even. I've been trying for years to deny that the night with him even happened. I never thought I'd be telling Drake what it was that made me shut down that night. The one thing that made me decide I never wanted to see him again.

Taking a deep breath, I blurt it out. "I have rules."

He blinks, his perplexity plain on his face. "Rules?"

An intense heat flushes my face as I continue. "When it comes to sex, I mean. I'm always the one to call the shots. I've never had sex within the confines of a relationship before. So I would always pick the guy. Make sure he fit my criteria, you know? And then I would tell him up front about the rules."

Drake's brow furrows as he tries to understand. "But you never told me about any rules, Mea."

Groaning, I throw my head back. Drake's hands settle on my shoulders, smoothing down the wrinkles of my agitation. "I know! That's the thing. With you, it's always been different. That day at the garage that we met, I was completely out of my element. That level of pure attraction that I felt toward you...it was something completely new to me and I had no idea how to handle it."

Drake sits up. I bounce on his lap a bit, but he steadies me with his hands as he draws me closer to his chest. And that chest distracts me for a minute as my eyes rove with hungry interest over the hard muscles and sprinkling of dark hair.

"Electric. That's how I always thought of it. It's how it's always been between us." Drake moves his head around, trying to find my attention once more.

I bob my head in the affirmative, grateful that he understands. "Yeah, I guess it has, hasn't it?"

My hair is all over the place, and Drake smooths the wild locks back from my face.

"You didn't tell me your rules that night. Tell me now."

Biting the corner of my bottom lip while I consider, I nod. As I talk, my heart rate picks up its rhythm, pounding an unforgiveable cadence against my ribs. "Um, I just have a few. First, I choose a guy who hasn't been drinking."

Drake's eyes narrow right before a deep sense of shame pours out of his shocked gaze. I say nothing, only watch him as he takes this statement in. Finally, he nods, swallowing hard. His Adam's apple bobs in his throat, and it sounds like he choked on it when he speaks. "Go on."

I sigh. "Next, I always provide protection. And the guy has to wear it."

His face is a mask of stone, I can't read anything in it. But his hands still touch me, holding me, soothing me. So I continue.

"The last rule...is that the guy I sleep with can never, ever be on top."

It's like I dropped a hammer in the room. Drake pulls back from me like he's been slapped. "I wasn't drinking that day."

I watch him with wary attention. "I know that. That's why I slept with you."

His voice rises slightly. "And we used a condom."

"Yeah." My stomach is clenching and unclenching, balling my muscles up and then expanding them again in a repetitive motion.

"But...I rolled you over that night. It was so damn good, Mea. You felt amazing. And I rolled you over just before we finished. Are you telling me..." His voice trails off, and he coughs, as if he's trying to expel something.

I don't say anything, only watch him. I imagine my expression is sad; I'm heartsick. Despairing. I'm already grieving the loss of him, because there's no way he'll want to be with me now.

And then he's clutching me to his chest with a ferocity I don't understand.

"I'm so, so sorry. I didn't know the rules."

I wrap my arms around his neck and pull back so I can look him right in the eye. "I know that. It wasn't fair to hold you responsible. Up until that moment, it was the best experience of my life. I was loving it. I was into it, right there with you. It's the messed-up shit inside my own head that messed me up that day. Not you. It's not your fault."

His eyes are almost savage as he shakes his head. "You're not messed up. I wish I had known, but whatever's going on inside your head is because of a ghost. It's not your fault either."

I think about that. Because of something he hadn't even realized he'd done, I pushed Drake away. And then I treated him horribly afterward because I couldn't stand to look at him and remember that day. But it's not because I was scared of him. It was because I was scared about the way he made me feel.

Out of control.

Drake reaches inside my head and plucks out my thoughts, as if I'd spoken them aloud. "You're in control here, baby." He leans back against the pillows, never dropping my gaze. He holds me captive with his eyes, and his hands are strong and sure as he hands me the condom. Positions me on top of his ready hardness.

He waits.

Glancing down, his dick jumps against my most sensitive spot and I'm a live wire again. With just a few words he's said everything I'll ever need to know. I slide the condom on his tip and roll it down over his impressive length.

I lift myself up, and then slowly sink down on top of him. We both groan at the sweetly illicit contact. I can see every muscle in Drake's jaw twitching, and feel his strain as he holds himself back.

His hands gently cup my bottom as I lift up and fall back down again. "This is your ride, sweetheart. And it's perfection."

Letting my eyelids flutter shut as a flurry of pleasure drifts though my body, Drake's gentle command has them flying open again. "Look at me, Mea."

I do, and I begin to find a rocking rhythm. He hisses out between his teeth, but he doesn't make a move to unseat me or flip me over. He just keeps holding my gaze. I watch with fascination as a bead of sweat, evidence of his effort, rolls down his chin and drops onto his chest. It disappears into the hairs there. I lean forward and lick him, following the same trail the bead of liquid just had.

"Fuuuuuck," he grinds out. "Mea."

I bob faster, feeling the rigid hardness inside me stretching me out, filling me up. I could be floating. I could be flying. I'm empowered, because I'm not forcing the control here. It's not something that I've designed because of my rules and manipulations and independent decisions.

I have control because Drake freely handed it to me.

And I'm only just beginning to understand the difference.

Finding myself through Drake's eyes, discovering who I am from the way he views me, I ride him until I've climbed so high there's no other option but to fall. Drake's gentle hands find my breasts, and he tweaks my nipples between his thumb and forefingers. His eyes are still locked on my face, and there's a sense of wonder and longing in them I can't quite understand. But when he speaks, I know I'm home.

"I got you, baby."

At the peak of pleasure and the brink of something unknown, I crash down under the weight of waves of ecstasy. I lean forward, collapsing onto Drake's chest. His hands smooth up my back as his body shudders beneath mine and my name slips from his lips.

When he's still, except for the heaving of his chest, he moves me so that I'm lying beside him. Then he slides off the bed and into the adjoining bathroom. When he returns, he's carrying a wet washcloth. With steady and gentle hands, he flips me onto my back and proceeds to clean me up. When he's finished, he returns the towel to the bathroom and slips back into bed.

Pulling the comforter over us, he pulls me against his chest. His lips brush against my head.

We don't speak, because at the moment nothing more needs to be said. He just told me more with his body than any man has ever said to me with words. He showed me how he feels and what he thinks with his caramel eyes as I broke apart above him, and that was more than enough.

Snuggling in close to his side, drawing in the warmth from his body, I sleep.

"A pub crawl?" The excitement in Berkeley's voice is matched by the rosy flush in her cheeks, and I know my idea for my best friend's last girls' night out before she gets hitched is a good one.

"With ghosts," adds Greta. "It's Savannah; don't forget the ghosts."

Berkeley claps her hands together, glee apparent on her gorgeously perky features. "Oh, my God."

Rolling my eyes, I guide her toward the limo waiting for us. It idles on the curb in front of the house with suited driver standing in wait. It meant taking money out of my savings, contributing with the other girls for this special night, but when it comes to Berkeley and Greta, every cent I spend is worth it. Their friendship is invaluable to me.

"And if you're worried about your man, don't be. He's taking the crawl starting at the other end of the tour. We arranged this especially for you two with the tour company. So you'll get to kiss at the bar in the middle, and then keep on truckin.'"

She squeals in delight as she ducks into the limo. Grinning wickedly at Greta, I accept the white-and-pink "Bachelorette" sash she hands me, along with the tiara. Berkeley's been sort of a princess her whole life, but tonight we'll be turning her into a whole different sort of royalty.

"Put these on!" I thrust the dress-up items in her lap as I climb in beside her. The driver closes the door behind Olive as she brings up the rear, and she takes it upon herself to pull a bottle of champagne out of the automobile's mini-fridge.

"Well, girls…should we get this party started right?"

Handing us each a flute, she pours the bubbly liquid into our waiting glasses. "Thank you for letting me come on this trip with you. I'm having so much fun getting to know you all. Cheers to new friends, new beginnings, and a new chapter for Berkeley!"

Raising our glasses, we all yell, "Cheers!"

"So," Berkeley begins, leaning back and making herself comfy in the leather seat. "Mea."

Her whiskey-colored gaze lands on me and I know I'm in trouble. I've given Berkeley that look myself so many times before I can read it like my favorite book. She's out for information, and if she doesn't get it she'll only settle for blood.

"Hmm?" My nervousness at whatever she's about to ask is only amped up by the vibration of my phone in my clutch.

I realize only then that it's the first time today that I've thought about Mikah's call last night.

My stomach muscles harden into a wall of coiled steel, and I have trouble catching my breath. Spending the afternoon with Drake kept the fear and the dread at bay, but now it's back full force. I'm left reeling from the ferocity of it and I wish so badly that Drake was here to be my escape again.

"Mea?" Berkeley's face changes expression as soon as she notices my impending panic. "What's wrong?"

Shaking my head, I gather myself along with a deep cleansing breath. I can't allow this to ruin Berkeley's night. Whatever Mikah has to tell me can wait until her special occasion is over.

"Nothing. Everything is fine. Are you ready to get your drink on?"

Her normally large eyes narrow. "I looked for you this afternoon. I didn't want you to be bored or lonely, but you weren't in your room when I checked. Where were you?"

Olive's gaze shifts from Berkeley to me with interest, and Greta's elbow lands in my ribs.

"You're holding out on us? Were you with a certain hulk of a mechanic, oiling his engine?" She bites the inside of her cheek to keep from laughing, but a giggle escapes anyway.

"Greta...please don't ever, ever make an analogy again. Ever!" She blushes at my playful scolding but holds her ground. She and Berkeley are a united front on this one, and I can't escape the limo.

I huff out an impatient breath. "We're all adults here, right? What happens in Savannah stays in Savannah."

"Mea! You know that if it were either one of us you'd need all the details. I demand to know what's going on with you and Drake. Is it just sex? Or do you like him?"

Her question firmly plants a picture of what Drake did to me earlier in his bed at the front of my mind. Thoughts of my fingers twisting in his hair, tugging on the strands until his urgent groan met my ears. Thoughts of the way his glistening skin felt sliding against mine in the most intimate possible way. Thoughts of the feelings he evoked in my body when his hands and his tongue and his cock brought me to the brink of pleasure more than once.

I use a hand to fan myself, and Berkeley zeroes in on the motion, a blond poodle with a bone she can't put down.

"I knew it! You are definitely screwing him!" Her triumphant voice fills the limo and the other girls' heads snap to attention. "But…you have rules. You never sleep with the same guy twice. And you never spend time with the guy. Because we're all friends, Drake is automatically different, right?"

I tilt my head to the side, considering. *Is that the only reason things are so much more with Drake? Because we have the same circle of friends and we're familiar with each other?* The way Drake makes me feel: safe, surrounded by warmth, keyed up with sexual energy…those aren't familiar emotions for me. He's the only one who has ever inspired them. And I know, deep down inside my soul, that it's not just because we've known each other for a few years now.

It's more than that.

Greta's searching my expression, and sees something in it that makes her reach out to squeeze my shoulder from her place across from me. "How do you feel about him, Mea?"

Shaking my head slowly, I gaze at her in utter disbelief. "I didn't mean for this to happen. I tried as hard as I could to prevent it, to stay mad at him for something that wasn't even his fault. But he got to me...somehow."

Berkeley's voice has gentled, and she grasps my hand in hers with fierce friendship shining in her eyes. "And?"

I have to admit it. For myself as much as for my friends. "And I think I'm falling for him."

17

Drake

It's my turn to buy Dare's drink, so I grab his order request and head for the bartender in the back of the old, classically "haunted" Savannah dive. I had my doubts when Mea first suggested this idea, but I have to admit it's turning out to be a great night. We let the girls leave first in a limo, and then we followed in a stretch Hummer to the opposite end of the riverfront.

Knowing that in a little under an hour I'm going to see Mea's gorgeous face lighting up everything around her again is enough to have me sweating in anticipation. After our afternoon together, my body is spent in the best possible way, and my brain? Filled with memories of how amazing she looked while she fell into pieces in my arms.

I know how lucky I am. I know that although Mea might not be a stranger to sexual partners, the fact that I got to see her all vulnerable and free the way she was today is something that I should cherish. I'm always going to remember the way she looked. Always going to want to replicate the way I made her moan.

And the way she made me feel? It's unmatched by anyone who's ever come before her. I know for a fact that no matter where I go or whom I'm with, I'll never have another experience like that one. That's why I'm going to try my damnedest not to let her go. I need to be enough for her, and I want to be more than she needs.

The female bartender heads over with a flirty grin. Leaning over the bar, she sends me a wink. "Your turn to buy, huh?" She glances over at Dare, who's clearly been having a good time tonight, and then back at me. "He's the groom? Let me guess…" She allows her eyes to slide around my torso, taking in my build and flicking over my face before she finds my eyes once again. "Best man?"

I'm surprised, but I don't let it show in my features. "How'd you guess? And yeah…he wants a Killian's."

She turns to grab the bottle of beer, and when she slides it across the bar to me she grins. "It's my job to know. You, though…you've caught my attention. Want to swing back by here after your party is all done?"

I've never really been a player; it's not my style. I've been with women, sure. But I don't jump from woman to woman like some of the guys I know. And to each his own, I don't judge anyone for their choices. I've just always known that in life, a revolving door of women, isn't for me.

"Sorry." I grace her with a rueful smile. "I've got plans after this party."

She leans into her hand and offers me a sad half-grin. "She's a lucky girl. What can I get to top you off?" She gestures toward Dare's beer.

I look down at the sole beer in my hand, and then look back up at her. "Nothing. I'm good."

And I am…good. One beer, just like the me before I lost my mom. Alcohol doesn't drown out the pain. It just numbs it for a little while. But now? I know there's a better way to deal with things. Especially knowing that being drunk meant I wasn't there for Mea when she needed me.

Never again.

Pulling a folded bill out of my jeans pocket, I leave it on the bar and rejoin my group. Jeremy and Chase seem to be getting along really well, laughing at the same types of jokes and ribbing Dare with everything they have. Ronin, quieter than the other guys, eyes me as I return. I don't know Ronin well, but I've noticed that his eyes miss nothing. He's shrewd, and he has a reason for every move he makes.

There's been more than one friendly gathering where I noticed Ronin and Mea with their heads together. I'm a guy, and I can read the hungry expression in another man's eyes when it comes to a woman. Back then, there was nothing I could do about it. I'd be restless as hell, wanting to slam my fist into his face just for talking to her with intent, but I couldn't without looking like an asshole.

That's not the case now. Mea is mine.

I hand Dare his beer along with a clap on the shoulder, and then I take up a relaxed stance beside Ronin. He acknowledges my presence next to him with an incline of the head, but we both stare straight in front of us.

"What's up?" I stuff both hands into my pockets, for lack of anything better to do with them other than clenching them tight.

Ronin takes a sip of his highball, swallowing before he speaks. "So. You and Mea? This a new thing?"

My blood heats up as it races through my veins, but I fight to keep my cool. Ronin is asking. There are a lot of guys who wouldn't do that. They'd just try and take what they want. So I nod.

"Yeah."

He flicks his mossy eyes toward me quickly before looking away again. But I don't miss the seriousness in them, the question in his gaze. "Casual?"

I shake my head. He needs to be well aware of where I stand with Mea. Because no guy with brains in his head would turn down a prize like her if he thought he had a chance. "Not for me." I look at him when I say it, and he turns his head so that our gazes meet.

He stares at me for a minute, and I don't back down or look away. When he finally gives me one brief nod of his head, I know we have an understanding. "Treat her right."

Blowing out a quiet breath through pursed lips, I give him a curt nod. "Plan to."

Our tour guide returns to us then, leading us out of the bar and onto the brightly lit, busy Savannah riverfront street.

"The next place is extra creepy," he informs us as we walk. He's really gung-ho about the ghost thing but can also read the vibe from our group. It's telling him that we don't give a shit about ghosts or haunted bars, but we like a good drink from a good pub, so he's left us alone to enjoy that for the most part.

It's not lost on me that I've only had one beer tonight. I don't have the strong urge to get lost inside a glass of whiskey, and I know exactly the reason why. The sweet obscurity of Mea is still swimming through my system, and its power gives me more strength than a drink ever could.

It gives me hope. Just because my mother was a drunk and now she's gone, it doesn't mean that I now need to turn to alcohol to cope. It just causes more problems, especially with Mea. I've always wanted my own life separate from the shitty one she gave me, and I've made that in Lone Sands. The fact that she passed away rocked me through and through, but I can't change who she was or what she lacked as a mother. I can only live for today, and right now a big part of my today includes this small tornado force of a woman.

We pause outside the next stop. "This is the Tucker Inn," our tour guide informs us. "It's said to be haunted by the ghost of a lonely man who used to frequent the pub at the turn of the century. Come on inside and we'll tell you the rest."

The dude is so excited about the prospect of this ghost that he speeds inside. Jeremy is shaking with laughter, and Grisham elbows him hard in the ribs as he leads the way into the dim tavern.

We hear the girls before we see them. They're making a ruckus right at the front of the place. Apparently, the little group has been taking turns buying Berkeley her drinks as well, because she's spinning in a slow circle in the center of them, wearing a pageant sash and tiara. When she spots Dare, she books it across the bar and leaps into his arms.

Catching her easily, he buries his face in her neck and begins murmuring something that I can't and probably don't want to hear. Removing my eyes from the spectacle, I search out Mea.

She's a fucking temptress in tight black jeans and a pair of black, scuffed-up cowboy boots. Her top, flowing around her like it contains currents of its own energy, hangs off of one shoulder. It exposes creamy mocha skin, and my feet carry me toward her before I realize I'm moving. Her eyes lock in on me, drinking me up the same way I'm swallowing mouthfuls of her vision like a man dying of thirst.

"Hey, you," she murmurs as I wrap an arm around her waist and pull her soft curves right up against me. She sighs as the fingers of my other hand trace tiny pictures on her bare shoulder.

"Hey, sweetheart. Miss me?" My voice feels like its buried somewhere under stacks of sandpaper.

My dick twitches when she stretches up on her tiptoes to whisper in my ear. Her lips touch my skin, and I'm a live wire. Ready to burst into flames with a mere touch.

"I don't do clingy, remember?" Her husky voice is everything.

I want to pull her to a dark place in the back of this bar and let her tornado suck me up.

"I remember." Then my mouth catches hers, and the sexy slide of her plump bottom lip against mine makes me groan.

Too soon, we have to pull away. Both of our tour guides have chosen that moment to gather our group and tell a ghost story.

"The ghost that haunts this bar is affectionately known as

Lonely Joe. He fell in love with the bar owner's daughter, who lived in the apartment upstairs with her family. She worked in the bar, helping her father with the bartending and other bar duties. They had a torrid affair, but when the bar owner found out, he put the kibosh on the whole thing. The daughter was heartbroken. She jumped off the balcony at the top of the bar. After she died, Joe disappeared. No one ever saw him again. But ever since, customers and workers here have claimed to hear and see his ghost, still waiting for the woman he loves to come downstairs again."

Beside me, Mea shivers. I pull her closer into my side.

"That's a horrible story," she says aloud. "Way too sad."

Greta peeks out from under Grisham's arm and agrees. "I want to cry."

"Well," says the tour guide with a knowing smile on his face. "Spirits are the best way to remedy that. Everyone head on over to the bar to grab a drink."

The group settles around the bar, ordering drinks. Mea's phone vibrates from where my hand rests on her hip. There's a stubborn set to her jaw and a determined gleam in her eyes as she ignores it.

"What's up? Are you going to check your phone?" I keep my voice low, so that only she can hear my question. I'm more than a little curious at her reaction and the tension rolling off of her right now.

Shaking her head, she avoids my eyes. "Not now. I'll check it later."

I spin her around so that she's facing me, searching her eyes.

"Is everything okay? Remember what we did in my bed this afternoon? Me and you aren't limited to spending time in the bedroom together. If something's wrong, I want to know about it."

Pulling the corner of her lip into her mouth, a war rages in her eyes as she debates whether or not to tell me something that's clearly tearing her apart.

"Mea?"

Shaking her head quickly, her curls fly in a wild frenzy around her head. "Not here," she whispers. "But…I do want to tell you, Drake. I want to tell you everything."

The way she says "everything" feels like the word weighs a hundred pounds leaving her lips. She's hefting the weight of it; I can almost see the heaviness of it on her shoulders as the toes of her boots scrape against the wooden planks of the bar floor.

I smooth my hands up from her shoulders to her face, cupping it between them like something precious. "I'm right here. We can talk later. You gonna be okay the rest of the party tonight?"

Blinking up at me, I can see the steel she uses to cover up whatever's creating a storm of turmoil inside her. It's like a coat of armor she wears to protect her heart; she's so used to hiding behind it that it takes almost nothing for her to shutter herself in.

We turn to join the group, and I take her hand in mine as we walk toward them. I squeeze it just to remind her that I'm here and she's safe with me, and she glances up at me with a small smile. It's only a fraction of the normal Mea grin, but it tells me what I need to know. She's strong, and she won't let anything get in the way of her best friend's happiness.

Even if it means she has to bury what makes her heart beat fast with fear. What makes her body heavy with sadness. What makes her expressive, chocolaty eyes glaze over with pain.

Fuck. How long has she been dealing with whatever this is on her own? She carries it on her shoulders, and from the looks of her, she's close to breaking.

I make a vow to myself right then and there. Whatever her secret is, it's going to be deep and dark. It terrifies her; it chases her in her dreams at night.

I'll fight it for her. I'll be the light in that darkness if it takes every last breath I have in order to do it.

18

Mea

I wait until I'm back at the rental house, alone in my bedroom with Drake, before I check my phone. Drake watches me while I pace the room like a wild animal trapped in a cage. My phone is caught between my hands, but I haven't looked at it yet. I'm counting my steps, gathering every ounce of courage I have before I finally flip the phone over in my hands and read the screen.

Drake watches me, silent pleading in his eyes. But I haven't told him about my father yet. I don't know the right words to say or how to launch into a story that grotesque.

I have Daddy issues. You know, the first man who's supposed to love you and protect you? The one who is supposed to fight the monsters away? Well, mine was the monster. And I'm the one who had to put him away.

It's no conversation starter, that's for sure.

There are six missed calls from my brother. And three texts.

I open the first text message.

Call me.

The second text message is a bit longer.

I don't want to text this, Mea. Call me.

My stomach plummets toward the floor. My fingers tremble along the warm metal of my phone as I open the third text. I read the two words there and can't control the strangled cry that leaves my throat.

He's out.

Drake is off the bed and across the room in a second, pulling the phone from my hand and pulling me into his arms. Over my shoulders, he reads the text. I can hear the confusion in his voice as he grinds out his question. "Who's 'he'? Out of where?"

I try to take a breath, but no air flows into my lungs. I realize I must be having a panic attack at the same time that Drake does. He lifts me into his arms and places me on the bed before he crawls in beside me. Pulling me to him, he strokes my hair as my entire body convulses with terror. Cold, hard terror that steals your breath and your words.

"Shhh, baby girl. I'm here. No one will hurt you, I swear to you. I'm right here." He murmurs the words and ones just like them over and over again. I have no idea how long it takes for the attack to subside, but when it does my body is empty and cold. My limbs are weak and heavy. But at least I can breathe again.

"It's my...it's my father."

Drake stiffens, but he doesn't stop his comforting stroking. He waits for me to tell him more.

I run my hands along his bare chest. As soon as we came into my room, he stripped off his shirt, dropping it on the floor before sitting on my bed. I'm so glad for the bare skin contact now. It's as soothing as his voice and the cloak of his arms around me.

"He's been in prison since I was fifteen years old. When I was thirteen and a half, I told a teacher that he had been...assaulting me...for the previous two years."

Drake takes a deep breath beneath me. I hold mine, waiting for his reaction.

I've never told anyone this. Especially not a man. It's humiliating, and it makes me feel dirty just speaking the words. Thinking about them is difficult enough, but thanks to the therapy my aunt and uncle made me endure for two years when I arrived at their home, I had developed skills to cope. The nightmares stopped, or at least became extremely rare.

"Mea." I've never heard his voice sound this way. It's as if he's been swallowing broken glass. It sounds like it hurts him just to speak. "Did he hit you?"

I shake my head. A tear leaks out of my eye and lands on Drake's chest. And then another. And another. "He was always kind of a control freak, you know? My mom...I remember her being so wonderful and normal when I was younger. But she developed mental illness when I was around seven or eight. And she just kept retreating into herself more and more until she was barely there at all. She would still move around the house, but I never heard her voice. She never looked at anyone. Now, I wonder if her illness wasn't spurred on by a desire to escape him." I sniff, trying hard to stem the flow of tears that are so freely falling now.

Drake's hand rubs small circles on my back. He doesn't speak, just listens.

"He wasn't violent. Not like you're thinking. But he would drink…and then his temper was worse. I would always shelter Mikah from it as best I could. But when my mom disappeared…he had appetites that weren't being satisfied anymore. One night he came into my room and told me it was my job to take her place."

"Fuck." His body jerks like he's been punched. Gently, he slides me off of his chest and stands. Pacing the room much like I had just moments ago, I watch with every single muscle inside of me tightening into painful coils. He reaches the small roll-top desk and leans over it, pressing the wood with his big, strong hands.

Shaking his head back and forth, back and forth. "No, baby. No."

I just watch him. I can't tell him it isn't true. As much as I want to. And watching the way it's killing him…it's killing me.

Then, he pounds both fists against it, making me startle. "Fuck!"

Standing up straight again, he runs both hands over his head a couple of times before turning to face me. He strides back toward the bed and climbs on it, situating me against his chest again.

"I'm sorry," he whispers, his voice broken. He turns his head and rubs his nose along my jaw, inhaling me deeply. "I can't stand the thought of him hurting you. Your father...the man you were supposed to be able to trust above all others."

Nodding, I wipe the tears away from my eyes. Drake reaches up, helping me to clear my face of the wetness. "Every fucked-up thing about me today is because of him."

There's a ferociousness in Drake's voice when he answers me. "There's nothing fucked-up about you. I've known for a while that there was something beneath the surface that made you who you are. But you are amazing in *spite* of him. Believe me when I say that."

His words bring a tiny ray of light to my heart where before it was lost in darkness. "Thank you."

"Why did your brother's message say that he's out, sweetheart? I need to know the answer to that."

The question brings my terror screaming back to the surface. It wraps around my throat, threatening to squeeze the life out of me. "He was up for parole. I thought there was no way in hell he would get it, Drake. Especially not without his family there to support him. But he did. And now he's out on parole."

Drake sucks in a sharp breath. "Are you afraid he'll come after you?"

"Just the thought of him makes me scared. My nightmares of him are nothing compared to the real, live man. He stole something from me back then that I can never get back. And

I can only imagine that years in prison haven't helped him get better. He was probably thinking about ways to hurt me worse."

"Baby, it's okay. I'm right here. He can't hurt you. He'd have to go through me, and that's not gonna happen. Why do you think he'd want revenge?"

The word *revenge* makes me shudder. *Is it too much to hope for that my father will get out of prison and start his life over again somewhere new? That he won't ever try to find Mikah and me? That he'll just walk away and leave us alone?*

"The last time that it happened…" My voice trembles and I *hate* it. I've spent years turning myself into someone strong, someone confident. Someone who couldn't be hurt because no one would ever get close enough to cause me pain again. And here I am, falling apart at the very thought of my father. "Mikah was only eleven. But he was always this scrappy kid who wasn't afraid to take on the world. He walked into my bedroom. He knew right away that what he was seeing wasn't right, and he started yelling at our father to get off of me."

Drake hisses, the sound slipping through his teeth. "I can imagine his fury."

"I was so afraid for Mikah after that. Our father was too unpredictable. Our mother couldn't save us. So I went to school the next day and told a guidance counselor what was happening. We were taken out of our home and sent to live with our aunt and uncle in North Carolina."

I feel it when Drake drops a kiss on my mess of curls. His hands are so steady on my skin while he comforts me. I never imagined that I could feel this protected while talking about my father and what he did to me.

"Mikah and I both testified in his trial a little over a year later. It sealed his conviction."

"You changed your name when you moved." It's not a question. My mind flashes back to the Emily girl I knew back in Kentucky all those years ago, and who I'd run into again last night.

I nod against his chest. "Yes." My voice cracks on the word, and Drake's arms tighten around me.

"Baby girl," he murmurs so quietly against my hair. "I'm so sorry. I won't let him hurt you anymore. I promise you that."

With every heartbeat I hear thrumming in Drake's chest, I feel the earnestness he experiences when he tells me he'll keep me safe.

"I know you will. I just have to calm down and keep living my life. Just because he's out doesn't mean he's a threat to me. I just have to keep living."

It's a mantra I remind myself of over and over again as I drift off to sleep in Drake's arms.

Just keep living.

19

Drake

I'd call the Bachelor/Bachelorette Party Weekend a success. Both Dare and Berkeley seemed happy with the events we'd thrown together and to have the opportunity to spend time with our tight-knit group and each other in one fell swoop. As February runs into March, it takes all of the winter air with it and brings about a change in the world I should be used to seeing by now.

In Lone Sands, a true spring or fall is a rare find. When winter ends with a string of mild weather, it rolls out the red carpet for summer. And as soon as the weather begins to warm, the tourists start their weekend trips to the perfect seaside retreat.

Something about that weekend—I'm not sure if it's the fact that I messed up and realized I never wanted to do it again, or the fact that she shared something so intimate with me that brought us closer together. I don't go a day without seeing her now, and most nights are spent together in my bed. It feels right. Having her beside me, where I can keep an eye on her and keep her night-mares away, is a new purpose for me.

It's always busier at the garage at this time of the year, and that's something I'll never complain about. It gives me a lot less time to finish up my Yamaha, but it puts extra change in my pocket, and that's never a bad thing. The motorcycle will wait, and I don't have much left to do on it before it's done, anyway.

Now that it's warm enough, we keep all the garage bay doors wide open so that the warm air can flow in around us while we're working, and we've turned off the space heaters for the last time this year. One morning when I'm hard at work on a stool beside a Buick, Mea strolls into the garage through one of those open doors.

Someone's tool clatters to the floor as she walks in, and I can't blame whatever fucker dropped it because, *damn*. She's got her hair piled up on top of her head in the style I think borders on erotic, letting the stray spirals flutter around her flawless face. She's wearing tight yoga pants that call far too much attention to her sexy curves. Her tight little waist is barely covered with a workout top, and I know she's just finished teaching yoga for the day. There's a big brown bag in one hand and an electrifying smile on her lips.

Hoover clears his throat and stands up from his bench, and I shoot him a look that I want to send a message. He's not looking at me, though. He's staring at my girl, and I can't fucking blame him.

"Hey, you." It's her standard greeting for me, and her chocolate gaze leveled at me tips Hoover off that this isn't just a customer. He turns his shocked gaze on me.

"Hey, sweetheart." I approach her, pull her to me gently. I brush my lips quickly against hers, then pull back and glance down at the bag.

"What are you doing here, baby?"

Without pulling her body away from mine, she looks up at me, and her smile alone is almost enough to do me in. Every time. I can't resist the wild wind that sucks me in every time I'm with her, and I don't want to try. I'm a willing sacrifice to her cyclonic power, and as usual, it's wild, wild, wild.

She indicates the brown bag. "Brought you lunch, you big lug. I seriously don't know what's wrong with me. I've never brought my man lunch before. Guess I've never been able to call any man 'mine' so I'm all excited about it."

The inside of me melts. Fucking melts. "You callin' me your man?"

Pulling back all the way this time, she mock punches me in my arm. "Who else?"

Javier, coming up beside me, leans an arm on my shoulder as he stares between the two of us. "Day-um, boss. I swear if I weren't taken, I'd steal your girl."

Rolling my eyes, I jerk a thumb toward Sosa. "Mea, Javier. Javier, Mea. Don't worry baby, he's not stupid enough to touch you."

Javier grins, pushing off my arm so that I have to brace myself not to lose my balance. "Shawn wouldn't like it if I tried to add a third, anyway. He's fucking selfish that way." With a laugh, he goes back to his station.

Mea stares after him, her eyes filled with pure delight. "I love him. Can he be my best friend?"

Shaking my head, I pull her past the prying eyes of the guys and lock the door of my office behind us. Setting the bag of food down on my chair, I lift Mea up easily and sit her on top of my desk. She leans back on her arms, and gives me one dark, provocative look.

I'm standing between her legs in a heartbeat. Unbuttoning my dark gray coveralls, I let them hang down around my waist as I capture her face in my hands. Cradling it, I bring her mouth to mine.

Mea uses her nails to rake a path up my back, pushing the fabric of my wife beater up as she goes. Letting one hand drift around to the back of her neck, I hold her to me while I find the hem of her shirt with the other. Pulling apart, she lifts her arms and I pull the shirt off over her head and toss it over my shoulder. Pulling back from her, but keeping my eyes locked on her gorgeousness, I let the coveralls fall. Stepping out of them, I pull the tank over my head and drop it before shedding my boxers. Then I reach past her to open my desk drawer. Grabbing my wallet, I rip a foil packet from its pocket and tear it open.

She watches me, a hungry expression on her face while she sits on the desk. When I'm fully bared to her, it's clear from the sight of my throbbing erection that I can't wait much longer to be inside of her. She hops down off the desk and makes quick work of her stretchy black pants, and then the black thong panties she's wearing underneath.

My eyes drift closed as she takes the condom from my hand and rolls it, agonizingly slowly, down my shaft.

"Damn, baby. Should have spent more time undressing you." Moving toward her, I lift her into my arms. Spinning her around, her back bumps against the office door. Pinned there, she trains kisses down on my shoulders while the softest part of her lines up in perfect symmetry with the hardest part of me.

Groaning, I bury my face in her neck. Her spicy smell overwhelms me; I could be on fire. "Do you know what you do to me?"

Whimpering as I begin to rub the long hard length of me against her, she bites down on my shoulder in a way that I never thought I'd love. Sex with Mea is freedom.

"Wait." My voice is a pant. "Is this...okay with you? In my office, against the door?" I search her face, looking for any sign that she's not completely with me. There isn't one, but I need to hear it from her mouth that she's completely comfortable with what we're doing right now.

"This is...new for me, Drake. But with you, I know I'm safe. My rules don't apply here. Not anymore." She holds my gaze, and I know she's being open and honest with me.

When I enter her, it's with the most unbelievable melding of bodies, and the way her insides clench around me creates a display of fireworks behind my closed eyelids.

"Perfect, baby. Always perfect." My voice is a pant as I pump in and out of her.

There are times for savoring a woman. For making her feel safe, for making her feel loved. There are times to take it slow and times to make sure every single inch of her is taken care of before you dive in. But with Mea's unexpected visit and the way she made my insides light up when she sat on my desk made this not one of those times.

It's the time to take her fast, hard, and rough.

She cries out my name as I plunge into her, and the sound is so devastatingly sexy that I use a hand to cover her mouth as I continue to drive home. Her teeth scrape against my hand, matching the scratch of her nails against my back. When the muscles of her pussy clench tight around me, I grunt with the sheer pleasure of it. She's trembling, her slick body colliding with mine as she climaxes.

It's breathtaking.

Unable to hold on, I follow her as my own orgasm takes ahold of me, drawing me up tight and making me tumble over and over again in the place where perfect bliss lives.

For the next minute, the only sounds in my office are the breaths we take as we try to gather ourselves again. Finally, I let Mea go and she slides down my body, waking me up again to the sweet way her body sculpts against mine. I can't let her go far, sandwiching her in my arms between my body and the wall. She's tiny in the space before me, making me feel like the Incredible Hulk as I tower over her.

"Well, that's not exactly what I had in mind when I decided to bring you lunch." She lifts a finger to trace my lips, which makes me remember her words on a dark night in the Challenger.

"Don't put your fingers where they don't belong if you don't want them to end up wet and hot." My tongue darts out to lick her finger and she smirks, her eyes darkening.

"I like wet and hot."

Groaning, I pick her up and deposit her back on my desk while I retrieve my clothes and dress hastily. She dresses slowly, not taking her eyes off me in the process. Between us, electricity sizzles as we both replay what we just did over and over again in our minds.

I'm never going to look at my office the same way again. Mea has christened it her spot now, like so many other places in my life she's taken over.

As I finish buttoning my coveralls, I finally notice the aromas coming from the bag on my desk. "What'd you bring? Now I'm starving."

She pulls a spread out of the bag, hot deli sandwiches, pickles, chips, and fruit. We divvy the food up between us, and while I sit on my desk chair to dig in, I hate the thought of her being all the way on the other side of the big piece of furniture. So I pull her into my lap, situating her on one side so we can both enjoy the lunch she brought.

"You haven't heard anything from that bastard, have you?"

It's how I always refer to her father. He doesn't deserve the title, and I refuse to give it to him. He will forever be "the bastard." I can't stand the haunted look that appears in Mea's eyes whenever she talks about him, but I can't risk her not telling me if he attempts to contact her.

Ever since she told me what he did to her…that night in particular it took every ounce of self-control I had not to hunt him down and peel his skin off, bit by bit, just so he could feel an ounce of the pain he inflicted on his daughter. I always knew…there was something underneath every smile, every care-free look, every laugh. The nasty demon known as her father has been hiding just under the surface, haunting her. For years.

When I'm alone, it's harder. There's nothing stopping me from finding him, except the fact that Mea would know. And she'd worry about me. If I can spare her one more second of worrying in this lifetime, I'll do it.

But if he *ever* decides to attempt to walk back into her life or make contact with her in any way, he's a dead man. I'll use every single connection I've made over the years as an army Ranger and through the Night Eagle Security team to make sure he never sees the light of day again. And sacrificing my own freedom to make sure he never hurts her again?

It's nothing to me.

She gives a quick little shake of her head. "Nothing." Pulling the corner of her bottom lip into her mouth, she nibbles on it, pulling my focus there for a second while she's lost in thought. "I don't know what I expected, Drake. I mean, it's a good thing, right? That he hasn't found me? But it wouldn't be hard. I changed my name, but he knows that they would have sent us to live with Aunt Tay and Uncle Wes. They were the only relatives we had."

I stay silent, listening to her vent her worries. But I'm glad I made sure she stayed close to me during lunch. The contact is comforting for me as well as for her.

"Do you know that Mikah and I had never even met our aunt

and uncle? My father alienated my mother from her own sister."

Shaking my head, I lace my fingers through hers and lift our joined hands to my lips. "Men like him…they have to control it all. If they don't, they can't function. My mom dated a few like that when I was growing up. Your mother was a victim of his, probably more than you even know."

"She died…" Her voice has dropped to a whisper, one broken and full of years of perfected sorrow. "She died a few months after. After Mikah and I were sent to live in North Carolina. My aunt brought us back to Kentucky for a quick funeral, but I still don't know exactly what happened to her. I always thought…she just ended it all. There was nothing left for her."

I rest my chin on her shoulder. "I'm sorry she had to endure what she did. And I'm sorry that you had to be so damn strong all the time…it wasn't fair for a kid. But, Mea…I've never known anyone with more strength than you. And I served with men who could bench-press two or three of you. You are the strongest person I know."

She leans back against me, allowing me to fully wrap her in my arms. She fits there, against my chest. I don't know if I believe in the idea of two people being created to be together. I'm not even sure if I believe there is a higher power that created us all. Not with the childhood that I had. And now that I know Mea, I'm even less sure that God would allow a child to suffer as much as she did.

But if I did believe in any of that, it would be pretty damn hard to deny the fact that she is my perfect complement in every single way. Now that we've both stopped dancing around each other and have realized that we're better together than we are apart, I can't believe I spent the past few years keeping my distance.

What a waste.

"Sometimes, being strong is exhausting." Her confession sounds like something she's never said aloud. Her voice is weary, down to the very core of her. Her body sags against me, her head heavy against my heartbeat. But I know without a doubt how true her admission is.

"And those are the times that you lean on me, sweetheart. Let me be strong for you."

I will be strong enough.

20

Mea

A few days after I brought Drake lunch at the garage, I'm sitting in Wilmington's trendiest wedding boutique sipping a mimosa while watching Berkeley be fitted for her wedding dress. The frothy drink tickles my lips. On this Saturday morning, Berkeley isn't the only bride-to-be donning a white gown, but in my opinion she's definitely the most beautiful.

"Holy hotness, girl." I eye her from top to bottom with true appreciation. "Every guest on that beach is going to hold their breath when they see you coming down the aisle."

Berkeley turns this way and that, admiring her choice of dress in the three-way mirror while the seamstress looks on with happiness behind her.

"It's amazing, Berk." Chase's wife, Shay, joins us today, and she looks positively radiant with her short, stylish garnet-colored hair and rockabilly flair.

Greta admires Berkeley's dress with equal admiration. "I swear.

Dare is going to have trouble standing there waiting for you to come to him. He's going to want to leap over wedding guests to get to you."

Berkeley's lush curves are encased in an off-white fit-and-flare gown made of the softest crepe satin. The material fits flush on her torso and drips with the most delicate embroidered lace I've ever seen. The satin flares out at her knees, rippling into waves of silk that pool around her feet and trail out into a perfectly formed train behind her. More lace finishes the hem of the gown, framing the entire thing with pretty accents.

She turns around, and we all sigh at the appearance of the backside. The scooped back is dramatic, reaching down to the top of her tailbone. An illusion back gives a sense of modesty despite the plunging drop, and it's littered with rhinestones and pearls. Wide lace straps finish out the stunning, runway-ready look.

Standing, I place my glass down on a side table. I glide over to my best friend and gather her into a tight hug. My own set of tears begins to prickle the backs of my eyes, and I blink rapidly to keep them at bay

"You are more than beautiful," I whisper. "And I'm so, so proud of you."

Two more sets of arms fold around us, and then we're all entwined in a tangled mess of a group hug. When we finally separate, the seamstress is fluttering around with a look of pure terror on her face and Berkeley is ordering us to go and change into our dresses.

In my own dressing room, I slip on the champagne-colored gown Berkeley chose for me. It's flirty and fun, because…well,

Berkeley. The strapless top is made from silky beaded satin. It stretches taut over my breasts when it's zipped, and the fluffy tulle skirt flares out at my waist and ends just at my knees. I try on the heels we picked out to match the dresses, strappy stilettos the same color as the dress.

As we all stand in our matching dresses, being nipped and tucked by the seamstress, we discuss the upcoming nuptials at length.

"Only three weeks to go." Berkeley sighs, with a blissed-out smile on her face. It's the expression I've come to know and love whenever she's talking about Dare. He's truly the love of her life, and he makes her happier than I've ever seen her before.

I give an exaggerated sigh, checking out my legs in the mirror. I might be the shortest girl in the wedding party, but the heels are doing killer things to my calves. "Only three weeks to come up with a sufficiently embarrassing toast for the reception."

Berkeley gasps. "Stop! My parents will embarrass me enough, don't worry." Her eyes widen as she notices the way I look in my bridesmaid's gown. "Oh, my God! Your boobs look ah-mazing!" She sings the last word, her voice traveling up to a higher pitch.

Checking the mirror, I smile. "Is it the dress?"

Greta turns in the mirror so she can see the sparkling back of the dress. "Must be, Mea. I mean, you're actually in danger of spillage."

Grinning, an impish surge of devilry bounces around inside me. "So, will Drake want to rip this dress off me before the night is over?"

All three girls burst out laughing. I shoot them my most calculating grin. Shaking their heads, Greta and Shay head for the dressing rooms to change out of their gowns. As I'm stepping down off the box, Berkeley grabs my hand.

Her smile is warm and genuine. "Seeing you with Drake makes me so happy, Mea. It makes me feel like I don't have to worry about you, you know?"

Warmth flushes my cheeks and I squeeze her hand. "Why would you worry about me?"

She sighs, searching my eyes. "Because on the outside, you're always so sure of yourself and confident, and you act like nothing can ever hurt you. But deep down, I know you deal with stuff. Maybe even more stuff than the rest of us. I just hope that you'll really open up to Drake. He's such a good guy. If anyone can protect you and help you deal with your demons, it's him."

Her ability to see right through the walls I've thrown up around me over the years to protect myself from harm and from humiliation scares me. Berkeley has been there for me ever since I moved to North Carolina. It never mattered to her that I didn't come from money the way she did. It never fazed her that her parents hadn't approved of our friendship. She was always honest with me, and she stuck by me no matter what.

One of these days, I would need to open up to Berkeley and Greta the same way I did for Drake. They deserve to know me, really know me.

And I'm surprised to discover that I want them to.

I don't want to hide behind walls anymore. I want to open myself up to these people I've come to think of as my family.

And with shock, I realize that Drake is the one who's made me okay to do that. His becoming my soft place to land has made everything in my life seem easier. It doesn't feel like I have to climb a mountain all alone anymore.

He's changing me, and I like the person I'm becoming.

"So, this is your baby." The understanding in Drake's voice is warm honey, poured all over my heart. "This is awesome."

After our dress fitting, I grabbed some lunch with the girls. Berkeley's mother joined us. She'd seen the dress during Berkeley's original shopping trip, and the experience was so stressful for Berkeley she'd declined inviting the woman I've always called the Ice Queen back for the fitting. During lunch she grilled us about the dress and the way it fit. And then she proceeded to exhaust the finer points of the wedding details until Berkeley felt as though the event was a noose hanging around her neck rather than the upcoming happiest day of her life.

I've never been so happy to see a lunch date come to an end. I hightailed it out of there, exuberant to know I'd be spending the evening with my two favorite men.

"You think so?" I worry my lip, watching his reaction closely as he evaluates the space I've chosen for my yoga studio.

I scan the mostly empty area. The space is actually two retail storefronts combined to give me enough space for a yoga studio, changing room, office, and front reception area. The space is pretty much empty, but the money I'm saving will actually turn it into the yoga studio I've been dreaming of.

Drake slowly spins around, taking in my dream with a pensive look. He walks around the entire thing, touching walls and visually measuring.

"I've already leased it," I offer with trepidation. "That's where all of my money is going right now. It's why I live in a craphole. So I won't lose this space. It's too perfect to let go of. Even though I'm not ready to open yet."

His warm brown eyes are full of perceptive compassion. "That's a strain on you, isn't it?"

Shaking my head, my curls whip me in the face. "It doesn't matter. This is my dream."

He comes toward me, not stopping until he stands just before me. Wrapping his hands around my waist, he pulls me in close. "I understand dreams. That's all the garage was before I got it up and running. But this?" He gestures around him at my future business. "This won't take much. Will you let me help you?"

Will you let me help you?

Over the years, the answer to that question has always been a firm no. I learned early on that the only person who I could really count on to help me was myself. I hate the thought of being someone else's burden. I hate the thought of having to depend on anyone. And the thought of owing someone something? It makes me absolutely nauseated.

But when I stare into Drake's ridiculously handsome face, and his huge, strong arms wrap around me, I feel like maybe leaning on him won't be the end of me. Like allowing him to help me achieve my goals won't mean that I owe him…it'll mean that we did something amazing together. And I want that.

It scares me how much I want that.

"How would you help?" My tone is cautious, testing out what he's thinking before I agree to anything.

Drake glances around again, moving me to stand beside him as he assesses the space. "I'm pretty good with my hands."

I swat him on his backside. "I know."

Glancing down at me, his smirk turns sexy and carnal. The heat of it embraces me, wrapping me up in flames. Suddenly, just looking at him makes me breathless and wobbly, my knees weakening as I imagine what he can do to me.

"And," he continues. "I can ask some of the guys from the shop if they can help me install the floors and mirrors you need. You can use the money you've saved up so far to buy your yoga equipment."

I'm nodding, following his intentions closely. "That'll get so much of it done, Drake. Thank you."

"And you let me invest the rest."

That sentence stills me. I blink a few times to make sure I'm seeing and hearing what I think I'm seeing and hearing.

"You want to give me the money to finish this?" My voice lifts to a higher octave on the last word. I hop on the balls of my feet and detach myself from Drake's arms.

He follows me, studying my face as he nods. "I didn't say 'give.' I said 'invest.'"

"They're the same thing!"

Grabbing my hands, he forces me to stop bouncing and look at him. Really look at him. "We can do this together. I want to see you achieve this. And it's the perfect location. If you want to pay me back, you can."

The resolve in his voice and his eyes tells me he's very serious, and that there's no way he'd ever take a cent I tried to pay him back for his kindness. "You're for real?"

His lips curve upward in one of his gorgeous grins. "I'm so for real."

Letting the elation grab me, I squeal and leap into Drake's arms. He catches me with ease, hugging me to his chest with his hands cupping my bottom. Pressing my lips to his, I kiss him with no holds barred, showing him with my lips what my words can't possibly say. When I pull away, his mouth is swollen and pink, and his eyes are hooded with latent desire. "I accept. Thank you so much, Drake."

He leans forward and catches my bottom lip, sucking it into his mouth and pulling a moan from deep inside me. He presses the heated center of me against the growing bulge in his jeans, and I wrap my arms even tighter around his neck. My fingers play in the soft hair at the nape of his neck.

"This is gonna be incredible. Promise you that, sweetheart." His tone has gone all husky and low, sending the flow of blood in my veins toward the ache between my thighs. I rub against him, and his answering groan sends sparks of gratification through my body.

"Mea." Gravel coats his words. "Stop. I can't take you here, so don't tempt me."

I move my lips along his rough-shaven jaw, stopping to nibble on his ear. His arms tighten around me. "Why can't you take me here?"

He growls. "Because I'm not throwing you down on a cement floor, that's why. And we need to go meet your brother."

With a whimper, I unwrap my legs from around him and he sets me down on the floor. I'd almost forgotten that we're meeting Mikah for dinner and drinks. Butterflies dance in my stomach at the thought of these two important men in my life meeting for the first time.

"You're right. Rain check?" I head for the front door.

Drake follows. Opening the door for me, he palms my ass as I walk through it. "Later, sweetheart, you're mine."

His suggestive promise thrills me, sending chills dancing across my skin.

21

Drake

The young man sitting at the high-top table stands as we approach. Mea wraps him a fierce hug as soon as she's close enough, and I take a second to evaluate Mikah Jones.

He's tall and slender, not as tall as my six foot three but close to it. Other than the height, he's Mea's male twin. His hair is short and a mess of wild dark brown curls, his skin matches her bronzed tone exactly. Deep, dark green eyes are spaced widely under bushy black brows. His mouth is curved into a tender smile as he hugs his big sister.

"Hey, sis. You doing okay?" His drawl is distinctly southern, a mixture between his Kentucky heritage and his North Carolina upbringing.

Mea pulls back and holds him at arm's length, her shrewd gaze scoping him out from top to bottom. Then she slaps him, hard, on the arm. "I feel like I never see you anymore! A kid moves to Wilmington, only forty minutes away, and never looks back!"

Mikah flinches, grabbing his arm in dramatic fashion as he scowls at her. "Damn! A man be busy! I've got things to do!"

I step up beside my girl, holding out a hand for Mikah as I wrap the other arm around her waist. "Sweetheart, don't beat your brother up before I can meet him."

She rolls her eyes, but gestures toward me. "Baby brother Mikah, this is Drake. Boyfriend Drake, this is Mikah."

He shakes my hand, but his eyes zero in on my arm wrapped loosely around his sister and the way she's snugged into my side just because of my closeness.

From what I know about Mea, she's probably never brought a guy to meet the most important man in her life. At twenty-five, she's never been in a serious relationship. If I were Mikah, I'd be looking myself over carefully, too, wondering *what's so different about him?*

We all sit down at the table, me sliding Mea's chair out for her and scooting her back in before I take my own seat. And all the while, Mikah's careful gaze watches my every move. I can't blame the guy. He and his sister have protected each other since they were kids. I'm sure that doesn't stop now just because they're all grown up.

The server marches over to us. He's clearly slammed, this being a Saturday night at the beach in March, and his brisk tone reflects that. Mikah and Mea both order a beer, but I decide to stick to water.

Mea glances at me and gives me a warm smile. The fact that she notices my change in drinking habits brings a reassuring comfort to my chest.

"So." Mikah leans forward, his eyes locking with mine. "How did you and my sister hook up, Drake?"

His question is so direct it makes me chuckle. He doesn't beat around the bush. He's like his sister in that way. For as long as I've known her, Mea's been a chick who can get straight to the point. I always knew that was a rare thing, and it's something I've grown to love about her.

Love?

The word floats into my thoughts out of nowhere. What did I think was happening here? I'm suddenly afraid. The last woman I loved broke me. Over and over again. Until one day, I had to leave her and never look back.

The pain must be showing on my face, because Mea nudges me gently. "Drake? What's wrong?"

Clearing my throat, I shift in my seat. "Nothing. I'm fine." Directing my gaze at Mikah, I answer his question. "Mea and I met a few years back, when she brought her car to my garage for an oil change. Then we crossed paths again when her best friend and mine got together."

Mikah eyes me thoughtfully. "Right. Berkeley and Dare. You and Dare served together?"

I grunt in the affirmative. "Ranger battalion."

Mikah looks impressed. At that moment, our server returns to take our dinner orders. After he leaves again, Mikah leans back in his seat. It's the first time since we sat down that he's relaxed a bit, so I take it as a good sign. And then Mea's little hand finds my thigh under the table. My body tightens up immediately. When she begins kneading my muscle in a sensual way, my dick hardens at the same time that my balls draw up nice and tight. I try to keep the strain from showing on my face.

She's wearing a sneaky little smile that tells me she knows exactly what she's doing.

This is war. If she thinks she can make me look like a horny teenager in front of her brother, I can come up with a game of my own.

As Mikah and Mea start discussing his job as a junior longshoreman in Wilmington, I casually drape my arm over the back of her chair. Using my fingers, I begin to trace small circles in the area that I know to be the most sensitive: the back of her neck. She jumps slightly, and I let my fingers dip just below the neckline of her shirt.

I watch in fascination when she tucks her bottom lip into her mouth, sucking on the corner of it the way she does whenever she's feeling something intensely. It always adds fuel to the fire always burning inside of me when I'm around her. She's so fucking sexy in ways she has no clue about.

"So, Drake." I force my eyes to leave Mea's mouth so I can focus on Mikah. She takes the opportunity to slide her hand farther north on my thigh. I try not to wince.

"You own a garage? I've never been taught much about cars, but I'm still into them. Bikes, too."

My eyebrows shoot up in surprise. "Yeah? I'm restoring a classic Yamaha motorcycle right now. You should come by sometime and help me out. Maybe I can get done with it faster, and you'll learn something new."

Mikah's eyes light up, and Mea groans.

With a smile for both of us, she turns shining eyes my way. My heartbeat rockets at the sight of it. I let my fingers entwine in her hair, any thought of teasing her in front of her brother nonexistent now. My lips curl into a real smile, returning hers.

"I think you just made his month." Mea sounds thrilled.

The rest of the dinner goes smoothly. Mikah and I are getting along really well, and I can tell by Mea's sunny smile and easy laughter that she's happy about it. Never having had siblings myself, I admire their relationship. They seem to know everything about one another, and get each other on a level no one else does. It's enlightening and intimidating.

I refuse to take any arguments from Mikah when I pick up the tab. I throw my credit card down on the table just as Mea excuses herself for the ladies' room. As soon as she's out of earshot, Mikah's expression goes serious as he looks at me.

"Has she told you about our father?" His eyes flash at the mention of the man.

Feeling everything inside me tighten at the mention of the man who hurt her, I nod. "Yeah."

Mikah's brows lift in surprise. "She did? She never tells anyone about him."

I lean forward and clasp my hands together on the table. Looking him straight in the eye, I match the seriousness of his tone. "Mea's important to me. I'd like to think I mean something to her, too. So, yeah. She told me. It was hard to hear, Mikah. Really fucking hard."

There's a hard glint to his expression now. "I was too young to protect her back then, you know? But a day hasn't gone by that I wish I hadn't killed the bastard. If he ever thinks about contacting her again, I will."

There's not a hint of humor or casualness in his tone. Mikah is dead serious about his threat, and I can't blame him for wanting to hurt the man that hurt his sister.

I have the same strong desire.

"He hasn't contacted her, Mikah. She'd tell me if he had."

Mikah leans back against the back of his chair, rubbing his thumb along his jaw in agitation. "Good. You'll let me know if he does?"

I hesitate. I would never do anything that hurt Mea, or that put either one of them in danger. If Mikah is serious about his threat against their father, I don't want anything to push him into action. His safety and security are important to Mea, and that makes it important to me, too.

But as a man, I can understand his need to protect her. If I had a sister, and I knew that a man had hurt her the way Mea's dad did to her…I don't know what I'd do. I have enough trouble picturing how helpless Mea was to save herself from a monster like that. I can't imagine feeling responsible for a sister that way, too.

So I agree to Mikah's question. "Yeah. I'll let you know."

We drop the subject when Mea returns to the table.

But the conversation with Mikah doesn't leave me right away. It's something that replays over and over in my mind, even hours after the dinner is over.

"Do you know…" My breath comes faster as I slip Mea's short little dress over her head. My heart is a caged animal in my chest, fighting to break out when she's bared to me. My girl always keeps it simple, but the sight of her in her emerald-green cotton bra and matching black panties suck all the air from the room.

Instead of falling back onto my bed, she grabs hold of my belt, making quick work of the buckle before she starts in on the button of my jeans.

I keep my eyes locked on her tiny, deft fingers. There's no hesitation in her work. "…how much…"

She slips my old faded jeans down over my hips. Her eyes are liquid fire.

"…I've needed to get you naked tonight?" I finish in a pant.

Mea nods, her tongue darting out to lick her lips when she realizes there's nothing under my jeans. She follows their procession down my legs, falling to her knees in front of me as I step free from the denim.

Looking up at me through her long lashes, she smirks. "As much as I have." Then she takes my dick into her strong, steady hand.

"Fuuuuck." I want to drop my head back, let it loll along my neck, but I can't take my eyes from the gorgeous sight before me. She strokes her hand up and down my length. My senses are going crazy just watching her. I don't know what's sexier: her enthralled gaze while she watches what she's doing, or the satiny feel of her hands as they stroke me.

Dipping her head, she takes me into her mouth. Every single muscle in my legs tightens on instinct. The last thing I want to do is lose my release right now. Not like this. But *damn*.

"Holy fuck. You're killing me, sweetheart." I grind out the words.

She lets go of my erection, and as I pop out of her mouth she shoots me a wicked grin. "Then don't hold back. I can take it."

Winding my fingers through her curls, I hiss through my teeth as she sucks me deep. Her head bobs as she pulls me in and out of her mouth, the warmth and the wetness driving me wild. I can't help but thrust my hips in time with her action, until my toes begin to curl and my eyes start to roll back in my head.

Jerking out of her mouth, I pull her up and into my arms. She grabs my face in her hands and kisses me. She ravages my mouth, and I groan at the way her tongue tastes. The mixture of my salt and her sweetness is a drug. I'm addicted to her.

I know that I'll never be able to kick the habit.

Turning with her in my arms, I lay her down on my bed. For a second, I just stare down at the beauty she creates just by being there. Her hair fans out around her, a mess of wild, tangled curls against my sheets. As I watch, she grabs the sides of her panties and wiggles out of them. I can't take my eyes off of her, even after she tosses them to the floor. She does the same with her bra, and she's completely bared to me.

Her eyes take on a vulnerable sheen. Pulling the corner of her bottom lip into her mouth, she worries it while she stares up at me.

I go to her like I'm caught on a line, sliding toward her on the bed. When I'm hovering above her, I hold my weight and stroke her face with one hand. My hand nearly engulfs her.

"You are so beautiful." My whisper is ragged, raw. She brings something out of me that I never knew existed. It's a primal need to show her how important she is…how she's turned my world into something I barely recognize anymore.

If it weren't for her, I might still be allowing alcohol to dull my pain. She gives me purpose.

"Baby." Her arms go around me, pulling me tighter to her warmth. "Is this okay? With me on top?"

When her eyes fly up to meet mine, I know she hadn't noticed our position, the relevance of it. She stares up at me with something like devotion in her eyes.

Devoted? To me? It's a foreign concept. No one has ever been devoted to me. My mother sure wasn't. The bottle, her next score, was always way more important than raising a young son. My brothers in arms…they respected me, they appreciated me for the fact that I'd die for them and they'd do the same for me. When I rose in rank, they even respected me. But devotion? That's totally new, and I'm humbled enough by the emotion in her eyes that a lump forms deep in my throat. I dip my head down until my forehead meets hers. Our breaths mingle; we share the same air.

Her whisper breaks me. It puts me back together again.

"I trust you."

It's different this time. When I enter her, my entire heart feels the aftermath. Her storm eats me up, it swallows me whole. This woman who has turned my life upside down twice now is undoing me bit by bit, and there's nothing I can do to stop it if I wanted to.

I don't want to.

Her body folds around me, her slick heat wrapping me up in comfort and heat and wild, wild energy. She arches, a gasp leaving her lips as I find a rhythm. And then I can't help but take her hard and fast, because that's the way we relate to each other best.

"Oh, God. Drake." Her voice rises, and it's a sweet, sweet sound.

Her fingernails scrape my flesh, and I plant my head in the soft place between her neck and her shoulder. Nipping at her skin, she moans, and the vibration of it resonates in my cock. I let my lips rest against her throat, and it moves as she swallows hard. The pulse racing just beneath the surface of her skin makes the frantic pace of our bodies that much more intense.

"Mea." Her name is a prayer.

Her walls start to clench and tighten around me, her inner muscles in furious turmoil. Lifting my head so I can see her like this, like *this* is the best thing that's ever happened to her, I reach between us and pinch her clit between my fingers.

"Drake!" she screams.

My breath catches in my throat as she comes apart, holding her tighter against me as she shakes and writhes underneath me.

"Always so beautiful, baby. Every fucking time." With a growl, I pump into her until my seed is spreading warm and free out of me and into her.

My seed.

My body goes rigid; every muscle clamping down in an effort to deny what I just did.

Mea's quiet gasps blow heat against my shoulder, and I let my head fall against her chest. Pulling out of her slowly, I lay hold of myself above her so I don't crush her with my weight. She strokes me so softly, her fingers tracing sensual circles against my fiery skin.

"What is it?" She can sense that something's wrong, and I won't hold back from telling her the truth.

"I just came inside you. So sorry, baby…I forgot…" I fumble with my words, trying to find it in me to actually feel sorry when in reality nothing has ever felt that good.

Her tender strokes don't change. "It's okay, Drake."

Lifting up to look at her. "Yeah?"

She smiles up at me. "Yeah. About a week ago, I decided it was time to go on the Pill."

Confusion washes through me as my mixed emotions create a turbulent ocean inside my brain. *What does that mean? Why aren't I panicked about this?* Never, ever have I come inside a girl without a condom. I can't even believe I let myself get that carried away. But that's what Mea does to me. She takes away my control. She makes me feel powerful and powerless at the same time.

The fact that she went on the Pill, for us…it makes me smile.

I lie back on the bed, trying to catch my breath. Mea rolls off the bed, and I watch her as she sashays toward the bathroom. Groaning, I want to follow her. But I force myself to stay put.

She returns a few minutes later, and snuggles back into the bed. I pull the comforter over both of us as a sated sigh leaves her lips.

"Thank you." The two simple words leave me reeling.

"For what?" The lump in my throat makes words difficult.

"For being a man I can trust. I *feel* you, Drake." She turns over on her side, her eyes almost glowing in the darkness of my bedroom.

Hearing my own words thrown back at me fills something inside me I never knew was missing. Not until Mea.

And even though I can't say it aloud, even though I'm not ready to admit it to myself yet, a mantra finds its way inside my head as we both drift off to sleep.

Falling.

Falling.

Falling.

22

Mea

The remaining weeks before the wedding fly by in a blur. The Carolina breezes become warm and fragrant as the crepe myrtle trees start to blossom.

Drake's kept his promise. He's been bringing two of the guys from his garage, Will and Hoover, over to work on my studio every evening after he closes up. I've made a habit of bringing them dinner each night. So far, barbecue sliders with the marinated pulled pork I made myself in my slow cooker has been their favorite. Will keeps hinting at how good it was, and I giggle every time Drake slaps him on the back of his head in response to his flirty begging.

The very next day after Drake offered to help me realize my dream, I gave Lenny and Boozer my notice at See Food. They were happy for me, and I promised that the restaurant would always be another place I can call home.

I can't remember a time when I've been so *happy*. There's a man in my life that's changed my perspective. Mikah is happy and thriving with his job and his life in Wilmington. I think he's even started dating someone, though he won't tell me anything about her yet. I know he will when he's ready.

My best friend is ecstatically planning to marry the man she loves, and my other bestie won't be far behind. I'm finally going to open the business I've always dreamed of owning, and I can claim to have done it independently. It's all I've ever wanted to do. Be able to take care of myself, because I learned the hard way that relying on someone else to take care of you is a dark and dangerous thing.

I'm terrified.

It's all *too* good.

It's all *too* perfect.

It's all *too right.*

It means it's only a matter of time before it all comes crashing down around me. It's what I've been protecting myself from since I was fourteen years old. Good never stays. Good disappears in the blink of an eye.

Good fails. Every time.

So while I'm pushing the thin strap of my black wedge sandal through the tiny metal clasp on my shoe on the night of Berkeley and Dare's rehearsal, an aching pain in my stomach makes me wince. I straighten and lift my arms over my head, attempting to stretch the pain away. I frown at my reflection in the mirror across Drake's bedroom. I'm wearing a poppy-red halter-top sundress. The tops of my breasts peek flirtatiously out of the V neckline. I've always had enough curves to be proportionate to my small stature, but I've never had a problem with spillage. I turn this way and that, trying to figure out why my dress isn't fitting the way I expect it to.

Drake's low whistle from behind makes me spin around. He's entered the room wearing casual gray slacks and a plain white button-down. The sleeves are rolled up just the way I like them, exposing his muscular forearms and the winding black tattoos that snake their way upward.

"You look beautiful, baby girl." His full lips curve up into a sweet-and-sexy smile.

My stomach flutters wildly when he calls me that.

Sauntering toward him, I stretch up on my toes to kiss him. Taking my hand, he gestures toward the back door. "Ready?"

We stroll out onto the back patio. Right away we're met by the cathartic sound of waves meeting the sand. I sigh, sniffing the air. "This deck is going to be my favorite place to be this summer."

Drake locks his door, and then takes my hand again. "Looking forward to that. There's gonna be a 'bikini only' sign hanging right over there." He points toward one of the lounge chairs.

He leads me down the steps and onto the boarded pathway to the sand. We walk along the quaint boardwalk, observing the private beach behind the row of cottages on Drake's street. It's a short walk; Dare and Berkeley live exactly three houses down. We open the gate leading into their backyard, which is decorated for the rehearsal dinner.

Colorful Japanese lanterns hang from the trees, and tiki torches line the pathway leading to their deck. There are Adirondack chairs scattered about, Dare and Berkeley's favorite form of seating. A long, rectangular table has taken up residence in the middle of the yard, and soft music is playing.

Berkeley and Dare are standing with Berkeley's parents, over by a buffet table laden with barbecue fixins'. We move to walk toward them when I suddenly realize something.

"Shoot. Forgot my purse." My mumble warrants Drake's attention, and he glances down at me.

"I'll get it for you." He turns to head back toward our house.

"Wait." I grab his arm. Normally, I'd be all for letting him return to get my purse. But my stomach is starting to turn, and I swallow back bile as I shake my head. "It's okay. I can get it. I'll be right back."

Drake opens his mouth to argue, but I turn quickly and half-walk, half-jog back down the beach. When I glance over my shoulder, he's watching me. I smile and wave, knowing he'll stand sentry there until I get back.

Traipsing through Drake's backyard, I grab his spare key from under a large stone and let myself into the house.

"There you are." My purse is sitting right on the bar top where I left it. My wedges move silently across the kitchen tile as I head in that direction. Then my stomach twists, lurches. Heaves. Changing direction, I lurch toward the kitchen sink. Leaning over the stainless steel, I lose the contents of my stomach into the basin.

Sputtering, I lift myself back up and rinse the drain. I lean with heavy hands onto the counter while I catch my breath.

"Dammit!" I slap the granite with my palm. "A stomach bug? Now?"

Grumbling to myself and moving slowly, I make my way to the bathroom. After I brush my teeth and wash my face, I walk with a steadier gait back to the kitchen.

As soon as I grab my purse from the counter, it begins to vibrate.

I pull my cell out and check the screen. Tapping the green icon, I put the device to my ear. "Aunt Tay?"

Aunt Tay's voice, usually cheerful even after a long day of working around the farm, drifts across the line, tight with worry. "Is this a bad time, sweetie?"

Taking backward steps until I reach a chair, I plunk down at the table. My stomach is full of turmoil today. Now it knits with dread. "What's wrong?"

Tay sighs. "He called."

No.

No.

No.

Finding my voice, it leaves my throat as a hoarse bark. "When?"

"Just now."

Closing my eyes, I picture Tay standing in the big, farmhouse kitchen. She's standing by the big, double-sided brick fireplace. Wringing her hands, twisting her fingers this way and that. Phone trapped between ear and shoulder.

"What...what did he say, Aunt Tay?"

Silence on the line.

"Tay? *What did he say?*"

My breath is hitched, caught somewhere between my lungs

and my throat. My spine straightens, an involuntary reaction to the fear racing along my back.

"Honey…he lies. All he wants is power and control. It's all he's ever wanted."

"Aunt Tay, you called *me*. What did he *say*?"

A deep sigh. "Let's meet, Mea. I can't do this over the phone."

Drake leans against the gate, his posture relaxed and lazy. But when he spots me approaching, he straightens. He studies me as I walk toward him, and as hard as I try, I can't school my features. Not for Drake.

"What's wrong?" He's beside me in an instant, stopping me midstride. His hands stroke my shoulders as he searches my face.

I smile even though it's weak at best. "Not now, okay? We have a rehearsal to get through. Then I'll tell you."

Drake doesn't move. His big body serves as a mountain in my path, blocking me from continuing any farther. "Just tell me one thing, baby. Did he contact you?"

His eyes are stern, hard. The usually dancing light in their depths is still and cold. He's serious and he wants an answer. Now.

I toss my curls and give him the most honest one I can at the moment. "No. He didn't contact me."

Drake's body sags as he relaxes each coiled muscle. "Thank God. You sure you're okay?"

His eyes are still full of concern, but relief is there, too.

I'm not okay.

Taking his hand, I lead him through the gate and into the gathering. "I'm fine."

The other guests have arrived, and we trek down to the shore, where the wedding is to take place the following day.

Dare and Berkeley will pledge their lives to each other while standing near the surf, the rollicking waves serving as the musical score during the ceremony. It's where they spent their first date. It fits.

Tonight, we'll practice for tomorrow. And then, to Mrs. Holtz's horror, we'll have a rehearsal dinner in Dare and Berkeley's backyard, barbecue style. It's something we love to do, and tonight will be no different. Except for the fact that the couple had the food catered in by the same company preparing the food at their dinner reception tomorrow night.

"You okay? Something seems…off with you." Carrying a plate laden with barbecue and slaw, Greta settles into the chair beside mine.

The rehearsal went off without a hitch, and now everyone in the wedding party has gathered in the backyard for a well-earned meal. I catch Drake's eye where he's standing chatting with Dare's brother Chase. His assessing gaze takes in everything about me: the way I'm sitting, my company, even my plate of food. I send him a reassuring smile, which he returns with one of his own.

I rest my head on the back of my chair. "Just tired. It's been a busy couple of weeks."

Greta takes a delicate bite of pork. Chewing, she studies me. "That's right. I need to come by and see how the studio is coming along. I'm so proud of you, Mea."

A smile threatens to split my face. My friends can always manage to mask any inner turmoil going on inside me. "Thanks."

My mind plays through the scenes from my week. Watching Drake and the boys install flooring into my studio. Directing where they should place furniture in the lobby and in my office. Screaming when they almost dropped one of my mirrors. Late dinners with Drake, cuddled up on his couch. I've been sleeping with him every single night. He pretty much hates the idea of me going back to my crappy little apartment, and I don't mind staying in his much nicer house. Especially when we're in his bed at night. One late night in his kitchen, when we'd just returned from the studio, something he said to me struck a chord in both of us. It changed the air sizzling between us from sexy and flirty to serious and life affirming.

"Nightcap?" I'm fussing around in Drake's liquor cabinet, trying to find something to mix with the soda he keeps in the refrigerator.

"How about some coffee?" Drake suggests. His hands find my waist, pulling me up to stand before him.

A small smile touches my lips. "You really have changed. No more drinking?"

He wraps his arms around my waist. "I'll have a beer every now and then. I'm no saint, baby. But for you…yeah. I'm different."

I unfold myself from his grasp and head into the kitchen, pulling out the single-serve coffeemaker. Putting a mug under the spigot and a tiny plastic coffee cup in the filter, I turn it on. While the coffee brews, I rummage around in the fridge, pulling out cheese to spread on crackers for a snack. When I turn, Drake is still standing against the counter, his eyes intently locked on me.

I stop. "What?"

He shakes his head, scrubbing a hand down the front of his face.

"This." He gestures around us. "You. In my kitchen. In my bed every night. Damn, girl. I never thought I'd love this so much."

I'm frozen, staring at him as he pours more of himself into me. He's perplexed, the little line in his forehead a dead giveaway.

"I just don't want it to end. I like you being here. I like the way I am when I'm with you. I like us."

Dropping the cheese on the counter, I go to him. I'm drawn in by his words, by the way his eyes are staring straight through me, by the way his dark and light mix together into a perfect cocktail.

"I like us, too. I'm sorry it took so long."

He hefts me up, plants me on the counter. Planting himself between my legs, his gaze turns dark and smoky. And I love his dark just as much as I love his light.

Greta and I both gaze over at Berkeley. Wearing a black maxi dress, her hair falling haphazardly over her shoulders in a cascade of blond curls, she's a vision. She laughs at something Jeremy Teague says to her, probably something completely inappropriate.

"She's so happy," I muse, transfixed by her. "I can't believe she's getting married tomorrow."

"I know." Greta sighs, her crystal-blue eyes soaking in our friend's joy. When she turns them on me, there's a glint in them. "So. You and Drake, huh? I always knew it."

I wave a flippant hand. "Oh, you did not. I was a master of deception when it came to Drake. No one knew."

Greta throws her head back and laughs. "You were! I thought you hated him. But it was all a ruse." She wags a "you naughty girl, you" finger at me.

Putting my plate aside, I lean forward. "I did hate him. At least I thought I did. For something that was so completely not his fault. After Berkeley's wedding is over, I need to tell you guys something I've only to this point shared with Mikah and now Drake."

Her expression changes, worry breaking free through the mask of happiness. Then the expression morphs into one of relief.

"You're finally ready." She breathes.

Then she leans forward and squeezes me up into the tightest hug we've ever shared. Kissing my cheek before she pulls back, she whispers in my ear.

"We've always been ready to know you, Mea. Just been waiting on you."

23

Drake

The wedding day.

Thanks to Will, my garage runs like clockwork even when I'm not around. I don't have to worry about my business on a day like this, when I'm supposed to be focusing on my best friend and his big day.

My thick fingers twist and slide around the green stem of Dare's boutonniere. The other guys are crowded into my living room. Berkeley and the girls are getting ready today at her and Dare's house. And I'm sure they brought the entire Lone Sands Day Spa to them.

When I finally have the damned flower pinned onto his lapel, I turn him so that he can check out my work in the mirror. He frowns, turning a little so he can see how his khaki linen suit works with the flowers.

I slap him on the shoulder. "Looks good, man. You about ready?"

We turn to face the rest of the room. All the guys are dressed in their suits and amped up. We're all ready to do this. The question is…is the groom?

I've never seen Dare like this. He's always been a deep-thinking guy, with a killer sense of humor. But today, he's nothing but serious. He hasn't cracked a smile, and he's checked over every single thing he's responsible for fifty times.

"Ring's in your pocket?" His voice is an octave higher than usual.

I step in front of him, placing both hands on his shoulders. "I got the ring. Now you gotta go get the girl."

"Speaking of girls…" Jeremy steps up beside us, a big grin on his face.

Glancing at me, his grin widens. "Have you seen Mea today? Man, I dipped into the girls' house this morning to drop off something Greta left at the security office. And damn, man. Mea looked *hot*."

The warning is my throaty growl, but Jeremy doesn't get it. Dare steps in front of me right before I launch. Jeremy backs up a step.

Dare speaks through his teeth. "Seriously, Teague? You want to provoke the best man on my wedding day by talking about his girl?"

I growl again.

Dare whirls on me. "Easy, Drake. You know Teague. He's an idiot. Ignore him."

Jeremy tries to cover his laughter, but he fails. As usual. "Sorry, man. My bad."

Taking a deep breath, I take a step back from the Jeremy situation and address Dare. "We need to get down to the beach."

The truth is, I saw her tits very clearly last night when she bounced on top of me. I felt them, I sucked them, and I admired them. They're amazing. And yeah, they do seem bigger. But maybe it's just that time of the month or something. I didn't ask Mea about it, because I didn't want to sound like an asshole. But I guess Jeremy doesn't have any qualms about that.

And now my train of thought is headed in a dirty direction. Shaking my head to clear it of all things Mea, I focus on Dare. "You ready?"

Dare looks me in the eye. "To marry her? Been ready."

I pat his back. "Then let's go do it."

Dare, the four groomsmen, and I make our way out the back door and down to the beach. The officiant, a high-ranking navy officer who has apparently known Berkeley since she was young, is waiting. I walk with Dare up the aisle, passing smiling wedding guests seated in white wicker chairs. We stop in our spots beside the officiant, and I give Dare a reassuring grin. He smiles back before focusing on the top of the beach.

As the processional begins, I hold my breath. It's not my wedding, but I'm still waiting for my girl to walk down the aisle. She wouldn't let me see her dress, and the suspense has me knotted up tight. A bead of sweat runs down my forehead, and I brush it away.

Grisham and Greta appear at the top of the dune. Looking like the picture-perfect couple they are, they walk down the aisle together. Splitting off at the end, Grisham kisses her on the lips before stepping next to me. She holds her brightly colored flowers close to her chest.

Ronin walks down with Olive, looking as serious as ever. Olive, on the other hand, looks like a bright and shiny model in a beach commercial. Her dark red hair is piled on top of her head and she smiles at the guests as she walks by them. They also split at the top of the aisle and Ronin joins our side.

Jeremy is next, with Mea on his arm. My stomach clenches at the sight of her, and my eyes narrow as I watch Jeremy's hands while they walk. If he makes one false move, I swear I'll take him out after this wedding is done. Mea smiles sweetly as she walks, but she's not nodding toward the guests on both sides of her. She's locked in on me, and the rest of the wedding disappears under her hot, chocolate gaze. She's a seductress, and I'm under her spell. Can't help it. Never could. She's stunning in a beige gown, her long, curved legs moving to keep up with Jeremy's long strides. When they reach the end of the aisle, she winks at me.

I mouth the word "later."

She pulls her bottom lip into her mouth and I stifle a groan.

Chase and Shay walk down the aisle together, with their toddler daughter between them. She's all decked out in a frilly dress, tossing flower petals out of the little basket she's clutching in her chubby hands. She's taking her job seriously, making sure each petal makes it to the ground before reaching in to grab another handful. The guests are in a quiet uproar at the sight of her toddling down the aisle between her parents.

Once they reach the end, the little girl, Olivia, dumps her basket upside down. She glances at Chase, who's trying hard not to laugh at his daughter.

"All gone, Daddy!" she announces, clearly proud of the job she's done. Shay picks her up and carries her to stand beside the other bridesmaids.

The processional music fades away, the final notes lost somewhere in the rush of ocean meeting sand. I'm having trouble looking away from my girl, but as a singer takes his place at the front of the aisle, I have to check Berkeley out.

She's standing at the top of the dune, her arm locked tightly in her father's. Her eyes are locked on Dare, who straightens beside me. As she walks toward him, I rest a hand on his shoulder. He's trembling.

The singer, a friend of Berkeley's from college, is singing the steel drum version of "Over the Rainbow." I'm caught up in the moment just like everyone else, watching her drift across the sand toward the only man in this whole world who could hold her heart. Mea's eyes are shining with unshed tears. Feeling the heat of my gaze, she glances at me and beams. Something passes between us, then. *A promise?*

Could this be us one day? When I look at Mea, do I picture the rest of my life? Being chided by her sass, swept up in her perpetual tornado, loving her body each and every night? Is that something I want to hold on to?

The answer is an unequivocal *yes.*

I don't know when it happened, exactly. But sometime between the first time I loved her body and this moment, I fell headfirst under her spell. There's no other woman in this world that could keep me guessing the way she does. No other woman who could beckon me across a crowded room with one crook of her finger. No other woman who simultaneously makes me crazy with frustration and insane with greedy lust.

She's *mine*.

And I want it forever.

When asked to share their vows, Dare and Berkeley state that they've written their own. It's not surprising, since I think underneath all that broodiness my boy is actually a poet. Berkeley's an artist, she would never want to conform to the traditional vows. They pledge their lives to each other with beautiful, heartfelt words.

"I, Dare, take you, Berkeley, to be my wife. The first and last person I think about each and every day. The mother of my future children. The love of my life. The first day I saw you I decided you were an evil vixen siren who'd been sent to mess me up for anyone else. It was partially true. You're definitely a vixen, and I answer to your siren's call. But evil? Never. You're the sweetest, most thoughtful, kindhearted woman I've ever met. When I fell in love with you, Berkeley, I found my family. My home. And I promise that for the rest of my life, I will make that home the happiest place for the both of us. I will cherish you, honor you, respect you as my partner, and let you decorate every room in our house without a single complaint. I pledge my life to you today. Forever."

Hers is spoken through the haze of tears falling from her lovely eyes. "Dare, the day I met you, I pegged you for a dark and brooding army egocentric." The wedding guests burst into laughter.

"But I was wrong. You taught me that judging someone by past prejudices can be fatal. No matter what I thought of you then, I couldn't get you out of my head. And I still get those same butterflies whenever you walk into a room. You're my love, my partner, and my hero. I pledge my life to you now. I promise to always be the person you can turn to in times of distress. I promise to be the mother to your children. I promise to love you through every peak and every valley this world might bring us. But most of all, I promise to be your compass, so that you'll always know where to come home."

The ceremony ends shortly after, with Dare dipping his new wife to kiss the hell out of her in front of family and friends.

I pull Mea closer to me as we wander over the dance floor. The soft strains of a slow Bruno Mars hit waft through the air, but I barely hear the music. My senses are overwhelmed with her. Her smell invigorates me, the feel of her body pressed against mine is a drug. Her head rests against my chest, and there are no wayward curls tickling my nose.

"I miss those curls," I whisper into her ear, loving how her body shivers in response.

She glances up, warm brown eyes meeting mine. "I straightened it this morning. You don't like it?"

I smooth a hand over her espresso-colored locks. When straightened, her hair falls over her shoulders in a thick sheet. She's gorgeous either way. "Love your hair, baby. No matter how you style it. Those curls just make you wilder. I like you wild."

Her lips curl, a seductive smile making the blood pump harder in my veins. "Oh, I'll be plenty wild."

Grabbing her hips I pull her against me so she can feel how much I want her to show me her wild. "Promise."

A soft gasp escapes her. Her voice is breathless. "I promise, Drake."

Promise. I should tell her...

My phone buzzes in my pocket. Without taking my arm away from Mea's curvaceous form, I pull it out and check the screen. Frowning, I show it to her.

"Who's that?" Curiosity is evident in her tone.

"It's a lady I know from my hometown back in Georgia. Took care of me a lot when my mom…couldn't. Hold on one second. I need to answer it." I kiss Mea's cheek and walk away from the dance floor, heading outside the big white tent set up on the sand for the reception.

"Ms. Ebbie? Is everything okay?"

"Hello, Drake, dear. I'm sorry to bother you, but there's something I thought you should know."

My brow furrows, concern and confusion sweeping through me. "It's okay, Ms. Ebbie. You're not bothering me. What is it?"

Her elderly voice wavers a little as she speaks. But knowing Ms. Ebbie, she walked a mile through town today making sure someone who needed something got her help. "Well, when the movers were packing up your mama's house, I went on over to make sure there was nothin' in there you might want someday."

I smile, because of course she did. Ms. Ebbie was always thinking of others, and it doesn't bother me in the least that she took it upon herself to save mementos in case I'd want them. "Did you find something you think I need?"

She sounds unsure. "Well, I know you never knew who your daddy was, Drake. There was a shoebox in your mama's closet that held some things…important things. There's a picture of your mama when she was pregnant. I thought it was her bein' pregnant with you. But the man standin' next to her in that picture ain't your daddy. I don't recognize him at all."

"What are you saying, Ms. Ebbie?" Suddenly, my palms are sweaty. But my body feels cold all over.

"I was there when you were born, Drake. Helped your mama through that labor. But I wasn't there when you were conceived, was I? I think the man in this picture…he's your real daddy."

I use my free hand to cover my forehead. Squeezing, I want to push the information she just told me right out of my head. My voice comes out as a rough whisper. "Why would you think that?"

"On account 'a there's also an envelope in this box with a DNA test inside. I won't open it, Drake. That's for you to do."

I squeeze my eyes shut. *Maybe if I keep them closed, this will all fade away. This can't be happening right now.* "Does it say anything? On the back of the picture?"

"It does indeed. It says 'Me and Richard.'"

"Richard? I don't know any Richard. Do you?" I blow out a heavy breath and start to pace the sand.

"Drake…I think you need to come home. Sort this out."

Stopping, I spin toward the opening of the big, white tent. "I don't think I can do that right now, Ms. Ebbie."

Her voice is weary. "And that's your God-given right, honey. But it'll be here waitin' on you when you're ready."

Sighing, I drop the phone. Grabbing both sides of my hair, I yell over the sound of the music coming from the tent. "Fuck!"

When I retrieve the phone back out of the sand, my voice is resigned. "Thanks, Ms. Ebbie."

Instead of going back inside the tent, I trudge toward the ocean. My mood is drastically different now from before I took the phone call. My brain is swirling with the implications of what the older woman just told me.

Is it true? The man who left me and my mother when I was a baby, and then spent most of his life in and out of prison afterward, isn't actually my father?

Growing up, I'd asked my mom about my father. It's a question all little boys want to know the answer to when they realize that other boys in their class at school have dads who live with them and play with them and love their mothers. My mom, probably drunk when I asked, snapped at me that my dad didn't love either one of us and he was sitting in a prison cell upstate. She said he was a bad man, and I never asked about him again. I didn't need to. What she told me was enough, and I put my focus on my schooling and on making sure she didn't choke on a puddle of her own puke.

But what if the photo Ms. Ebbie found was of my real dad? What does it mean? Did my mother meet him before the man I thought was my father? Or did she have an affair with another man? Why didn't he stay? Why didn't he help her?

The questions keep rolling in, and my anger ratchets with each new wonder. The moon is directly above the waves, shedding cool white light on the rollicking water. I stare at it until my eyes burn with the effects from the salty spray.

"Drake?"

Mea's voice doesn't make me turn around. I don't want her to see me like this. I feel out of control, violent. I feel like I could crush something with my bare hands.

For the first time in a long time, I want a drink.

But I know now that it won't help. It'll only numb me. What I really need is standing right beside me.

Mea touches my shoulder. "Drake—"

I silence her with my lips. Kissing her hard, I draw her against me until I'm squeezing her so hard she gasps. When she opens her mouth, I take the chance to ravage her hot, wet mouth with my tongue. She responds, stroking me with her sweetness and coating me with her honey. Her storm brews just beneath the surface, threatening to pull me into its orbit and keep me tethered to her.

When her fingers tangle in my hair, I lift her up. Carrying her toward my own backyard, I forget about the dwindling wedding reception and anything else but the fact that I need to be alone with her.

My lips fused to hers, I follow the path and open the gate to my backyard by memory. Fumbling with the lock on my door, I let us inside and kick it shut behind me.

We make it as far as the kitchen table. Mea slides down my body, and I reluctantly let her lips leave mine. With frantic, hurried movements, she yanks open my white dress shirt. Buttons go flying, but I hardly notice the soft *pings* as they hit the tile floor. She slides the fabric over my shoulders, exposing my chest. Reaching around her, I unzip her sexy little dress. The sound of the zipper is erotic and makes me even more desperate to slide inside her heat than I already am. Turning her around, I push her down with one palm until she's leaning against the kitchen table. I slide her dress down over an ultrasexy pair of lace boyshort panties. After she steps out of the dress, I push those down, too, baring her perfect, round ass to me.

"So fucking sexy." I don't recognize my voice. It's rough, it's frenetic. I need her more than I need another breath.

Reaching between her legs, I find her slick folds hot and ready for me. Groaning, I insert one finger inside her and then another. She moans, bucking back against me with a furious need of her own. I don't care about control. I've tossed it out in order to succumb to how much I need her right now.

Unzipping my slacks, I let them fall down my legs. There's no other barrier keeping her from me, and it only takes a second for me to slam into her from behind.

"Yes, Drake." Her gasp of pleasure spurs me on.

Pulling back out of her, I pound back home. Over and over again, in and out. My body becomes slick with sweat, a drip of it runs down my temple. Mea reaches back to meet me, the sound of her ass slapping into my hips is going to slowly drive me insane.

"Remember this, baby. Remember me." My words are released on a groan. She starts to quake around me just as my balls tighten in anticipation of my own release.

Our panting breaths have taken over the sound waves in the kitchen, and I'm captured by the wild grace that this girl brings to my life. I'm struck by the fact that I'm about to leave her for God knows how long, and I'm not even going to be able to explain. I'm leaving her with this one rugged memory, and I'm a bastard because I didn't take her to bed and love her right. This is what I needed. But it's not what she deserved.

My body shakes and shivers as my release rises and builds, and when she cries out her own uncontainable pleasure, I come hard and fast.

And then I slide out of her, staggering backward until I reach the kitchen counter. Glancing down, I pull up my pants and fasten them while Mea slowly rises from the table.

I don't know what to say. I definitely can't say what I was thinking earlier, during the wedding. Now isn't the time. Not when I've got more fucked-up shit swirling around inside my head.

"Stay with me tonight." More demands. I can't seem to help myself.

She gathers her dress into her arms, her expression wary. Nodding her head, she walks toward the bedroom.

Following her, we climb into bed. Mea runs over so that her body is facing mine. She reaches out a finger, traces my lips. Her touch is soft, gentle. Loving.

Love.

Love.

Love.

My phone buzzes in the pocket of my pants on the floor. Thinking it could be Ms. Ebbie again, I pull it up and check the screen.

"Ms. Ebbie?"

"No, I'm sorry. This is a paramedic. I found this phone on the lady we just brought to the hospital, and this was the last number she called."

Sitting up, I shake my head slowly. "She's in the hospital? What happened?"

The paramedic's voice is sympathetic. "Stroke. If you're a loved one, you should probably get to the hospital."

The call disconnected. I know that Ms. Ebbie has a daughter who lives in Texas, but I can get there faster than she can.

Turning to Mea, I kiss her lips.

"What's wrong? Who was that?" Her voice carries a note of alarm.

I raise my hands, tugging at my hair. I take a deep breath.

Without looking at her, I speak. My voice is raw. "I have to go back to Georgia."

Confusion makes her voice rise. "Why? For how long?"

Standing, I shake my head. "Don't know for how long. A lady who used to take care of me a lot when I was growing up just had a stroke."

Quickly, I explain to Mea about Ms. Ebbie and how important to me she is. I also tell her what Ms. Ebbie said to me when we spoke earlier.

Mea sits up and swings her legs over the side of the bed. "I'll come with you." She turns to face me. When I glance at her, I see her eyes shining with determination. She's so beautiful my heart cracks a little bit just looking at her.

"You can't, Mea. You're getting the studio ready to open next month. And I'm not sure how long I'll be gone. You need to stay here."

Hurt and rejection. That's what I see in her eyes. Inflicted by me.

I look away, because the sight of her staring at me like that is too fucking much.

"Do you think that while you're there, you'll look in that box? I want to be there for you." Her voice trembles slightly.

"I'll be back, Mea. I just need to go and do this now."

I reach for her. Even when my mind is full of tumult, and my spirit is curdling with poison and anxiety, I need to touch her. As I caress her face, she closes her eyes briefly. When she opens them again, they cut me with shame.

"I just need to stay with Ms. Ebbie until her daughter gets there. I...I don't know about the box."

"I know you have to go, but I don't want you to." Her voice is dim, depleted. She's asking for this, and she means it. But I can't give it to her.

"Mea...I have to. I wouldn't be leaving you if she weren't in the hospital. The guys will look out for you while I'm gone."

Mea's eyes are wide. Her hand cups my face. Something inside of me goes soft at the soft contact. But I swallow down the tenderness, because if I don't get out the door now, I won't go at all.

And I owe it to Ms. Ebbie to be there for her.

"I'll be here waiting for you when you get back." Her voice is soft and sweet.

"Will you stay here? At my place? I can make sure Grisham and Greta are checking in on you while I'm gone. I need to know that you're safe. And if you need me, call. I'll be in the car and on my way back to you."

She nods. "I'll stay here. Don't worry about me."

She wraps her arms around my waist. Burying my head in her hair, I take deep, even breaths.

She'll be safe while you're gone. You won't be gone long. She'll be fine.

Those thoughts turn into a chant for me as I grab a duffel bag, and kiss her good-bye.

24

Mea

When I woke up to the morning sun streaming in through the window, my first thought is that Drake is gone.

Hugging his pillow to my chest, I allow myself to become overwhelmed with the rising emotions. Crying, my tears soak Drake's pillow.

I don't know if I'm crying because he's gone, or because the prospect of sleeping without him tonight is unbearable.

Maybe it's because I never got to tell him that Aunt Tay had heard from... *that man*. I won't call him my father. He doesn't deserve that title. But I know he wants something, and I'm going to have to face it alone now. Not with Drake, my big, strong protector, by my side.

You're strong, Mea. You're in control. You always have been. A few months of happiness with Drake didn't change that.

Maybe it didn't, but it allowed me to believe I didn't have to be so strong by myself all the time.

A bright spot lights the darkness of last night's events. Drake opened up to me about his mother, about his childhood. His past is a subject he's never previously broached, and I'm proud of him for divulging what he went through. I'm proud that he picked me to share it with. I have a feeling not very many people know the inner workings of Drake Sullivan, much like they don't know the pulleys and gears that make me tick.

Maybe last night didn't sever a bond. Maybe it made ours stronger. He'll come back to me.

Rising from the bed, reluctant to leave my moment with Drake's ghost behind, I plod toward the bathroom. I turn on the shower as hot as I can stand it, and then step back to study myself in the mirror as it heats. Stripped down, my body looks properly ravaged from my time in the kitchen with Drake last night. Just thinking about it brings a rosy glow to my cheeks and a pulsing ache between my legs.

Last night he was needy, and he was rough. But he was mine, and I wouldn't have him any other way.

Mine. I smile in spite of the despair lurking just beneath the surface. I pull the pins out of my disheveled hair, knowing that as soon as it gets wet my wild and crazy curls will be back. *Maybe I'll text Drake a picture of the curls he loves so much.*

The mirror begins to fog, and I step into the shower. Taking my time, I wash Drake's scent from my body, hoping it won't be long before he's all over me once again. The steam rejuvenates me, makes me feel powerful and in control once more.

I'm going to need that power and control during my coffee date with Aunt Tay this morning.

Once toweled off, I dress quickly in yoga pants and a soft cotton tee before leaving Drake's room and padding down the hallway. As soon as I enter the kitchen I'm bitch-slapped by the powerful scent of bacon. Greta stands over the stove, frying up breakfast.

"Greta?" I clutch my stomach, and as she turns around, her sculpted eyebrows knit with concern. Covering my mouth, I rush back through the bedroom and into the bathroom. I only just make it kneeling in front of the toilet before I'm throwing up.

Retching and heaving into the toilet when you haven't yet eaten for the day is a miserable experience. The heaves just keep coming, keeping me coughing and doubled over. My throat burns and my eyes sting. Greta is behind me, pulling back my still-wet curls and speaking to me in a soothing voice.

"It's okay, Mea. I've got you."

When my body finally finished the wracking, wretched up-chucking, I stand on wobbly legs and lean over the sink. Taking a few deep breaths, I fill the cup beside the sink with water and rinse my mouth out. Greta's eyes follow me in the mirror as I load toothpaste onto my toothbrush and stick it in my mouth.

But at the first taste of my toothpaste, my face drains of color and my stomach roils again. Quickly pulling the toothbrush from my mouth I rinse it and slam it back into the holder beside the sink.

What the fuck is going on?

Weakly, I turn to face Greta, leaning against the sink for support. "Um, hey?" I wave a halfhearted hand. "Thanks for holding my hair."

Her eyes hold massive amounts of concern, wide and knowing. But her mouth twitches ever so slightly as she nods. "What are best friends for?"

"What are you doing here?" The melancholy I'm feeling at the loss of Drake seeps into my voice.

Greta notices. "I'm making you breakfast, silly. Drake stopped by early this morning…gave Grisham and me a key, since we're only a few minutes away. If Dare and Berkeley were in town, I'm sure he would have given it to them. But they left early this morning for their honeymoon."

I nod. "So you know he's gone?" My voice breaks on the last word.

Greta's face melts into a soft place to fall. "Oh, sweetie. Yeah, he told us he was going out of town for a bit. What happened? He looked wrecked. Did you two have a fight?"

The tears erupt from my eyes before I know what's happening.

I pride myself on my ability to keep my emotions in check. The fact that I'm now reduced to a quivering mess is a problem for me. Because *I don't do this.*

"No," I sob as Greta's arms wind around me. "We didn't."

Between sobs, I explain Drake's connection to his friend Ms. Ebbie and why he had to go.

Greta smooths my hair as she squeezes me to her. She just hugs me while I cry, and I find out that's exactly what I need. To cry.

When I don't have any tears left and my sobs have subsided, Greta pulls away from me and steps back. Her eyes scan me from head to toe, like she's looking for something. Bewildered, I stare right back.

"Do you want some bacon?" she asks suddenly.

My nose wrinkles automatically. "Uh, no. And I don't think I want to come out until you're done cooking it."

Her lips curl into a slow smile. "I thought you loved bacon."

Rolling my eyes, I lean back against the countertop. "You are being so weird right now, Greta. Is your own wedding planning going to your head? We can have a girls' night tonight if you need to unwind."

With an intense focus, Greta reaches forward and grabs both my breasts in her hands. As I yelp, she squeezes.

Jumping, I swat her hands away. "Ouch. Dammit, Greta! What the hell is wrong with you?" My girl's clearly lost her marbles.

Greta is staring at me hard, like she's attempting to laser some sort of information from the inside of her head into my own. I just stare at her, a blank, mute stare.

Then she spins on her heel to leave the bathroom. "Don't leave this house. I'll be right back. I'm gonna toss the bacon on my way out. Open some windows, and that should help with the smell."

She marches out of the bedroom. It takes a few minutes for me to follow, and I do what she says. I sprint around the house, opening every single window. Standing in the middle of the living room, I inhale, smelling nothing but clean, salty ocean air.

That's so much better. But then I scowl. Since when does bacon make me sick? I was sick yesterday, too. And why do my boobs…Oh, God.

No.

No, no, no.

When Greta returns, I'm pacing the living room like a caged tiger waiting for feeding time. She tosses me a brown paper pharmacy bag. My stomach clenches with some unnamed emotion. I snatch the bag out of the air and run to the bathroom.

Two minutes. Two minutes. Two minutes.

I sit on top of the toilet, staring across the room at the offensive white stick sitting on the countertop. Mocking me.

Two minutes is a long fucking time.

When the timer on my phone begins to beep, I leap off the toilet and snatch the thing off the countertop. I stare down at the two tiny pink lines.

Two tiny pink lines.

Two tiny pink lines.

I stare. And stare, and stare and *stare.*

I don't know how long I stay in that bathroom. And Greta must know that I need a few, because she doesn't pound on the door like I know she wants to.

I'm pregnant. I'm going to have Drake Sullivan's baby.

Dropping the stick, I cover my mouth with both hands.

I'm pregnant.

What does it feel like to be in shock? If I had to guess, it would be shallow breathing. A difficulty catching one's breath. A cold sweat breaking out all over the skin. Disorientation.

Check.

Slowly, I open the bathroom door and walk into the bedroom. I scan the room. Even though Drake and I have been sharing it, it's still so very Drake. Dark wood furniture. Slate gray comforter.

No curtains, so that the sunlight and views of the ocean can be seen clearly from anywhere in the room. Clean, modern designs.

That's Drake.

Will a baby fit into his life? Will he want this?

Because, I realize through the haze of shock and awe that covers me, I do. *I want this baby.*

I don't even realize tears are streaming down my face until they drip down my chin and onto my shirt.

In a daze, I leave the bedroom and walk right into Greta's waiting arms.

I cry, and so does she. She hasn't even seen the stick, but she knows. Pulling back, I hand it to her.

She glances down at it, and then bursts into a fresh wave of tears.

"You're pregnant." She hiccups. "You're pregnant!"

I sink down onto Drake's big brown leather recliner. "I'm pregnant. Oh, my God."

She sits on the ottoman, her eyes scanning me carefully. Her eyes are shining with happiness. "Are you okay? How do you feel?"

"I feel…" I glance down at my stomach. My hands go there, caressing the little life inside me that I hadn't even realized was there. Growing. Something inside me breaks apart then. It might be my soul splitting in two. Half for me, half for the tiny life growing inside me.

I look back at Greta, wonder in my voice. "I'm having his baby."

Her expression lights up in a radiant smile. "You are."

And then she launches herself at me, and we're hugging and crying and laughing all at once.

When she finally pulls away, she picks up my phone from the arm of the recliner and hands it to me. "Call him, Mea. Tell him. He's going to want to come back for this."

I throw the phone back down like it's burned me. Shaking my head with strict vehemence, I know that telling Drake right now is out of the question. "No." I grab her arms, squeeze them tight. "And you have to promise me that you won't tell anyone. If you tell Grisham, he'll tell Drake. I can't tell him this over the phone."

Shock permeates her features. She tosses her long, sleek dark hair over one shoulder in agitation. "But, Mea! He's going to *want* to know this!"

"*No*, Greta. I will tell him when he comes back. End of conversation." I lift my chin, and Greta sees it and resigns to my stubbornness.

She sighs. "Fine. I think it's the wrong choice. But it's your choice to make."

We sit in silence for a minute, breathing in the salty breeze and thinking our own thoughts.

"What are your plans today?" Greta finally asks.

That question shoots me right back into the here and now. I grab my phone, look at the time. "Shit. I have to go. I'm meeting Tay for coffee."

Greta narrows her eyes. "Your aunt? That's rare. What's going on?"

I rise from the chair, one hand automatically going to my stomach to rub it gently. "I'll tell you tonight, okay? You know how I told you there were some things I wanted to share with you? Come over and hang with me tonight. After coffee with Tay, I'm teaching yoga at the gym until early evening. Then I'll come back here. Drake left me his key...he wants me to stay here while he's gone."

Greta nods. "Yeah, that's what he told Grisham this morning. And of course I'll come. I'll bring Eggs."

I smile at the thought of Greta and Grisham's boxer puppy running around the house while I tell her the deepest, darkest part of me. He'll make everything seem a little bit sunnier.

"Sounds good." I give her a quick hug, grab my purse off the counter, and rush off to my meeting with Aunt Tay.

I'm going to have a baby. Drake's baby.

25

Drake

As I'm sitting in the hospital waiting room in Georgia, something feels wrong. Missing.

I've been in contact with Ms. Ebbie's daughter in Texas. She is arranging care for her children and will be on a flight as soon as she can. Until then, I'm here for the old lady as long as she needs me. She's been awake, but the doctors are still running tests on her condition.

As soon as her daughter arrives and I know she'll be okay, I can go back to the girl I'm in love with.

In love with.

It's the fucking truth. I love her. With everything in me. I'd put myself between her and anything that might be coming for her. And that's how I know. Risking my life for someone? That's love.

And I'd do it for Mea without thinking twice.

"Mr. Sullivan?"

I stand when a doctor in a white coat enters the waiting area.

"Yeah."

The doctor consults his clipboard. "You aren't Ms. Ebbie's emergency contact."

Clearing my throat, I nod. "Yeah. I know. I'm just here until her daughter can make it. But I know Ms. Ebbie very well."

The doctor nods. "Well, her condition is stable, but we would like to let her rest for now. Her daughter will be able to see her when she arrives."

I let out a relieved breath. "Good. That's good. Thanks for letting me know."

The doctor exits, and I decide to head for the house. Maybe I can do something useful, like grab some pajamas for Ms. Ebbie or something.

Ms. Ebbie lives next door to my mom's house. Climbing out of the Challenger in the driveway, I stare at the small, one-story home where I spent my childhood. There are no good memories here.

And yet I'm pulled toward it without even planning to go in.

Sighing, I walk up the drive. Letting myself into the house, I note that it's empty. The moving company packed everything up and placed it in storage. At some point, I'm going to have to dump it or sell it. I'm just not ready to decide either way right now. I stand just inside the front door, looking around as memories bombard me from all sides.

I close my eyes, remembering. Ms. Ebbie would try her damnedest to make sure I knew I was loved when my mother was unable to do it. She would hug me, she would tell me she was proud of me when I got all the answers correct on my homework.

She would try to shield me from the full brunt of the effects of my mother's drinking.

Walking over to the pile of boxes, I notice one is set aside.

Shaking my head, I mutter, "Thanks, Ms. Ebbie."

The box doesn't look familiar to me.

But then again, I didn't have time growing up to go searching for clues to my heritage between cleaning up vomit and keeping my head above water.

I take a deep breath. And then I pull off the lid of the box.

Right on top is the photo Ms. Ebbie called me about. I pick it up, feeling the old photograph in my hands. It's definitely my mother. Long, dark hair. She was beautiful when she wasn't carrying lines from years of alcohol abuse. Her dark eyes are crinkled at the corners. Happy. She's staring down at her swollen stomach, her hands lovingly caressing the bump.

Me. That bump is me.

I'm blown away by how happy she looks. And Ms. Ebbie is right. The man standing beside her, with one large hand covering hers, isn't the man my mother always spoke about as being my father. She had a photo of Timothy Sullivan stuffed inside her nightstand. Sometimes she'd pull it out and curse his name for leaving us.

Flipping the picture over, I run my thumb across the scrawling writing.

Me and Richard.

The picture is dated a few months before I was born.

This guy…he *looks* like me. Same eye color. Same big build.

I riffle through the box, searching for the DNA test that Ms.

Ebbie mentioned. I find the envelope with the return address from a lab and pull out the document inside.

Scanning it quickly, I come to the same conclusion that Ms. Ebbie did. My mother requested this DNA test. She submitted three DNA samples: one from Timothy Sullivan, the man I thought was my father; one from another male, who I'm assuming is this Richard from the photo; and one from me. The test is 99 percent conclusive. The DNA from the man I thought was my father is not a match for mine.

Richard is my father.

So many thoughts chase one another through my head at that moment. Who is this Richard? Why wasn't he ever in my life? It seems apparent that the man who was married to my mother at the time likely found out that I wasn't his son. So he bailed. And Richard must have known. This picture with my mother proves it.

And in this picture, they appear to be so in love. Their hands are together, over her stomach. It looks like they both loved *me*.

What the hell happened?

I need more answers. So I grab the box and head for the hospital.

When I arrive, I ask at the nurse's station for the room where they've placed Ms. Ebbie. And I tell them I'm her son.

Because now isn't the time for technicalities, and they'll still only let immediate family see her.

Pushing open her door, I see she's still, lying under the blankets. She looks small, frail, something Ms. Ebbie's never been.

Her head turns toward me as I pull a chair beside the bed.

I reach for her wrinkled hand and clutch it.

"You look good, Drake." She coughs.

Her words are slightly slurred, the wrinkled skin on one side of her face drooping slightly.

"Thanks. There's a girl back in Lone Sands who has something to do with that."

Ms. Ebbie beams up at me. "I'm glad to hear it, boy. A good man like you needs a good woman in his life. Now, tell me what was in the envelope in that box."

I arch one eyebrow. "How'd you know I opened the box?"

She pshaws. "Can see the confusion all over your face."

"What am I supposed to do now, Ms. Ebbie?" I'm practically begging her to solve this problem for me.

"There was some talk, years ago." Ms. Ebbie coughs again. "There was a woman who was close with your mother while she was pregnant. They'd been friends since grade school. But after your ma fell apart, this girl felt she had to step away. I think if you go see her, she'll have a story to tell ya."

I glance up. "What's her name?"

"Sheridan. Sandy Sheridan. And she lives over on Oak."

The turquoise blue front door creaks open. A slight, mocha-skinned woman stares out at me. Her long black hair is swept up into a ponytail, and impossibly dark eyes stare out at me.

"Can I help you?" She leans against the jamb. Her hand grips the edge of the door, ready to slam it shut against the towering, muscled, tattooed stranger standing on her doorstep.

"Ms. Sheridan? Sandy Sheridan?" I try to keep my tone gentle so I don't scare her.

Her eyes narrow anyway. Taking a step back, she prepares to close her door. "Do I know you?"

Shaking my head, I try to appear as unintimidating as possible. I lower my voice, adopting a gentler tone. But I can't hide my gruffness. It's a part of me. "My name is Drake Sullivan. Miranda Sullivan was my mother, and Ms. Ebbie told me you used to know her."

Her eyes widen, and she glances behind me. Her house is on the very edge of town, explaining why I never ran into her. She's completely unfamiliar to me.

Stepping back from the door, she gestures inside the house. "Come in."

She leads me into a casual sitting room just off the foyer. A striped sofa takes up much of one wall.

"Please," she says without a smile. "Have a seat, Drake."

I do, folding my hands in my lap and scanning the room.

Sandy sits down across from me, in an adjacent armchair. She mimics my posture, leaning forward. She searches my face. When recognition washes over her features, I sit up straighter.

"You have her eyes, you know? They used to be alert and clear, seeing everything. Just the way yours are now." Sandy's voice is full of the memories showing up as moving pictures inside her head. She loved my mom, at least at one time. It's there in her eyes.

"You knew her well?" I try to keep the ball of emotion at bay, but damn this is hard. I've buried feelings about my mother for so many years that now they're rushing to the surface, tiny air bubbles of emotions that I can't ignore.

Sandy tucks a strand of hair behind her ear. "We were best friends in high school. Before that, even. Can you tell me why you're here? Is there something you want to know?"

I allow the silence to stretch between us before I run both hands over my face. Sighing, I nod. "Yeah. My mom kept this photo in a box in her closet. It's her when she was pregnant with me. But it's not Timothy Sullivan, who I thought was my father, in the picture with her. Do you have any idea who that man could have been?"

Her expression doesn't change, and I know she was expecting the question. She's not surprised by it, nor does she have to sift through her memory to find the answer. She holds up one finger, leaving the room. I stand up and begin to pace. My body can't stay still; it's full of nervous energy that forces me to move. When Sandy returns, she startles when she finds me prowling her living room like a caged panther.

Moving back to my seat, I incline my head toward the large book in her arms. "What's that?"

Taking a seat beside me on the couch this time, she smooths a hand over the front of the burgundy book. "It's our high school yearbook." She opens to an earmarked page full of smiling faces. Senior portraits. She points toward the picture of my mother. Glancing at it, my heart constricts. God, what must she have been like at this age? Full of life, full of hope? A different person from the broken woman who raised me. Her eyes were bright and shining, her smile beaming out from the page.

"She was beautiful, wasn't she?" Sandy's voice is sentimental. "Charmed every single person she came in contact with. But it was this year that she met Timmy. And he was bad news for her."

I look sharply at her. "What do you mean?"

Sandy's gaze is steady, intense. "I mean they started dating, and it was like he took possession of her. He wanted her all to himself, didn't want to share her with anyone else. Not even me, her best friend. We tried to tell her that he was no good, but she didn't want to listen. I think she saw something light underneath all his layers of grime, and she thought she could shine him up until he was brand-new again. But it wasn't possible. Not with Timmy Sullivan.

"She married him right out of high school. He went to work at the tire plant, but he wouldn't let her work. She was home all the time in their little trailer out by Route 11, and none of us knew what to do to help her. Her mother, your grandmother, tried to go over there one day and pack her bags. Timmy came home and kicked her out, told her he never wanted to see her on his property again."

My jaw is clenching so hard my teeth are starting to ache. "Did he hit her?"

Sandy's eyes fall downward. "I'm guessing he did. If he didn't, he sure put the fear of God in her, and that was enough. I would call her, but she'd beg me to stay away.

"One Friday, Miranda called me. She said that Timmy was going to lay pipe for another company for the next week, and she just wanted me to take her out of there for a while. I was ready to get her as soon as he left, and she stayed with me. It was like old times…well, almost. She was still Miranda, but Timmy had dulled her shine. She was the same, and yet she wasn't. One night we went over to Athens for a girls' night out, and she met a man there. If she had only let Timmy go back in high school, she could have had a chance with this one. I knew from the moment they met that they were perfect for each other. He was going to college at UGA, and he was a real good guy. They exchanged numbers that night, but Miranda didn't tell him she was married."

My mind is swirling, a tangled mess of confusion. I'm trying to grab hold of this story, comprehend what it all means, but it's so hard. I can't imagine what my mom was like back then, stuck in a marriage to a bad dude like Timothy. A man she didn't love. A man who hurt her, scared her, intimidated her.

And no one could help her.

The situation was like stacking kindling on a fire, slowly but surely. No matter what happened, as soon as someone lit a match, the whole damn thing was set to burn.

"What happened between them?" My voice is ragged, dry. I cough, trying to clear my throat.

Sandy notices. "Would you like some water?" Her tone is sympathetic. It must be showing all over my face what this story is doing to me.

Nodding, I try to give her a grateful smile. I think I fail.

When she returns with the water, she settles back onto the couch. Turning the yearbook to another page, she pulls out a photo of my mother and the man she met in Athens.

She hands the photo to me. I study it, marveling at how happy she looks. She's riding him piggyback style, and her chin is resting on his shoulder as they both smile.

"I took that," offers Sandy. "They were so happy. And I kept

Miranda's secret. I never told him what her real life was like back here."

I must look bewildered, because she rushes on. "Timmy took a job with the company laying pipe permanently after that week. So he was gone for two weeks at a time. During those two weeks, Miranda would spend every second she could with Richard."

I look up, startled. "Richard?"

She nods. "Richard. That was his name. And…as you can probably expect, Miranda got pregnant with Richard's baby."

I suck in a sharp breath. *Me. She got pregnant with me. Richard is my father. Where did it all go wrong? Why didn't he try to help her? Why didn't he stay with her?*

Staring at the picture of my mother, I can only imagine what her life would have been like if she had left Timothy and stayed with Richard.

"Well, naturally, she couldn't hide a pregnancy. She had to come clean to Richard about Timothy and her life here in Blythe. He felt lied to, cheated. And I guess in a way that was true. But Miranda's heart belonged to him. He just couldn't see it at the time."

Rage fills me, and I suck in a deep breath so it doesn't explode all over Sandy Sheridan's living room. "He ditched her?"

She shakes her head, her expression forlorn. "He couldn't. He loved her. He tried to talk her into leaving Tim, moving to Athens with him. He was going to finish school and make a life for them."

I lean back against the couch. Suddenly, I'm weary. This story is making me feel tired, and sick, and just strung out. I was only a blip on the radar at that point, but I'd never known any of this

as a kid growing up. And I was so miserable with my own circum-
stances, I never stopped to think how miserable she was. About
how she got to the place she was in.

"What happened?" I whisper.

Sandy places a hand on my knee. She seems to realize that I'm
falling apart on the inside, and one reassuring squeeze from her
hand is enough to give me a little fortitude. She continues.

"She told Timmy that she was leaving him, and that the baby
wasn't his. He threatened to beat that baby right out of her if she
tried to leave him. I would have thought that he'd let her go, once
he knew that the baby she had growing inside of her was another
man's, but he wouldn't. He just held on tighter, wrapping a noose
around her neck so tight that she could barely breathe. He told
her that if she left him, he'd hunt her down. He'd kill her, the baby
growing inside her, and the man who put that baby there. It was
enough to terrify her. It was enough to make her stay."

Sandy brushes a stray tear that had left her eye and had begun
to coast down her cheek. She sniffs. "She broke it off with
Richard. She feared for his safety, she feared for yours. She knew
Timmy well enough to know he'd never let her go. So she sent me
to Athens to tell him that she'd lost the baby, and she didn't want
to be with him anymore."

And there it is. That's the reason he never came looking for me.
That's the reason he never stepped up and became a father. That's
why he never lifted a finger to help my mother.

He didn't know.

It's like a drumbeat pounding inside my head. I have a father
out there, and he thought I died when I was still inside my

mother's stomach. Nausea rolls inside me, and I take deep breaths to try and keep it down. I take another sip of water. Cough.

Sputter.

Swallow.

Repeat.

"What about…what about after I was born? Tim left her, right?" I don't recognize my own voice. It's full of rage. Of hatred. Of despair. All the emotions I'm feeling are rolling around inside me like an unsettled sea, threatening to pull me down into the deep, dark depths.

Sandy can't stop the flow of tears now. "He was such a bastard. He made sure she severed all ties with the people who loved her. He made sure she couldn't depend on anyone but him. He watched her suffer. He watched her die inside because she couldn't be with the person she truly loved. And then, a year after you were born, he left and never looked back. He was picked up a few months after that for armed robbery, and I hear through the grapevine that he's been in and out of prison ever since."

"Shit." It's just a breath of a word. "Why didn't she go back to Richard after that?"

"She thought about it. She went looking for him, brought you with her. But he'd graduated from school and had started living and working in Athens. He was engaged to someone else. She was heartbroken, and she left before saying anything to him. Then she came back to the house where she raised you. It belonged to her mother, who died right before you were born. She was a wreck then, and none of us could ever help dig her out of it. So we eventually just stayed away."

I stand up then, because if I don't move I might burst into flames. Angry, raging flames that'll burn up anything and anyone in my path.

"I'm so sorry, Drake." Sandy's voice drops to a whisper. "What she was like after that…she was never the same person. She didn't want my help or anyone else's. So I stayed away. It broke my heart, but I stayed away."

I give her a hard look. "Yeah, I was pretty broken, too. But I guess you couldn't have known about that, because you 'stayed away.' Thanks for the information. I have one more question."

She looks miserable. "Anything."

"What was Richard's last name?"

She looks into my eyes, sees the intention in them. "His last name is Walsh. Richard Walsh."

I don't know what I said to her after that. I just knew I needed to get out of there, breathe some fresh air, and let the thoughts floating around in my brain either eat me alive or guide me toward my next step.

As soon as I slam the Challenger's door behind me, I lean my head against the steering wheel and roar. It's a scream of pain, of regret, and of loss. It's a shout of pure pain for my mother, for the life she was deprived of. If Timothy Sullivan wasn't sitting somewhere in a prison cell, I would have hunted him down in that moment.

But as it is, I can't get to him. So I beat my hands against the steering wheel of my car, and I roar.

I roar until the shouts turn to sobs.

26

Mea

Wrapping my hands around my decaf latte, I allow the steam from the mug to waft up and warm my face. Despite the end-of-March warmth outside, I'm shivering right down to my bones. Without even thinking about it, one hand drifts down to my belly. I rub it gently.

When Aunt Tay sits down in front of me, I smile at the woman who opened her home to me when I was just a messed-up teenager she'd never met before. Sure, we were family, but I will never be able to thank her enough for taking in Mikah and me.

"How are you, Tay?" I ask, my voice sounding haggard and weary to my own ears. "It couldn't have been easy, hearing from that man."

She shakes her head, shuddering at the very mention of my father. "He's an awful man, Mea. I'm so sorry I didn't rescue you from him sooner. I didn't know…"

I place my hand over hers. "I know you didn't. Now tell me what he said to you."

She takes a deep breath. Scanning the coffee bistro, she notes that it's mostly empty. The patrons are taking advantage of the weather and sipping their drinks and eating their sandwiches outside today. We're almost the only customers inside. She lowers her voice anyway.

"First, he put on his charming act. He was contrite, saying that he learned a lot while he was locked away and that he knows how many wrongs he has to right. He asked for me to give him your contact info so that he could apologize for the pain he caused you."

Now I'm even colder than I was a few minutes ago. I rub my arms, trying to circulate my blood so that they don't go numb. There's no way Carlos Sanchez wants to "right his wrongs." If he wants to know where I am, it's for no other reason than to hurt me.

Again.

Again.

Again.

Closing my eyes for a moment, I try to gather myself. I haven't been to a doctor, and I know I can't be more than a month along, but stress probably isn't good for the baby, right? I have to think about more than just myself now.

"You didn't give him my number or tell him where I am, right, Aunt Tay?"

She shakes her head, a violent motion that sends her long dark hair flying. Her skin is a shade darker than Mikah's and mine.

Our mixed heritage makes our tones lighter than hers, but the family resemblance is still there.

"Of course not. I would never do that, Mea."

A small bit of relief finds its way into my heart. "So then what did he do? That had to make him angry, right?"

"Well…" She hesitates. I look at her closely, because there's always a tell when she's trying to hide something. When her eyes shift off to the left, I sit up straighter. "What aren't you telling me?"

"When he called, Mikah was at the house. He was helping your uncle paint the porch. They heard my shouts when your father got me all riled up, and they came rushing in."

Dread settles heavily in my stomach. After I talked to Aunt Tay, I was planning on ordering her not to say anything about this to Mikah. He's so protective of me, especially after what happened all those years ago. I never wanted him to find out that our father had called Aunt Tay.

"Once he discovered who I was speaking with, he grabbed the phone before I could hang up. I think your father baited him easily. Mikah yelled, and he listened. And then his face went pale and he hung up the phone."

This isn't good. This is so bad. This is beyond bad.

"What'd he say to Mikah, Aunt Tay?" I whisper, horror filling me. I don't want Mikah anywhere near Carlos. Never again. He might be out of prison, but I just want the two of us to keep living our lives independently of that man. No matter what he tries to pull, we're adults now. We don't have to be reeled in by him. Not anymore.

Aunt Tay shrugs helplessly. "He wouldn't say. He just said good-bye to your uncle and me, apologizing for not finishing up the paint job. And he left."

Sliding my mug away from me, I bolt to my feet. Aunt Tay stands, too.

"Where are you going?" Her tone is alarmed. "Mea?"

"Thanks for telling me this, Aunt Tay. I need to go find Mikah before he does something stupid." I reach across the table, hug her quickly. Then I rush out of the coffee shop.

Sitting in my car, I push Mikah's name in my contacts. The phone rings, and then it goes to voice mail.

"Dammit!" I swipe my finger across the screen until I get to Drake's name. Lifting the phone to my ear, I wait to hear his luscious caramel voice, my balm, come over the line.

Drake's voice mail answers.

Close to tears, my fingers fly across the keys as I text him.

Please call me.

Placing the phone in the cup holder, I buckle my seat belt and head back to Drake's house. When I pull in, I notice with relief that Greta's still there.

Stubborn girl isn't going to leave me alone until Drake knows about this baby. I smile, because I'm relieved that Greta's here. I want to tell someone about what's going on, and I don't want to fly off the handle and make a bad decision. Especially not now.

But Mikah's my baby brother. And if he's in trouble, I will always go to him.

I fly through the front door. Greta is sitting at the bar in the kitchen, drinking a cup of coffee. When she sees the look on my face, she hops down from the stool and approaches me.

"What's wrong?" Her tone is full of fear. "Are you okay?"

I gesture toward the couch. "Please sit down. What I'm about to tell you requires you to be sitting. And maybe drinking something stronger than coffee."

Her eyes wide, she glances at her mug, and then at me. "I'll take my chances. You're okay, though?"

"I'm okay right now." I reassure her. "But a long time ago? I wasn't."

Greta sits on the couch, her feet tucked under her, both hands covering her mouth. All I can see is horror, shock, and revulsion in her wide blue eyes. That's why I don't tell this story. That's why, for all these years, I've kept it locked up tight inside me. It took a lot out of me, you know? Keeping something like that bottled up? It changes you. It makes you dark, cursed.

When I finish, I look her straight in the eye. I don't look down at my hands in shame. I don't hide from my past. I don't cower or hide.

Because what he did to me isn't my fault. And the people who truly love me will still love me when they know about my past. They won't hold it against me. I won't disgust them. They won't try to pity me.

Drake taught me that.

"Is that...it?" she whispers. Her eyes are filled, like they have been for the past thirty minutes, with tears.

"Isn't that enough?"

"Of course…I mean…oh, God. I…don't even know what to say. To think of all the times I had the nerve to complain about *my* father. Mea, you must have hated me!" Her shame is cutting her deep. Her chest is caving in from the pain of it, and I go to her now. Because I'm ready to hug her.

I sling my arm around her shoulder, and she immediately curls into me. "Of course I didn't. Because that was *your* struggle. Just because it was different from mine didn't make it any less real. And you had no idea. I couldn't talk about it then. Drake made me stronger. He made me feel safe enough to share. And now I need your help, because I'm afraid Mikah will go after him."

Greta sits up straighter. "Would he?"

I stand, frustration eating me up from within. I take a page out of Drake's book and pace the room. Wearing a line into the carpet. Tugging at my hair. "I think he would. He told me he'd never let him hurt me again. I believe he meant it. And Carlos is making himself a threat again. Mikah will never allow that to continue."

Greta's eyes narrow. "What do you want to do? Have you called Drake?"

"He didn't answer. He's got his own family stuff going on right now. He didn't even say when he'd be back, or how long it would be until I heard from him. I can't wait. I need to find Mikah."

Greta's face is set, determination apparent in the steely blue of her eyes. "I'm not letting you go looking for him by yourself."

I offer her a small smile. "I was hoping you'd say that."

"And I'm calling Grisham." She pulls out her phone, her slender finger swiping across the screen while she studies her cell.

Mine dings from somewhere inside my purse. I grab my purse from the coffee table, searching through it until I find the thing. Pulling it out, my heart leaps when I see Mikah's name on my screen.

I love you. I told you once I'd never let him hurt you again. I'm keeping that promise.

"Greta!" I scream. My blood races toward my head, causing me to feel dizzy and disoriented. My hand shakes as I hand my phone out for her to take. She's midconversation with Grisham, and she tells him to hold on as she reads Mikah's text. When her face pales and her lips stretch out into a grim line, I know I'm right to jump to conclusions.

Mikah has gone to confront Carlos. For me.

27

Drake

Even though it's dark when I leave Sandra's house, I drive the hour straight to Athens. Checking into a hotel, I pull out my phone. I'm still not right in the head from the revelations I discovered about my mother. I never had a clue what she went through when she was young. Her life just went so horribly wrong. And all it would have taken was one different decision on her part, in any number of places, to force a change. I flipped through scenarios again and again in my mind as I drove.

But I know that it doesn't matter. Any way I figure it, she still comes out the loser in the end.

Tomorrow, I don't know how I'm going to do it, but I'm going to find my father. I'm going to search for Richard Walsh until I find an address, and then I'm going to knock on his front door. I owe it to my mother to meet him. To tell him I exist.

I'm sure my showing up is going to do all kinds of fucked-up things to his day. I imagine he has a family. A wife. Kids.

Kids?

That would mean I have siblings.

Damn.

This is a mind fuck I'm in no way prepared for.

Once I check into a hotel and drag myself into my room, I flop onto the bed and pull my phone from my pocket. There's a voice mail from Will, undoubtedly giving me a rundown on the day at the garage. There's also a text from Mea.

Seeing her name on my screen does something drastic to my insides. It soothes me and ratchets me up at the same time. I close my eyes, picturing her lying here beside me. She'd offered to stay by my side. I should have let her.

I didn't want her to walk blindly into the fucked-up situation with my mother and who might or who might not be my father. I knew it would mess with my head, force me to face demons inside me that I didn't want to face. I didn't want to go through it with Mea at my side, because I've never wanted to be anything but strong for her.

And right now? I feel anything but strong.

As I'm thinking about her, the strong urge I harbor to visit the bar downstairs dwindles. All I want to do is hear her voice. See her face. Feel her fingers grazing against my skin.

Fuck.

I miss her.

Holding my phone up in front of my face, I read her text.

Please call me.

Frowning, I sit up in bed. That doesn't sound good. Checking my phone, I see that I have a missed call from her. Hours ago.

"Shit." I punch a finger on her name, waiting for her phone to ring.

It goes straight to voice mail.

A whirlwind of unrest is starting to stir in my stomach. Tumultuous. Chaotic. I gave my key to Grisham and Greta, so calling them means finding out what's going on with my girl.

Regret floods me, making me wish I'd never left her. I should have brought her with me. I should always have her by my side.

Especially with the bullshit going on with her father. *She said he hadn't contacted her. Has that changed?*

Now I'm up and off the bed. The chaos inside of me amplifies. I hit Grisham's name on my Contacts.

"Man," he answers on the first ring. "I was just about to call you."

His tone is grim, dancing just on the verge of alarm. I know Grisham pretty well, and the dude is an ex-navy SEAL. He's unflappable. Nothing scares him, unless it has to do with his fiancée.

"What the hell is going on there? Where's Mea?"

"Where are you?" Grisham's voice comes across as a growl, and I hear the distinct groan of an engine in the background.

"I'm in Athens, Georgia. About five and a half hours away." Panic rises in my throat, tasting like bile. Too far. Too far. *"Where's Mea?"*

"Get your ass in your car. Or to an airport. Whichever is the fastest way to get you to Kentucky."

I'm already off the bed and pulling my boots back on my feet. "What the fuck? What happened? Where's my girl?"

Grisham's voice is clipped. "In the car somewhere ahead of me. I'm guessing they had about an hour head start on me."

"They?" The hotel room door slams behind me. My heartbeat is rioting in my chest, wreaking havoc against my rib cage. My duffel bag bounces against my thigh.

"Greta wouldn't let her go to Ashland alone. Apparently, Mea has a crazy-ass father who was just released from prison."

"Fuck! Yeah, I know that, Grisham." I toss a few bills on the front desk as I breeze past it. The shocked faces of the employees don't slow me down. I'm out the front door and eating up the concrete between the Challenger and me in less than a minute.

"You knew that, and you left her alone?" Grisham's tone is incredulous.

"No," I growl. "I didn't leave her alone. I left her with you and Greta."

Silence on the other end of the line. Finally, I hear Grisham take a breath.

I punch Ashland, Kentucky, into the Challenger's GPS and rouse the engine to life. Later, I'll change it to a more specific address. Right now, as it is, it has me crossing the state line in six and a half hours.

Not fucking fast enough.

"Tell me what's happening, Grish. Why is she going there?" *Without me?*

The answer to that is clear. She called me. She texted me. I wasn't available.

I wasn't there for her when she needed me.

"Greta is keeping communication open with me. They're fine. They're in the car, driving. Mea is worried that Mikah went after her father."

"What?" I picture my conversation with Mikah at dinner in my head. He loves his sister. That much was crystal clear. He also had a lot of guilt about not being able to protect her all those years ago. *But why now?*

"Grisham, I need you to tell Greta to get me Mea on the phone. Need that to happen now. Or I'm gonna lose my goddamn mind." I'm somewhere between a complete meltdown and a full-blown panic attack. I just need to hear her voice. I need to know that she's okay. And I need to tell her to stop and wait for me.

"Will do." Grisham disconnects our call.

I wait, and while I wait, I stare miserably out my windshield. There's nothing but dark asphalt and black sky beyond me. Somewhere out there, the girl I love is driving into who knows what kind of situation with a psychopath. I don't want her anywhere near him. I don't want her anywhere in his vicinity.

Slamming the steering wheel with my fist doesn't make me feel any better. But I do it again, anyway.

When my phone rings, I press ANSWER on the screen on my console.

Mea's beautiful voice fills the interior of my car. It pushes the air back into my lungs. "Drake?"

She sounds scared. Really fucking scared.

"Baby, yeah. It's me. Are you okay?" I swallow hard, attempting to block my fear from reaching her.

"Where are you?" Her voice trembles, letting me know that she's on the verge of tears.

But despite her fear, she's still driving into a situation she knows could be dangerous. For her brother. She's so goddamned brave. She's a warrior. Always has been.

Right now, I wish she weren't.

I try to keep my voice soothing. Even though on the inside I'm agitated. I'm restless, disturbed. Anxious. "On my way to you, sweetheart. You want to do me a solid and pull over somewhere safe for the night? That way Grisham and I can meet you?"

I can picture her shaking her head, and I curse under my breath. "No, Drake. Mikah might be in trouble. I need to get to him."

I don't want to rile her up while she's driving. It's late and she must be tired, but I don't know what to do from so far away. I'm helpless, and it's killing me.

"Okay. But if you get tired, pull over. You and Greta can switch drivers if you need to. I'm on my way, and Grisham is right behind you. Listen to me, Mea. We talk every hour while you're on the road. You hear me? Every. Hour."

She sniffs, but her voice sounds stronger, more determined. Her tornado, whirring around her. Gathering strength. "Okay."

"Promise."

"I promise, Drake." A soft smile in her words. I can see it even when she's not with me. Sweet. Fierce. Turbulent.

"Love you, baby girl."

She gasps. "That's...that's the first time you've ever said that to me, Drake."

"Not the first time I've felt it. And it won't be the last time I say it." *That's a motherfucking promise.*

"God, Drake. I love you. I wish you were here right now." Another voice tremor.

A solid ball of emotion catches in my throat, choking me up and propelling me forward. Fear coils spindly fingers inside me. Reaching. Reaching. Reaching. My foot stomps down harder on the gas, and the speedometer jumps. "I'm right here, sweetheart. See you soon."

After the longest, most nerve-wracking road trip in my life, I pull into Louisville. The sun is just coming up over the hills, the sky a serene burst of pinks and oranges that should make me feel ready to face a new day. Only I don't feel anything but tortured as I barrel through town, looking for the truck stop where the girls and Grisham have stopped to clean up and grab coffee.

Mea's little car in the parking lot is like a beacon for me, pulling me in. Grisham's bright yellow Jeep is parked on the other side. Slamming my door shut, my boots hit the pavement. The bell above the door to the truck stop jangles loudly as I enter, a harsh and jarring sound too rowdy for the otherwise quiet morning.

"Drake!"

My girl is a sight for sore eyes. It's only been a day since I've seen her, a day and half since I've held her in my arms, but *damn.* I welcome the turbulence of the swirling wind that always surrounds her as she runs and launches herself into my arms. Catching her easily, I cradle her to my chest, inhaling her scent on her neck, her hair, her cheek.

"You scared me, baby girl. Never again. Got that?" I murmur into her skin while I smell her, just reassuring myself that she's real and she's here. And she's mine. Darkness and light churn together around us, pressing us more tightly together. Her body pressed against mine? Nothing has ever felt so good.

"You came." Her words are more like a gasp, and they're awed. Disbelieving. I pull back, staring into her eyes.

"Sorry I made you doubt that I would. I left because of the fucked-up shit going on in my head. Not because of you. You're perfect. Don't doubt that." I nuzzle my nose into hers.

She sighs. "I'm worried about Mikah, Drake."

Putting her down, I reach around her to shake Grisham's hand. Giving him a meaningful look, I hope all of my thanks are conveyed to him. He made sure she was safe when I couldn't. I'll always owe him for that. Shooting Greta a quick smile where she stands beside her fiancé, I turn back to Mea. My big hands cradle her face.

"We'll find him. Do you have any idea where the bastard is staying? Would Mikah know?"

Tucking a wayward curl behind her ear, she clears the haze of exhaustion from her face. Now that I know she's safe, I can really assess her. She has dark shadows under her eyes. The red blood vessels smattering the irises indicate extreme tiredness. She keeps rubbing at them, which spreads a trail of mascara haphazardly across her face. Her hand clutches her belly, like she's having anxiety pains there. My heart squeezes looking at her, wishing I could scoop her up in my arms and force her to take a nap.

"I talked to Aunt Tay," she relays. "She told me that the only place she thinks he would stay is with his parents—my grandparents—here in Louisville. That's why we came here."

I nod, tucking every bit of information into my mind. "Do you know where they live?"

Nodding, she turns toward the door. "Let's go!"

I tug her gently back to me. "Not happening. I want you and Greta to go get a room and stay put while Grisham and I check it out."

The firm set of her chin is my first clue. My second is the way she narrows her eyes and stares with rugged determination right into mine. "I will not step aside while you go look for my brother. I'm coming, too."

Greta pipes up. "She'll go crazy, waiting in a hotel room for you, Drake. She won't sleep. She's better off with you."

Turning away from them, I run both hands through my hair and tug on the ends. I want to roar with frustration, but I hold it together somehow. A rising tide of aggravation, helplessness, and anxiety is rising, threatening to overtake me at any moment, pulling me down into the dark depths of emotion. I take a deep breath and turn back to face her.

"Let's go."

Indicating that we should all go in the Challenger, I place Mea in the front seat while Greta and Grisham climb into the back.

Then we weave through the quiet streets of the Louisville suburbs. I follow the directions Mea gives me, turning onto residential streets and stopping at red lights. The Challenger handles the streets like a champ, but the noise it makes probably has all the residents checking out their windows for the offensive sound.

Crawling slowly down the avenue Mea has declared as her grandparents', I approach a quiet, two-story Colonial-style home set back on the tree-lined street. The Sanchezes, according to Mea, are a retired elderly couple. Mea had never spent much time with them growing up, but from what she said they were probably devastated when their only son was arrested and imprisoned for such an abhorrent crime. It just goes to show that love for your child never changes and never waivers, no matter what he's done.

Mikah's car, a black two-door sports coupe, is parked at the curb.

Before the Challenger is even fully stopped, Mea leaps out her door and is running toward the house.

Cursing, I exit the car, hurtling behind her. Grabbing her in my arms, I pick her up off the ground and hold her to my chest. Her legs kick out wildly as she screams.

"Drake! Let me go! Let me *go*!" Her voice is vehement, potent, wild. She's a strong little thing, I'll give her that, but my arms are like iron around her and I'm not budging. There's no way in hell I'll let her go barreling into that house all by herself. If it's up to me, she's not going in there at all.

Just behind us, Greta's gentle voice attempts to calm down her friend. "Mea—"

The navy blue front door opens then. We all freeze, the spectacle we're creating in the front yard becoming clear as an elderly man calls out, "What's going on here?"

My hands tighten on Mea, but she steps forward, dragging me along with her. I can't hold her back without hurting her, and that's not a chance I'll take.

"Grandpa Sanchez? It's me, Mea." Her voice is tentative and sweet, a spoonful of honey wrapped in chocolate. "Is Mikah here?"

The man squints, leaning against the front door as he scrutinizes Mea. "Mea? My God. This week keeps getting better. Please come in off the lawn." He gestures toward us to come inside, but still I hold my girl captive. Grisham is standing beside me, his posture loose and ready for anything. One of his hands is slung casually around Greta's waist, but I know he'll turn deadly serious if he thinks there's even a hint of danger.

"Mea?" Her grandfather's voice carries the lilt of a Hispanic accent, and he's beckoning to her like any loving grandparent would.

Giving her some leeway, I slide my hand down her arm to grab ahold of her palm, holding it carefully in mine. When we reach the front steps leading to the door, I pause, my grip on Mea tightening. My mind is working at double speed, trying to take in our surroundings at the same time I'm evaluating the attitude and posture of her grandfather. I'm also trying my damnedest to keep Mea at my side, partially sheltered by my size.

But she doesn't currently have any regard for her own safety. She's only trying to get to her brother.

She puts one foot on the bottom step, and I halt her progress. Looking up at the old man, I call out to him.

"Morning, sir. Is your son inside?" Trying to keep my tone friendly is difficult, almost impossible. I don't feel friendly, I feel fierce. Protective. Feral.

His eyes widen as his head swivels in my direction. He's about to open his mouth to speak, when a shadow lands across the door beside him, and another man fills the doorframe.

This man, taller, broader, but vaguely resembling Mea's grandfather, lays a hand on the old man's shoulder. "Why don't you go on upstairs with Mama? Give me a few minutes to reunite with my children, Papa?"

I've never met the man before, and during Mea's stories she never described him. I think picturing him in her head was too horrifying for her, and so she never told me what he looked like. But I can *feel* it. Her fear, all wrapped up in her loathing, swirling around us like a cyclone of poison. Icy fingers of dread find their way down my neck, and I step completely in front of her as she shrinks back.

Grisham mimics my stance, stepping in front of Greta as he keeps his sights set on Carolos Sanchez.

Sanchez looms in the doorway, but he's attempting to keep his posture disarming, unintimidating. He doesn't intimidate me, but Mea's trembling body behind mine is a dead giveaway that he's scaring the shit out of her. There's no way in hell I'm letting her go inside that house. I thrust my chin toward Grisham, a wordless order to keep his eyes open while I turn my back on the enemy.

Cupping Mea's face, I bend down to her level and stare into her eyes. The melted chocolate color is so rich, so inviting, that I could drown there. But they're quickly filling with terrified tears, and her bottom lip quivers even as she tries to lift her chin. She's falling apart, and seeing her like this is doing two things to me. It's breaking my heart in two clean pieces, and it's making me more pissed off than I can ever remember being.

The rage is threatening to swallow me whole, driving through my veins with the pumping force of my blood. It's expanding my muscles, lengthening my limbs as I prepare to fight for this woman. Her fight is now mine, and I plan to take this son of a bitch down.

"I'm right here, sweetheart. He can't hurt you. Not this time." The underlying river of anger flowing beneath my words isn't lost to Mea. She focuses on me, nods. Her hands find my wrists, grab on tight.

Extending a hand toward Mea, Sanchez ignores the rest of us completely. "My baby girl."

A snarl rips from my throat. I turn to face him again, but Grisham reaches a hand toward me, as if to tell me to wait, to hold myself together.

"I informed your brother this morning that his being here would achieve what I wanted: your being here. Won't you come in to see him?"

Mea straightens behind me, she takes a deep, trembling breath. Her chest puffs out as she gathers her strength, her storm growing wild, wild, wild as she prepares to face her abuser.

"Is Mikah okay?" She steps out from behind me. Whatever she's done to gather herself, it worked. Her voice is strong, none of the trembles I saw just seconds ago. One hand drifts down to her stomach almost absently as she stares with hatred at her father.

Her father tilts his head. "He's inside. We've just been having a chat. I explained to him that all I want is to be in my children's lives again. I was gone for a long time; you can't know what that feels like. To be ripped away from your children. From your wife."

Mea's words are angry; she spits fire while she speaks. "Mom *died* after you went in! And what happened to her is your fault! I never want to see you again. I just want to get my brother and go!"

Carlos's eyebrows rise to his hairline. He's truly shocked, while he stares at her. He's attempting to put something together in his mind, but then he frowns with obvious dismay. "Is that what they told you? That it's my fault your mother's dead?"

Mea reacts like she's been slapped across the face. Her eyes go wide, and she grips her stomach like she's in pain. I take a step toward her, allowing my hands to caress her shoulders while I stare with venom at Carlos. All I want to do right now is pick her up and throw her in the Challenger. Lock the doors. Make sure she's safe. And then I want to rush the house and murder the man who continues to hurt her. Now with lies.

"Shut up! Just shut up." Her voice is lost on a whisper, carried away in the morning breeze. But Carlos hears it.

"Your mother was sick. I had nothing to do with that."

Mea begins to walk up the porch steps, calling Mikah's name. As a unit, we all move with her. Carlos finally glances at us. When he meets my eyes, his gaze hardens to a metallic glint. Waves of disorder and contention roll off of him. He reeks with it. His intentions, whatever they are, aren't good. They aren't genuine. He only knows one way to deal with Mea. And that's to hurt her.

Not this time.

I don't want her near that man. I won't allow it to happen.

"Mikah!" she screams again.

I grab hold of her, stopping her from moving any closer to the door.

"Mikah's in there," she says to me. Her eyes are just as pleading. "I have to get him."

Gripping her hand tighter, I shake my head. "No."

Carlos watches the interaction between us with growing interest. His lip curls in disgust as he zeroes in on my hand on his daughter's. The man is seriously twisted. Years in prison haven't mellowed him, haven't made him any less fucked-up in the head. He still views his daughter as his property. Something belonging to him that he can do whatever he wants with.

He chuckles.

My head snaps toward him, my hands balling into fists.

"Mea?" Mikah appears at the door. We all turn toward him.

Mikah is all amped up. He's fidgety, jumpy. He eyes Carlos, but he looks relieved when he spots me standing beside Mea on the porch.

"Are you okay?" Mea is asking him over and over again. But Mikah doesn't answer, just keeps staring daggers at Carlos, like his stare alone can knock the man off his feet.

"Hey, man." I keep my voice soft, because Mikah looks like he might go off the deep end with the slightest loud noise. "Let's get out of here, all right? Your sister is ready to go."

Mikah's eyes meet mine, and all I can see in them is despair. Dark, dark, desperation. I didn't notice the hopelessness in his eyes the last time I met him. I think the fact that he was away from this situation, hanging with his sister, living a good life, kept that muddiness clean. But now, I see that he has so much more darkness in him than his sister does. Where she's dark, she's also light. So much light lives inside of her, enough to drown out the twilight. Enough to lighten the murk.

But the same can't be said for Mikah. What happened to him when they were children, what he saw happening to his sister, changed him forever. It changed her, too, but maybe she didn't realize how much Mikah blamed himself for what had happened.

Seeing it all there in his eyes causes my stomach to cave in on itself. "Mikah."

He slides his gaze away from me. Then he kisses his sister. Right before he shoves her, hard, toward me.

Pulling a revolver from the back of his jeans, he points it at Carlos. His hands are shaking, not steady at all. But the steel in his eyes? It's unwavering. "You will never hurt her again. I won't let you."

In my haste to follow Mea from the Challenger, I hadn't grabbed my piece from the glove compartment. I have a license to carry, although most of the time I don't. I keep my pistol in my car where it'll be safe, and where I'll have it if I need it.

I need it now.

And I don't have it.

28

Mea

My eyes are lying.

That's not my brother, pointing a *gun* at the asshole we're forced to call our father. Nausea boils up inside of me, causing me to clutch my stomach. Nausea that tastes like fear when it reaches my mouth, threatening to overflow from me as vomit on my grandparents' front porch.

"Mikah." I lose the word on my tongue. It never makes it free of my mouth. I think it's stuck on a breath that I can't expel.

Everything happens so fast, too fast for me to comprehend. I'm shoved backward, behind Drake, as he takes a step toward my brother.

No.

No.

No.

"Mikah." Drake's firm voice. "This isn't how you do it, man. Walk away. He's not worth you losing the rest of your life to a cell."

When I peek out from behind Drake, I don't recognize my brother. His expression is so furious while at the same time serene. He's made peace with this decision. Nothing that Drake is about to say is going to change his mind.

He came here to kill Carlos.

For me.

For me.

No.

No.

No.

Mikah stands just to Drake's left, Carlos is frozen about fifteen feet away from us. He hasn't moved, he hasn't taken his eyes off my brother. And then he shifts his gaze to me. Hate. Spewing from his eyes like the blackest sort of tears. It's deplorable, the way he looks at me. Like I'm a piece of trash he tried to throw out.

"This is your fault. Remember that. All of this is because of you."

Drake stiffens like he's been punched. But my father's words don't affect me. Nothing he does from this point on can hurt me. And this is no longer about him. This is about me, trying to save my brother.

Stepping out from behind Drake, I sidestep his outstretched arm and step directly in front of Mikah. The barrel of his gun meets my collarbone. I barely register the feel of the cold, hard metal against my skin.

Only Mikah. This is about him and me.

"You have always been there for me." Keeping my voice steady,

I don't break eye contact with my brother. "And I need you. I need you in my life. I need you in my baby's life."

Patting my stomach with one hand, I keep staring at my brother. Waiting. Holding my breath. Searching for *him* behind the shroud in his eyes. He's in there. My father can't have stolen him from me.

Immediately, Mikah's eyes float down to my stomach. Then they fly back up to meet mine. He removes the gun from against me, because he never intended it to touch me, anyway. His voice rises.

"Baby?"

The strangled sound Drake makes beside me doesn't pull my gaze away from my little brother. Drake and I can deal with this revelation later. Right now, I need to get the gun away from Mikah. Before he does something he can never take back.

"My baby. Your niece or nephew. Right here." I grab his hand, pulling the gun from his grasp. He lets it go easily, he's so dumbfounded by what I'm saying. Placing the gun on the rocking chair beside me, I keep focusing on Mikah.

"You're pregnant." His voice is full of awe. Of joy. And I watch as the darkness recedes from his eyes. Sighing with relief I realize that my brother is going to be okay.

I can save him. *We* can save him.

A movement out of the corner of my eye makes my head snap to my left. Carolos has lunged for the gun, moving too quickly for anyone to stop him. When I glance at Drake, I realize he took his eyes off my father when I revealed the fact that I'm carrying his baby.

Whirling to face Carlos once more, I see he doesn't hesitate. "You were always a slut." He pulls the trigger.

I squeeze my eyes closed, waiting for the pain. The burn. However it feels when a bullet slices through the skin. But instead, all I hear is Mikah's grunt of pain.

When I hit the floor, it's with Drake lying on top of me. The only thing I see is his face above me. He's asking me over and over again if I'm hurt. If I'm okay.

Grisham is on the porch, wrestling with my father. I try to sit up, and Drake lifts me into his arms. Carries me into the yard.

"Where's Mikah! Where is he!" I don't recognize that voice. It's frantic. It's desperate. It's mine.

Greta is screaming as Drake lays me on the front lawn. He crouches next to me, poking and prodding my body, searching for a wound.

"Talk to me, baby girl. Are you hit?" Drake's voice is full of urgency. His warm brown eyes are wild, staring at me as he asks me over and over again if I'm hurt. When he presses down on my shoulder, I wince at the piercing pain.

Gasping, I put a hand to my shoulder. When I pull it away, it's coated with bright red blood.

I try to look toward the porch. The pain is intense, now that I can feel it, but the pain in my heart is so much worse. All I want is to see my brother, know he's okay.

Please, Mikah.

Sirens scream at the end of the street. Help is on the way. But all I can think about is if they're too late, I'll never forgive myself.

Grisham comes down the porch steps, leaving an unconscious Carlos on the porch.

"Is he dead?" Drake's voice is grim, distant. His eyes don't leave me. He has two hands on my shoulder, applying pressure to my wound. "Stay with me, sweetheart. You look sleepy. Don't go any-where."

I am so sleepy. I want to close my eyes and sleep for days. But I can't. There's something I need to know first...Someone I need to see...

But I can't remember any more. The world is going dark. I welcome the dark.

The dark feels good.

What's that beeping?

My eyelids are heavy; I struggle to open them.

"Mea? Baby girl...come back to me."

Drake's voice. He sounds scared. I force my eyes open, just be-cause I don't want him to be scared. He's never scared. He's calm, cool, and collected. He's the strongest man I know.

"Hey." His large hands are wrapped around one of mine. He squeezes gently, lifts it to his lips. As I stare up at him, I note that his eyes are bloodshot. I hone in on the scar by his left temple. His hair is falling over it, I brush it away. When I focus on his eyes, they're pained. Tortured. But beneath that, they're relieved.

"Where am I?" My voice feels like I swallowed a thousand rusty nails. And I want that damn beeping to stop.

Drake's hand smooths my hair back and he leans his forehead against mine. "You don't remember what happened?"

There's the torture in his eyes again.

*Wait...*My grandparents' house. Carlos.

"He grabbed the gun!" I jerk upright. And then pain blooms in my shoulder, forcing me to sink back down into the mound of flat pillows on my hospital bed. Because I know I must be in the hospital. I got shot. But it could have been worse...

"You landed on me." It's not a question; Drake launched himself on top of me and the bullet went through my shoulder. I have the pain to prove it. Where would the bullet have gone if...

"Mikah!" Urgency fills me with a rush of adrenaline. It courses through my body, racing through my veins and making me feel like I could stand up and run a race. "Where is he, Drake?"

Drake cups my face, stroking me softly with his thumbs as he stares into my eyes.

"Sweetheart...you need to calm down. The bullet that lodged in your shoulder just grazed Mikah. He lost consciousness from shock. He's okay...but he's going to have a lot do deal with."

Relief. I close my eyes as a wave of exhaustion sweeps over me. *Baby...*

My eyes fly open again. "The baby! Drake!"

My attempt to sit up sends pain slicing through my shoulder, and the previously steady beeping machines go haywire.

Drake pushes me back down, his hands gentle. "Mea! Calm down, please, sweetheart. The baby—our baby—is fine. You're both going to be just fine."

A nurse bustles into the room, shaking her head at me.

"You need to keep your blood pressure stable, my dear. Off to sleep you go." She uses a syringe to insert medication into my IV.

My eyes lock with Drake even as they begin to droop. "I'm pregnant."

His chuckle collides with his curse. "Yeah, baby. I got that."

"You...happy?" I sigh as I lose the battle with my sleepy eyes.

His lips brush against my forehead, my cheek, my nose, my lips.

His voice is the last thing I hear as I drift away.

"Yeah, sweetheart. I'm the happiest man alive right now."

Epilogue

Drake

Ten Months Later

The doctors in the hospital after Mea was shot told me that she and our baby are medical miracles.

That our baby shouldn't have made it through that kind of trauma early on in the pregnancy.

That Mea's loss of blood should have ended that precious little life.

But that didn't happen.

I'm more than grateful as I stare down at my daughter.

Mea, sitting across from me at the sidewalk café in Savannah, smiles. "I can't believe how good you are with her. She loves her daddy so much."

The little raven-haired beauty in my arms stares up at me, clutching my finger in her tiny fist and gripping it hard.

"She's so damn tough. Like her mama."

My eyes meet Mea's, and the searing need I have to protect this woman, to love her, to make sure she has everything she'll ever need, still burns strong inside me.

It'll never fade.

It's like she can read my expression, because she leans across the table and kisses me. "Still can't believe we're meeting your real father today. You ready for this? You never used to talk about your family."

I grab her hand, lacing our fingers together. Bringing it to my lips, I sigh. "I know. I didn't know how to, after knowing about your past. I grew up with a mother who only cared about how drunk she could get at any given time. She drowned everything she felt with liquor. My whole life, it was up to me to clean up after her. Or to call around town looking for her. The people in my town knew what was going on; they helped me out whenever they could. But it was tough. She told me that my father left when I was still a baby, and she was alone after that. I don't think she ever got over it, and drinking was the only way she could deal."

"I know how that made you feel." The little wrinkles in her brow that only show up when she frowns appear.

"But it's not like that anymore. I found my dad. We've talked. We've Skyped. I've e-mailed my little half-sister. And now this is happening. We're meeting them. And I get to show off my beautiful family."

"Then I guess we better take a minute and breathe deep, just so we're prepared."

Rolling my eyes, I oblige. There's no point in fighting her on the yoga stuff. We breathe deep for about a minute before I open my eyes.

"We good?"

"Drake?" The deep voice with a southern drawl matching mine causes both of us to look up.

There, standing beside our table, are Richard Walsh and his daughter, Phoebe.

My father. My sister.

I stand, passing my baby girl to Mea.

And then I embrace my father.

Releasing him, I turn to Phoebe. "Hey."

"Hey." Her tone is awkward, and she glances down at the ground. At nineteen, she's still young. This must all be totally weird for her. But after a second, she grabs me in a fierce hug.

"I don't know how to be someone's sister," she whispers. "But I'll try my best."

Holding her at arm's length, I shoot her a smile. "I don't know how to be someone's brother. But I'll fuck up anyone who messes with you."

"Drake!" Mea's warning tone grabs my attention, and I turn to her.

"Richard, Phoebe…this is my fiancée, Mea."

Mea smiles and waves one hand while cuddling our daughter with the other.

"And this"—I wrap my arm around her and gesture toward the cooing baby—"is my daughter, Graylyn. We call her Gray."

And from the looks of joy and awe in my father's and sister's eyes, I know that my daughter is going to receive more love than

I ever could have hoped for or imagined. Not just from me and my soon-to-be wife, but from my family as well.

It's going to be a good life.

Want more Drake and Mea? Leave a review and you will receive two bonus chapters of their story!

After you leave the review, just e-mail the link to authordianagardin@gmail.com and Diana will personally send you the bonus chapters!

About the Author

Diana Gardin was born and raised combing the coasts of southeastern Virginia. She is now a happy resident of South Carolina, as she married into an enormous Carolina-rooted family. She loves the beach; and even more than that, she loves to read while sitting on the beach.

Though writing was always one of Diana's passions, she enrolled in college to become an elementary-school teacher. After eight years of teaching in both Virginia and South Carolina, she decided to stay at home with her first child. This decision opened her eyes to the fact that she still very much loved to write, and her first novel was born. Diana is the author of several works of New Adult romance, including the Ashes series, the Nelson Island series, and the Battle Scars series.

Learn more at:
DianaGardin.com
Twitter: @DianalynnGardin
Facebook: facebook.com/diana.gardin